Second Chances

A Windsor Falls Novel

Kimberley O'Malley

Carolina Blue
PUBLISHING

Where Romance is True Blue & Red Hot!

Published by Carolina Blue Publishing, LLC

ISBN: 978-1-946682-05-5

For my children, Jordan Anastasia and Lucas Alexander. You are my miracles after years of heartache. May the world be a kind place for you. I wish you all good things with just a hint of struggle. How can you appreciate the good in your life without it?

Praise for
Kimberley O'Malley

Coming Home

"There was so much emotion in the story that you will definitely need to keep the box of tissues close by. I felt the heartache, joy, and love that the characters were feeling throughout the story. The author writes a beautiful story that kept me hooked until the end."

–Alpha Book Club

"Kimberley O'Malley really manages to captivate the reader with her words and descriptions. I felt their heartache and joy and loved the ups and downs."

–Texas Book Nook Blog

"Kimberley O'Malley has brought to life very multi-dimensional characters and given them a purpose. The world she has created is so vivid and really helps the reader feel like they are there with the characters. A strong and fast paced plot will keep you invested the entire way through."

–The Indie Express Blog

"Kimberley O'Malley has done an impeccable job of bringing to life some very compelling characters. There is plenty of drama laced throughout this wonderfully real novel and some heartache and emotional moments as well."

– Novel News Network

Taking Chances

"There is nothing like a hospital for the perfect background to emotional upheaval. I dived in with memories of Grey's Anatomy and ER running through my mind hoping that new ones would be created by Katie and Flynn."

-Nerdy Dirty and Flirty Book Blog

"This romance was sweet and believable. Major chemistry and attraction are a huge plus, but I loved the way that Katie made Flynn work for it. The plot is very well developed right along with the characters. They are real and have their faults."

-Texas Book Nook

"The story really grabs the reader's attention from the get-go. Kimberley O'Malley does a great job being descriptive and allowing the reader to feel like they are immersed in the story. I was surprised at how fresh and how many surprises there were in this story. What a wonderful job of keeping the reader invested in the story and its characters!"

-The Indie Express

"A wonderful witty sarcastic banter love story that shows you that patience and understanding is rewarded and taking risks is worth it in the end when it comes to love."

-Books Are Love

"Ms. O'Malley has a fan for life. Older characters, plots that actually make sense, smexy times, family, characters that you fall in love with, realistic dialogue, perfect pacing, interesting jobs, but above all…LOVE, LAUGHTER, and LIFE. You'll regret it if you don't pick it up."

-Harlie's Book Blog

Chapter 1

Charlie Avery slowed her pace from leisurely jog to brisk walk as her healing body protested her loop around Windsor Falls. The quaint town gave her hope. The sound of children's laugher, drifting on the Spring breeze, cultivated that hope more than she wanted to admit.

She slowed to a halt. Glancing around, she saw a small, neighborhood park. A dozen or more young children climbed on a jungle gym while others shrieked on the swings. She watched them with a touch of envy. To be so carefree was a gift.

Focused on that spot, a blur dashed into her peripheral vision. A petite, blonde child darted out into the road after an errant soccer ball. A car raced towards the child. Charlie had seconds to react. She sprinted towards the girl, diving for her moments before the car would have made contact. The momentum sent both rolling hard.

Pain exploded through her as they came to a halt in the gutter. But the little girl's condition was far more important. Charlie opened her eyes, her gaze met by a frightened, green one. The child, no more than six, lay very still in her arms. Never a good sign.

"Hey, honey. Are you okay?" Her heart slammed inside her chest and breathing hurt. But none of that mattered when the little girl opened her eyes and nodded her head. Charlie sat up, still holding her, to have a better look. By now, bystanders had gathered. She blocked them out. "I'm Charlie. What's your name?"

"Abby," whispered the little girl. Her eyes were very large in her dirt streaked face. "But I'm not 'supposed to tell strangers." Two big tears made their way down her face as Abby bit her lower lip.

If that was the worst thing on her mind, then we lucked out, thought Charlie. She smiled at the small girl. "Well, you're right about that, Abby. But this situation might be a bit different." Charlie took a deep, steading breath before continuing. "I'm a doctor. Would it be okay if I checked you for injuries?"

Abby nodded. The little girl cradled her left wrist with her right arm. Charlie scanned the gathered crowd. "Did anyone call 9-1-1? We need an ambulance."

"I did." Came a disembodied voice from the crowd. "I'm still on with them."

"Good. Tell them that I'm a doctor and that we only have minor injuries."

Not waiting for a response, she turned her attention back to her patient. "You are a very brave little girl, but I'm betting that arm hurts, doesn't it?"

More tears slid down her face. She nodded her head. "It does, Charlie."

"Hold it like you are while I look. I promise this won't hurt."

"Abby!" The shrieking sound stretched her already frayed nerves to the limit. She looked up to see a young Asian woman running towards the street. She held the hand of a carbon copy of her patient. But this one wore a dress.

Charlie plastered a huge smile she didn't feel on her face. "Hey. She's fine." She smiled down at her patient. "Aren't you Abby?"

Abby shook her head. "That's Miss Christine. She looks after us when we aren't in school. Today's a teacher day. Whatever that is."

"Oh, thank God. I only turned my head for a second, and Abby ran in the street." The young woman stopped talking. Sobs racked her petit frame.

"The car never hit Abby. But it looks like she may have broken her wrist when we fell. An ambulance is on its way." To prove her point, the wail of an approaching siren grew louder. "If you could call her parents, that would be great."

"We don't have parents. We only have a dad," piped Abby.

Before she could process that bit of info, the other little girl tugged on her sleeve. She turned to what had to be Abby's twin. She had the same blonde hair and bright green eyes. "You must be Abby's sister. She's going to be fine. Abby and I took a little tumble."

"I'm Kerry. I'm three minutes older than Abby." Her lower lip trembled and tears threatened.

"Oh, so you're the big sister. Well, why don't you come over here and sit with Abby? I'm sure that will make her feel better."

Charlie smiled for real as Kerry scrunched down beside her sister. The two were talking a thousand miles a minute. A sure sign that everything would be okay.

"Excuse me. Coming through."

Turning her head, she saw a uniformed police officer clearing a path through the crowd. Right behind him were two ambulance crew members, one dragging a stretcher.

She stood up and turned to greet the newcomers. "I'm Charlie Avery, and I saw the event. I happen to be an ER doctor."

The officer, Matthews by his name tag, approached her. "Can you tell me what happened here, ma'am?"

"I was running past this park when I saw Abby chase her ball out into the street. A car came speeding towards her." She twisted her neck to look but didn't see the car in question. "I grabbed her. I didn't know what else to do."

"It's true." Came a voice from the crowd, followed by murmurs. A small, elderly lady stepped forward. "I saw the whole thing. Pepe and I did." She motioned to a rather fat Chihuahua at her feet. "We were walking from the other direction, and that car passed us. Going way too fast, I might add. The little girl ran right out. The next thing I know, this lady, this hero, jumped in and snatched that little girl from a certain death."

The crowd had grown noisy, everyone agreeing with the story and wanting to add what they had seen. She didn't deserve the title of hero. People had died in Africa because of her. She held up a hand. "I did what anyone else would have done."

Officer Matthews shook his head. "Trust me. Not everyone would have run in front of a car. Are you okay, ma'am?" His eyes ran over her once.

"I'm fine. But Abby may have broken her right wrist."

The ambulance crew assessed Abby. The female one nodded. "Looks like a break alright, a simple one." She grabbed a short, padded board and placed Abby's arm on it to splint her injury.

The other approached Charlie. "Hi. I'm Mac." He stuck out his hand and she shook it.

"Hi, Mac, I'm Charlie. Thanks for coming."

Mac smiled. "No problem. Why don't we get Abby loaded up? Then, I can look at your injuries."

"I'm fine. Please take care of my young friend here."

Mac lifted Abby onto the stretcher. "Charlie, will you come with me. Please." Her voice trembled, and fresh tears slid down her face.

Charlie didn't hesitate. "Of course, I will Abby." She climbed up in the back of the ambulance and sat beside the little girl, placing a hand on her leg.

Charlie saw the nanny standing there, clutching Kerry's hand in a death grip. "Christine, call the girls' father please. And don't scare him. Abby is going to be fine. Tell him we're going to Windsor Falls Memorial."

She twisted around to Mac. "That is where we're going, right?" When he nodded, she turned back to the young woman. "Meet us there. And take a breath, Christine. She's fine."

"Uh, Charlie, you're bleeding." Abby's eyes rounded.

She looked down. Sure enough, blood trickled down both knees. She glanced at her elbow, which had started to sting. Blood and gravel clung to her skin.

Smiling for the frightened little girl, Charlie made light of it. "Oh, that's nothing, honey. I've wiped out worse on my bike." Although true, her whole body began to throb. The adrenaline was wearing off. Later, she'd be putting that deep, claw-footed bathtub in her room at the B&B to good use.

Mac checked vital signs and chatted with the little girl about soccer. Charlie sat back, keeping her hand on Abby's leg. She closed her eyes for a moment. Now that the crisis had ended, reality set in. The very, scary reality. What if she hadn't reached her on time? What if the car had been going a little faster? She was doing exactly what she counseled her patients to not do, but she couldn't help it. The image of this tiny, precious child running into the street burned into her brain.

She started at the small hand tugging on her sleeve. "Dr. Charlie?"

Opening her eyes, she squeezed Abby's leg. "Yes, honey?"

"Why do you have a boy's name?" Charlie and Mac both laughed out loud. Abby smiled. "I wasn't even trying to be funny."

Charlie smiled, this time all the way to her eyes. "My name is short for Charlotte. 'Charlie' is a nickname. Like Abby. My Dad always wanted a boy and got me. So, he called me Charlie, and it stuck."

Abby screwed up her face, deep in thought. "My Daddy always says you should like people for who they are."

"Your Daddy is very smart." She had spent her whole childhood trying to be what her father had wanted. She was a natural athlete, excelling at swimming and soccer. But her father had been the star quarterback at Clemson and would have gone pro if he hadn't blow out his shoulder. By the time she entered high school, her father didn't go to her soccer games because it wasn't a 'real sport'. That's when she stopped trying to impress him. Her mother only cared about her daughter becoming a debutante and marrying well.

"I hope my Aunt Elizabeth is working today. She'll fix my arm."

Charlie stared at Abby. "Your Aunt Elizabeth?" Could she mean *her* Elizabeth?

Abby cocked her head. "She was married to my daddy's brother, Connor. But then Connor went to heaven and Elizabeth was sad." She touched Charlie's hand when she noticed the look on her face. "But she married Sam. Kerry and I wore fancy dresses. Aunt Elizabeth is happy again."

What were the odds? "Honey, is your last name Fitzgerald?"

The ambulance pulled into the emergency entrance to the medical center. The little girl nodded as the medics removed her from the truck. Charlie followed behind them into the loud and busy ER. She grinned. The chaos felt like home to her.

She hustled to keep up with the stretcher bearing Abby. The sound of girlish shrieks of happiness helped her to locate her new friend. She turned a corner to see the unmistakable ebony curls of her best friend. The very distinctive baby bump that stretched the fabric of Elizabeth's navy-blue scrub top stopped Charlie in her tracks. She'd missed a lot more than Elizabeth's wedding while she was working in war-torn Africa.

"Is there something you forgot to tell me?"

Elizabeth whirled around, joy written across her face. She threw herself at Charlie, who hissed in a harsh breath at the impact. Her fresh wounds protested the contact, but Charlie hugged her friend fiercely. Finally, she took a step back and grinned at Elizabeth. "Only you could look that beautiful while pregnant. If I didn't love you, I might hate you."

Color splashes across Elizabeth's already glowing face. "This coming from the most beautiful woman to ever grace a pair of scrubs!" She leaned in and kissed Charlie's face. "I've missed you."

Charlie's smile faded. "I'm so sorry I missed your wedding, Elizabeth. You know I would have been here if I could."

Tears sprang to Elizabeth's eyes. Before Charlie could ask about them, Elizabeth burst out laughing. "Hormones. Another of the many, lovely things about pregnancy that you know about but can never appreciate until they happen to you."

Elizabeth was still talking, but Charlie didn't hear anything else she said. A tremendous wave of sadness almost toppled her. At the same time, her hands went numb and her heart threatened to burst from her chest. A steady stream of sweat trickled down her back. She clenched her hands into fists until the skin blanched white. She concentrated on the breathing techniques she learned. Deep breath in to the count of four, hold for eight, then blow out for another four. She had done this for several rounds when she realized Elizabeth was staring at her. Charlie could hear her calling her name, a worried tinge to her voice. But Elizabeth sounded though she were at the bottom of a well.

Not for the first time, she cursed what had happened to her. Charlie sucked it up and plastered a smile on her face. If it didn't quite reach her eyes, there was nothing she could do about that. 'Fake it until you make it', had become her personal motto over the past few months.

"What's wrong?" Elizabeth reached for Charlie's wrist, checking her pulse.

Can't fool a fellow ER doctor, Charlie thought grimly. Her pulse bounded in the one hundred thirties; down from much higher a moment ago. "That's a tale for another time. Let's talk about your niece."

Concern etched into the lines of Elizabeth's face. "Please, Elizabeth."

After a moment's hesitation, Elizabeth nodded. But her brilliant, blue eyes were shadowed. "So, Abby was telling me, at about a hundred miles per hour, that you're a hero. Care to share the details?"

Charlie grinned, relief flooding her. She recounted the events to Elizabeth. Her friend's face paled as she learned how close her niece had come to having quite a different outcome. "It's okay, Elizabeth. It could have been terrible, but it wasn't. A simple wrist fracture and some tales to tell her friends in school tomorrow. That's all."

But even as she spoke the words, she knew Abby's family would be upset. Elizabeth's first husband, Connor, had been killed by a drunk driver more than a decade ago. Elizabeth, more than most, knew how fragile life could be.

Charlie squeezed Elizabeth's hand in support. "She's fine. Now let's go see what the moppet is up to."

Elizabeth nodded and pulled back the curtain to Abby's room. Someone had cleaned the little girl's face and arms. Abby's smile was bright without the grime that had covered her face.

"Look, Aunt Elizabeth," cried Abby, pointing to her knees. Cartoon princess bandages covered both. "Aren't they cool? Kerry's gonna be jealous. And guess what! I get to pick the color of my cast if my arm is broked." She grinned, showing off the gap where one of her baby teeth was missing.

Elizabeth leaned in and ruffled her niece's blonde hair. "She sure will be. Now we need to take a picture of that arm to see if it's really 'broked'."

"That's my cue," called a young man pushing in a portable X-ray machine. "Hi, young lady. Can you tell me your name please?"

Charlie felt a twinge watching Elizabeth place a protective over the swelling of her belly. "And that's my cue, honey. Your about to be cousin doesn't want their picture taken today. So, Charlie and I are going to step outside for a moment. We'll be right back."

The two women walked out of the room and continued around a corner. Elizabeth frowned. "Of course, I have to pee again. Because it's already been fifteen minutes." She stroked a hand over her belly. "Peanut, you're killing Mommy." She laughed at the look on Charlie's face. "We decided to not find out what we're having, much to everyone's horror. So, for now, this little person is 'Peanut'."

Charlie pushed down the wistfulness. "Go to the bathroom. I'll wait right here."

Elizabeth had already moved off. "Be right back," floated down the hallway.

Charlie leaned against the wall for a moment to ground herself. One day, the feeling of loss wouldn't haunt her. She had to believe that. Angry sounds broke her reverie. Instinct kicked in. She followed the sound around the corner and back to the triage desk. And stopped. Her heart thudded at the sight of a very handsome man. He was also the source of the noise. She listened to the triage nurse attempt to calm him.

"Sir, you can't go back there. If you tell me your name, I can help you."

He pulled a hand through his raven hair. "I don't have time for this. I need to find my daughter." His blue eyes scanned the area.

"Maybe I can help." Two pair of eyes turned towards her as Charlie stepped into the fray. The nurse's were tinged with relief. Annoyance passed through his as the man swept his gaze over her. And dismissed her. She was a beautiful woman used to men taking a second look. Not this one, but then he did have more important things on his mind. Or rather, an important person.

"Are you Mr. Fitzgerald, by any chance? Here to see Abby?" Charlie spoke in a soothing tone.

The man took a deep breath and blew it out. "Yes, I'm Abby's father, Brendan Fitzgerald."

"I brought Abby in. I'd be happy to take you to her. I know she'll want to see you." She took him by the wrist, ignoring the warmth that spread up her arm at the contact. Without giving him a chance to argue, she led him away from the desk.

"I'm Charlie. I was there at the park. She's doing great. Her wrist may be broken. They were doing X-rays when I left her, but I think it's just a simple fracture. A few weeks in a cast, and she'll be good as new. Won't even have to give up swimming this summer."

Brendan stopped walking and planted his feet, no longer allowing her to shepherd him. She jerked to a halt. She craned her neck. At almost six feet tall, she normally didn't have to look up to meet someone's gaze. But Brendan had three or four inches on her, not to mention the work boots he was wearing. She remembered that his family was in construction. He looked the part, with well-worn jeans molding his legs. A forest green t-shirt with 'Fitzgerald Construction' written on it stretched across his muscular chest.

"Look, Charlie, I'm not trying to be rude, but I need to see my daughter. Now. Please let go of me."

Charlie looked down to where her hand was still attached to his wrist. She dropped it immediately, heat crept up her neck. "Sorry", she muttered.

"Brendan!" Elizabeth came out of Abby's room. Charlie smothered a grin when she watched her friend grab him by the wrist exactly as she had. This time, he allowed her to lead him around the corner like a puppy. There were only the sounds of quiet murmurs from Elizabeth and the occasional grunt from Brendan before they returned. Elizabeth grinned. "I was just reminding my friend Brendan that Abby has had a rough day. She doesn't need him going in there both barrels blazing. "Does she, Brendan?"

To Charlie's amazement, the big man ducked his head and mumbled, "Of course not, Elizabeth." She would have chuckled. But she didn't think he would appreciate that.

Brendan turned to Elizabeth. "I'm going in now." Charlie watched as he ducked behind the curtain. She resisted the urge to fan herself. That man was smoking hot.

Charlie felt Elizabeth watching her. "Don't even try to hide your reaction. Brendan is gorgeous. And he doesn't have a clue, which of course makes him even more so."

She tried to keep her expression passive but failed. "He is that. He has, um, classic bone structure."

Elizabeth giggled, holding her pregnant stomach. "I call bullshit, as we used to say." She glanced up and down at her, performing an initial assessment. "Now, let's get you cleaned up."

Chapter Two

"Daddy," Abby squealed. Never had one word sounded so wonderful. He leaned down and hugged his daughter, taking care to not bump her injured arm. Brendan sent a thankful glance heavenward. Someone had been watching over his precious girl today. He took a deep breath and schooled his features before straightening. The last thing he wan ted was for Abby to see the fear in his eyes.

"So, my friend, I hear you had quite the adventure today. Why don't you tell me about it?"

Abby did so, talking a thousand miles an hour, as she told him about the soccer ball and the speeding car. He tried to remember to breathe. He realized just how fortunate they had been. Losing Connor had been the bleakest day of his life. But losing his daughter was unimaginable. He swallowed hard while Abby chattered.

Brendan looked up when Elizabeth entered the room. "Look Abby, Aunt Elizabeth is here to the rescue."

His former sister-in-law chuckled. "I'm only the person with the news. Charlie is the hero." Elizabeth signed into the computer and pulled up Abby's results. "Now let's have a look, shall we?"

Brendan held his breath while she considered the image before her. Elizabeth pointed to a distinctive line with her pen. "Yep, right there. Simple fracture. Not on the growth plate." She turned to her niece. "In English, you get a cast for a few weeks young lady."

"Can I have green?"

Brendan couldn't help but smile. Abby only cared about the color of her cast, despite what happened. Thank goodness for the resilience of children.

"What do you think, Aunt Elizabeth, can she get green?"

Elizabeth laughed. "For being so very brave, Abby, you can have any color your heart desires."

He sighed with relief. He'd take a broken bone over what may have happened. He listened as Elizabeth talked about cast care and follow up with an orthopedist she recommended. He thought of his mother, Maggie. He and his five siblings put her through Hell when they were growing up. He guessed this was payback.

Brendan felt a tugging on his shirt sleeve and looked down into his daughter's beautiful, green eyes. She looked so much like his ex-wife that it broke his heart a bit. Jillian had been beautiful too, but only on the outside. Not for the first time, he was glad they were being raised without her influence.

"Daddy, I'm talking to you," whined Abby.

Brendan grinned. "Sorry, honey. Daddy was thinking about something. What did you say?"

"We need to get Charlie some flowers. Or chocolate. Or a puppy. Girls like those."

Both adults laughed at her words. His daughters were *obsessed* with the idea of a puppy. His long hours and single parent status had made him reluctant. But maybe it wasn't the worst idea. He was feeling generous today. *Charlie?*

"Who's Charlie, honey?"

Abby fixed him with a look, one mirrored by Elizabeth. Somehow, he was in trouble, but he had no idea why.

An amused Elizabeth answered him. "Charlie is the woman who saved your daughter today, Brendan. The tall blonde you were spectacularly rude to in the hallway."

Puzzlement became chagrin. He remembered his harsh words. She had been wearing a tattered t-shirt and running shorts. There were various scratches, bloodstains and dirt on her. She looked bedraggled at best. Homeless at worst. Shame raced through him. He hadn't given any thought to why she was in that condition. The tunnel vision of parenthood did that.

"You were rude to Charlie?" Abby's lip quivered. Her eyes brimmed with tears. "She's my friend, Daddy."

His heart squeezed. Nothing hurt him worse than his daughters' tears. "Don't cry, honey. I didn't mean to be rude to her. I was so worried about you." He stroked his daughter's hair, trying to comfort her.

"But you always say that even though we don't mean to hurt someone, it still hurts. You say that when Kerry and I fight."

He looked down into her serious expression. She was right. And he was screwed. He heaved a sigh. "When you're right, you're right. I owe Charlie an apology."

Elizabeth cleared her throat none too subtlety. "And a thank you. When Abby says Charlie saved her, she wasn't kidding. She grabbed Abby in the nick of time and kept her from getting hit by that car, Brendan."

His head whipped back and forth, first looking at Elizabeth and then Abby. "What? I didn't know that." He buried his head in his hands and groaned. "Flowers might be in order."

"And a puppy?" asked Abby.

Elizabeth laughed. "I don't think Charlie needs a puppy right now, Abby."

"You're right, of course, Elizabeth." He looked at Abby. "Where was Miss Christine when this happened?" He liked their nanny, but she could be a bit absent minded. She was a part time nanny, part time student at the University of North Carolina Asheville. Christine majored in early childhood education, one of the reasons he had hired her. Now that the girls were in school most of the year, he only needed help on odd days and in the summer. But if this was her idea of 'watching' the girls, he might be in the market for a new nanny.

Abby broke his train of thought, grabbing his hand with her good one. "Daddy, Miss Christine didn't do anything wrong. I promise. I ran out in the street after my soccer ball." Her lower lip trembled again, skewering him right in the heart. "I'm sorry, Daddy. Don't make Miss Christine go away. Me and Kerry like her."

"Kerry and I," he corrected. He squeezed Abby's hand. "Don't worry, honey. Miss Christine and I will have a chat. No one's in trouble." Turning to Elizabeth, he asked where he could find their 'hero'. "Abby, I'll be right back. Stay with Aunt Elizabeth for a moment, will you?" When she nodded, he left the room.

Brendan pulled the curtain closed. He took out his phone to make a quick call to the nanny. There wasn't any reason to drag Kerry to the ER. After calling the hysterical woman and assuring her that Abby was fine, he asked her to take Kerry to his mother's house. Then he called his mom. That one took a bit longer, as his poor Mom didn't know what had happened. When he was finished, he looked down the hallway. He had no idea what to say to this woman who saved his daughter. The reason may be understandable, but he still regretted speaking to Charlie the way he had. There might not be enough flowers in North Carolina for that apology.

Knocking on the partition, Brendan cleared his throat and entered the cubicle. He froze, air trapped in his lungs, when he saw Charlie standing with her back to him. She had removed her tattered shirt, standing in only running shorts and a sports bra. The golden, creamy skin of her back exposed. She must not have heard his knock, because she started to turn around and gasped when she saw him. She grabbed at the ruined shirt to cover herself. That was a shame, he thought. She was stunning.

"May I help you, Mr. Fitzgerald?" Her voice was cool.

He sighed. This might be tougher than he thought. "Please, call me Brendan." He walked further into the small space and extended a hand towards Charlie. "I came to apologize for my earlier behavior. And to thank you. But now I have to apologize for barging in as well."

She shook his hand. Brendan tried not to wonder at the sparks that crept up his arm when their hands touched. His hand felt cold after she let it go. "Uh, I really am sorry. For both things. And 'thanks' doesn't even begin to cover it." His bright blue eyes crinkled with his first true smile of the day. "But in my defense, I did knock."

Charlie toyed with the edge of her ruined shirt. "It's okay. I'm jumpy. The adrenaline is wearing off. I didn't hear you enter. And you're welcome, but I only did what any one else would have done." She shrugged back into the torn shirt, covering all that lovely skin.

Brendan knew for a fact that wasn't true. His ex-wife for instance had wanted to abort the twins when she found out she was pregnant. She would not have risked her life, not to mention her manicure, to jump in front of a car for Abby.

He took her hands in his and looked at the torn skin of her palms. "Thanks isn't enough for saving my little girl. I'm sorry you were injured. How can I help?"

She pulled her hands from his, as if uncomfortable. Her smile seemed a bit forced. "It's fine. Luckily, I know a great ER doctor. Not to mention the fact that I am one. Elizabeth wouldn't mind helping me with anything I can't reach." She gestured to a silver tray with sterile water and bandages on it. "I've got this."

"Still, they wouldn't be there at all if you hadn't saved my daughter's life."

"I wish I could have saved her from a broken arm. She may have tried to break her fall. If only I could have gotten her in my arms first."

His mouth gaped. "Are you kidding me? You're the reason she's alive, or at least not seriously injured." He shook his head. "I can't ever repay you for that, Charlie," he answered in a roughened voice.

Her smile reached her whiskey-colored eyes this time. "Then I guess it's a good thing I'm not looking for repayment. I'm just glad she's okay."

"That makes two of us. Elizabeth tells me you're in town for an interview. Good luck with that." Brendan looked at Charlie, really looked. Even wearing tattered clothing and covered in dirt and blood, she was amazing. Nearly as tall as him, Charlie had a willowy build. She could be a model. Not that he was interested in her in *that* way. No thanks. These days, Brendan didn't have time to think about any women.

Charlie interrupted his thoughts. "How's Abby? I was going to stop by and see after I finished up here."

Keep your mind on track, he scolded himself. "She's fine. Picking out her cast. Green's a safe bet. It's her favorite color." He laughed at the thought of her half of the room his daughters shared. Abby had insisted on decorating exclusively in greens of varied shades. "Obsessed with green is more accurate."

Charlie laughed, a light yet husky sound, that hit Brendan right in the gut. "I remember those days, although I preferred pink." Her wrinkled her nose. "To this day, I can't stand pink."

"I can't see that happening with Abby, but one can only hope. Nothing against green, but it gets to be a bit much with her. Anyway, I'll leave you to your wounds." He removed his wallet from his back pocket and pulled out a business card. "Here's my number. I owe you. If I can do anything for you, don't hesitate." He was careful not to brush his fingers against hers as she took his card. He didn't need further complications in his life. Even if she was gorgeous. Especially then.

With a parting smile, Brendan excused himself and left the room. Standing in the hall, he took a deep breath and blew it out. It had been a long time since a woman had affected him like that. He had forgotten that buzz of awareness. These days, he split his time between his work and his girls. Nothing came before them.

*****

Charlie's hands shook a bit when she took off her destroyed shirt again. Glancing down at the ugly surgical scars across her abdomen, she was thankful Brendan had not seen them. Tracing a tremulous finger along the puckered lengths, she thought about her days in Africa. She had gone there with such good intentions, but things hadn't ended well. Shaking off the memories, Charlie tended the minor scrapes across her belly.

If Brendan had seen her scars, he might mention it to Elizabeth. Charlie didn't want that to happen. She hadn't told her friend anything about her time in

Africa yet. Even her family didn't know most of it. Only what she wanted them to know. One day, she would tell Elizabeth. That's the kind of friendship they had. After all, she had been the first, and only, person in California to know about the tragedies in Elizabeth's background. But she couldn't share the truth of what had happened over the phone or email.

When she finished cleaning her wounds, she threw away the trash and went in search of her friend. Abby's room was empty. Good. She didn't need another encounter with Brendan today. The memory of him alone warmed her skin. His incredible body hadn't been hidden by the jeans and t-shirt. In fact, the material had only emphasized his muscles and long legs. Not that she cared. The last thing she needed was a man.

Nope. She was getting her life back and hoping to start a new chapter in Windsor Falls. She didn't need or want a man to complicate things. Not even a hot one like Brendan. Plus, Brendan was essentially family to her best friend. Charlie would run into him from time to time. If she had needs that she couldn't fulfill with her battery-operated friend, she would find a nice stranger to help her out. That worked in the past. After living through her parents' less than happy ever after, she wasn't eager to sign on.

She spotted Elizabeth, busy with a patient in the trauma bay. Walking to the triage area, Charlie saw the nurse from earlier. She approached her after she had finished with a patient. "Hi, do you remember me?"

The woman smiled in response. "Of course! You're the lady with the little girl. I heard what you did. Amazing!"

She grew uncomfortable when the woman gushed. "I was just happy to be there to help. Anyway, my name is Charlie Avery, and I'm an old friend of Elizabeth's. She's busy with a trauma right now, and I need to go back to the Inn and change." She gestured to her clothes. "Could you could give her a message for me. Please ask her to call me when she gets free."

Cindy, her name tag read, nodded. "Yes, ma'am. I'll be sure to tell her that."

"Thank you."

She headed outside and felt better when the sun warmed her skin. Chicago had been an amazing city, but she hated the winter. Being back in the South was the right choice for her. She made it to the ambulance bay when she realized she didn't have a car. The trip here had been a blur, and she had no idea how far or in what direction they had come.

What to do? She only had her phone. No money. No credit cards. Huh. Maybe Elizabeth could help her.

"Hey. I know you."

Charlie turned toward the voice. Mac, the paramedic from earlier, crossed the driveway. She squinted in the sun, but even then, he was hot. What was it with these guys from Windsor Falls?

She smiled at him. "Hi, Mac. I guess you remember me."

He stopped next to her, smiling. "You're hard to forget. It's not every day I get to meet a hero."

She groaned. "I wish people would stop calling me that. And you should talk! First responders, whether medical, police, or firefighters are all heroes in my book." Heroes didn't wake up screaming in the middle of the night, the cries of the dying dragging them from sleep. She was sure they didn't think about having a drink, or five, when the memories tortured her.

"Nah, I get paid to do this."

"True, but you choose to go out there, every day, and risk your life for others. That's a hero in my book." Mac started to squirm, and she laughed. "See. Not so easy, is it?"

He shook his head and stuck out his hand. "I don't believe we were properly introduced. Travis Mac Gregor, but everyone calls me Mac."

She shook his hand, hers dwarfed in his. "Well, Mac, I'm Charlotte Avery, but everyone calls me Charlie. Nice to meet you."

"You too. Are you new to town? You looked a bit lost standing there."

Charlie laughed at his observation. "Yes to both Mac. I'm an old friend of Elizabeth Fitzgerald or Bishop, whichever last name she's using now. I'm actually in town for an interview."

"Oh. That's right! You mentioned at the scene that you were an ER doc. That's great. You're going to love Windsor Falls. Ever been here before?"

"No. I got into town last night, and I haven't had a chance to look around." She swiveled her head to glance about. "Speaking of town, which way is it? I have to get back to the B&B to change."

"Come on, we can take you in the rig." He gestured to the gleaming ambulance idling off to the side.

"Oh, I couldn't do that."

"Absolutely not. My partner and I are heading back to the station. We're more than happy to help. Where are you staying?"

"The Blue Iris Inn, off the town square. I'm afraid my car and all my worldly belongings are there, so I'm happy to take that ride if you're sure."

A petite woman, in her early twenties with beautiful café au lait skin, came around the side of the rig. "Hey, Mac, are we ever going to grab lunch?" She started when she saw Charlie. "Oh, I'm sorry. I didn't know you were talking to someone." She looked closer, and Charlie saw recognition flash across her face. "Hey, it's you."

Charlie approached and smiled. "Yep, it's me. Charlie Avery, from the accident."

"I remember. Nice handling of that little girl. I'm Trina by the way."

"Nice to meet you and thanks. Happy to help."

"You did more than help, Charlie."

Mac turned to his partner. The difference in size made her laugh. He had to be a foot taller and at least a hundred pounds heavier than her. "Charlie is staying at the Blue Iris and needs a ride. You don't mind, do you?"

"Of course, not." She tossed some keys to him. "You can drive."

The three of them headed to the truck, Trina breaking off and opening the side door. Mac held the passenger door for Charlie and gave her a hand up. He winced at her scraped knees. "That's gonna hurt later."

"It already does. Everything does, to be honest. Looking forward to a long soak in the old-fashioned tub I have in my bathroom."

Mac grinned at her. "Is there room for two? I could tend to your wounds." He wagged his eyebrows at her.

"Goodness, Mac. She almost got hit by a car. Give her a break already." Trina poked her head between the seats and smiled at Charlie. "He's harmless. For the most part."

Charlie laughed and then wrapped her arm around her ribs when they hurt. "Oh, that wasn't a great idea."

Mac glanced in her direction. "Did you get seen while you were in the ER? You might have a broken rib or two."

"No, but I'm fine, thanks. It only hurts when I laugh. Or breathe. Just need a soak and a nap." She fixed him a look that women have been giving men for centuries. "And I can tend to my own wounds, thanks."

Trina snorted from the back of the rig. "Shot down again, Mac Gregor."

Mac stopped at the curb in front of the B&B. He grinned at his partner in the mirror. "Can't blame a man for trying, Trina." He got out and came around to Charlie's side, opening the door. She had almost forgotten the wonderful manners of Southern gentleman. He offered his hand, which Charlie took to steady herself as she slid out of the truck. Her legs were a bit shaky hitting the ground. She noticed there weren't any tingles when he touched her. Unlike someone else she wouldn't think about.

"Thanks guys. I appreciate the ride. I was sort of stuck back there."

"No worries, Charlie. It was our pleasure. Let me know if you need anything." Mac waved and jumped back in the driver's seat. Trina had stepped through and was now sitting in the passenger's seat. As they pulled away, she could hear them squabbling about lunch. That made her smile. Food was always important to medics and ER doctors alike. Because you never knew when you'd have the time to eat.

Charlie walked up the driveway leading to the B&B. She discovered this place on line. Their website charmed her. So did the name. She had always loved Irises, blue ones in particular. She had booked a room for two weeks. If she got the job, she would have to look for something more permanent.

The gardens flanking the driveway called to her. The spring flowers were a riot of blues, purples, yellows, and pinks. Charlie wasn't much of a gardener, yet another disappointment in the eyes of her mother. Anna Mae had beautiful, expansive gardens at their home. So beautiful, that the garden was on a walking tour of Charleston. Naturally, she thought without much heat. Anna Mae loved the attention. Somehow, saving lives for a living didn't compare. She mentally shrugged her shoulders. She learned a long time ago that she would never measure up.

Charlie breathed in the heady scents of the blooms before continuing up the long drive. She stopped on the front porch to look at herself. With her tattered clothing and dirt and blood streaked skin, she was uneasy entering through the front door. It seems Anna Mae's lessons had stuck after all. She briefly debated looking for a back door but dismissed the idea. Everything hurt too much. She'd hurry to her room, hoping no one saw her.

No such luck. A well-heeled couple in their sixties stood at the reception desk. For one heart-stopping moment, Charlie thought they were her parents. After all, the woman wore heels and pearls. All eyes turned towards her, and there was a distinctive gasp.

"Why, Dr. Avery, whatever happened to you?" Lorna, the woman who had checked her in last night, rushed around the side of that desk, a hand held to her mouth. "Are you hurt?"

Loathe to be the center of attention, Charlie smiled and shook her head. She could feel the dull red creeping up her face. "I'm fine, really. It looks much worse than it is."

The couple stood still, silent in their judgement, with only a single raised eyebrow between them. It was her childhood all over again. But after the carnage and loss she had witnessed in Africa, Charlie found she no longer cared. She could tell the story of the past few hours, but she didn't. Let them think what they would.

She smiled at Lorna. "A bit of an accident. Thank you for your concern." She left before Lorna could reply, walking up the curving stairway to the second floor and the sanctuary of her room. Once inside, she stripped to her underwear, balling up the ruined clothing and tossing them into the trash. She had a date with the claw footed bathtub.

The inn had supplied a lovely assortment of bath oils and salts. Charlie chose lavender oil and dumped some in the tub. She turned the water to just-short-of-boiling-your-skin-off and moved to the sink. Taking a steadying breath, she turned to the mirror. And gasped. Her long, blonde hair had started the morning in a simple French braid. That was long gone. Wild wisps of hair stood out around her head, giving her a mad scientist look.

And that was only the beginning. A trail of dirt streaked from her chin and disappeared into her hairline. The opposite cheekbone sported a scrape. she sighed. Nothing much she could about it. And she would do it all again to save Abby.

Charlie removed her underwear and trailed her fingers through the bubble filled water. Finding the temperature perfect, she lowered herself into the tub. *Yes.* The hot water bathing her bruised muscles was exactly what she needed. After leaning forward to turn off the tap, she slid down until the water reached her chin. Heaven, she thought, sheer heaven. A glass of wine would have been perfect. But that wasn't a good idea anymore.

She closed her eyes, leaned her head back against the rim, and thought about the morning's events. An image of Brendan Fitzgerald sprang to mind. He was a big man, something that she enjoyed. So many men were put off, even intimidated, by her height. But he had at least several inches on her and didn't come across as one so easily dissuaded. He was all lean, sinewed muscle and take no prisoners attitude. His earlier rudeness was completely understandable considering the situation. Charlie didn't have any children, but she imagined she would react the same way. Her pediatric patients often came along with apathetic at best, abusive at worst, parents. It broke her heart.

Her skin flushed thinking about Brendan's body. He had large, rough hands. Not the soft hands of a man who crunched numbers for a living. The warm water lapped around her. It didn't take an enormous leap to imagine those hands on her body. Everywhere. She shifted in the tub, less comfortable and more aroused.

It's been a long time, she told herself. A very long time. Yeah, that's the reason. It had nothing to do with Brendan's strong jaw line or chiseled cheekbones. Or his lips. Lips that, in the solitude of her bath, she could think about kissing. Nope. Had nothing to do with any of that. She had no business thinking of him in those terms.

Chapter Three

Brendan pulled into the driveway of his home and turned off the car. Turning in his seat, his heart clenched. Abby, utterly spent by the day, slept in her booster seat. His old sweatshirt acted as a pillow for her brand-new cast. Not only green, but in-your-face bright, Abby had giggled when the tech applied it to her broken arm.

He almost forgot to breathe as he took in the perfection of his daughter. Abby's platinum hair fell around her face and down past her shoulders, giving her a look of angels. Impossibly long lashes fanned her cheeks in sleep. Brendan sighed at the warmth that spread through his chest. Every moment of his life with Jillian was worth it just to watch his daughter sleep.

Brendan exited the car and walked to the mail box. Several bills, a flyer for Chinese food, and a letter with a Texas return address. He hadn't really kept in touch with any of his friends from there. Life had gotten too busy. That left his ex-wife, Jillian. Since he couldn't think of a single good reason to hear from her after all these years, he tore the envelope in half and tossed the pieces into the recycle bucket outside his garage.

Sitting on the porch steps, he took out his cell phone. He sent a brief text to Elizabeth, thanking her for her help today. Having her back in his life, all their lives, was a blessing. Brendan had always had a soft spot for Elizabeth when they were growing up. Not for the first time, thinking about the loss of his brother Connor saddened him.

Somehow, his girls had made it to six without anything more than some scrapes. Neither of the twins had ever visited the ER before today. He knew a fractured wrist wasn't a big deal, and things could have been so much worse. But he couldn't help feeling a bit sorry for himself. If his girls had a mother in their lives, maybe today wouldn't have happened. Of course, that was irrational. Children, even those with two parents, got injured. And the girls loved Christine. This wasn't her fault. He knew that. In his head. But it still hurt him, in his gut, to think about Abby's broken wrist.

Jumping up, he strode around his front yard, trying to clear his frustration. His life wasn't perfect. No one's was. But his was damn close. When he was younger, he only thought of escaping this small town. Now, Brendan couldn't imagine living anywhere else.

He grew up in the family business. His father, Joe, had built Fitzgerald Construction from a one-man operation to the sprawling, successful company it was today. All on his own back and sweat to provide for his growing family. Donovan, two years older than Brendan, had joined his father while still in high school, working summers on a crew. His two younger brothers, Connor and Aidan, had chosen other paths. His youngest sister, Riley, joined after college. She only waited until then because their parents insisted on her getting a degree.

Brendan had wanted nothing more than to see the country, possibly the world. Anything but stay in the tiny hamlet of Windsor Falls. Ironically, he had made his way across the country using the skills he learned at his father's knee. He worked construction wherever he landed for more than a few days. And he had loved it. Until Connor died.

He hadn't been here when Connor died. He was living in Houston, working on a skyscraper. He had pretty much settled there, as much as Brendan could settle anywhere. He had caught the first flight home to be with his family after the loss.

A few weeks later, when Elizabeth had fled to California and everyone else was expected to get on with their lives, Brendan had returned to Houston. Back to his job and life. But being back in Windsor Falls had reminded him of what a wonderful place it was to grow up. Houston, while beautiful and interesting, was impersonal to him. He had friends. Guys from the crew. But he didn't have anyone with whom he shared a history.

And that's when he met Jillian. The blonde, leggy oil heiress was exactly what he needed. Someone to belong to. Someone to build a life with. Or so he thought.

Brendan peered in at Abby, still asleep. When he looked at her, thoughts of Jillian evaporated like so much smoke. The past was behind him and no longer mattered. His daughters were everything to him. He worried about his daughters not having a mother. But they had positive female role models surrounding them. His sisters, Katie and Riley, and now Elizabeth, were the best aunts two little girls could ever ask for. And it went without saying that they were the light of his mother's life. Abby and Kerry would be fine without a mom. He would see to it.

An image of Charlie, unbidden and unwanted, flashed before his eyes. Brendan cringed when he thought about how he had spoken to her. There was a very large apology, and flower buying, in his future. But that meant seeing her again. Breathing in her scent. Wishing he could run his fingers through her silky hair.

He wasn't a monk by any means. He made sure his needs were met on occasion. But he kept it simple. He would never marry again, so he didn't bring any women into his daughters' lives.

But that didn't stop thoughts of Charlie from crowding his mind. Even under the dirt and torn clothes, her beauty shined. He had noticed. He might not do relationships, but he wasn't dead. But he could not avoid Charlie. Her friendship with Elizabeth made her a fixture in his life.

"Daddy?" came Abby's plaintive question from the car.

Glad for the reprieve, he jogged over. He opened her door. "Hello, Princess Abby. Awake from your slumber I see."

She giggled. "You're so silly Daddy."

Undoing the straps, Brendan lifted her out of the booster. He carried her as though she were made of the most fragile glass. He climbed the few stairs and strode to the door. Balancing his precious cargo carefully, he dug his keys out of his pocket and opened the door.

"Now, let's find you a comfortable spot." He placed her on the sofa and grabbed a pillow for under her new cast. He picked up the remote and turned on the TV, turning to The Disney Channel. Both girls loved it.

"What else can I get for you, Abby? Maybe something to drink? Is your arm hurting?" Elizabeth had given her some mild pain medication in the ER along with instructions to use ibuprofen as needed.

"Maybe some juice."

She was already enveloped in the adventures of the fictional characters. Brendan was relieved that she seemed unaffected by today's events. He hoped that continued.

"Juice, it is, my lady," he joked as he walked into the kitchen. Her laughter trickled after him.

*****

Charlie grabbed the gift bag from the passenger floor before getting out of her car. Her mouth dropped open when she saw the breathtaking vista that made up Elizabeth's front yard. The Blue Ridge Mountains stretched behind their home, built in a clearing. Beyond the front yard, the town of Windsor Falls lay below them in a valley. Elizabeth had mentioned the privacy they enjoyed. The nearest neighbor lived at least a mile away.

A door opened, and she turned towards the house. She spied her pregnant friend, flanked by three handsome dogs in assorted colors. Tongues lolling, the trio bounded up to her, all vying for attention. Charlie had always loved dogs but was never allowed to have one as a child. Too messy, according to her mother. She clapped her hands, laughing with delight, as all three swamped her.

A sharp whistle broke the chaos, and she whipped her head around as all three furry butts hit the ground. Sam, whom she only knew from pictures, came walking out of the garage toward her. Elizabeth stepped off the front porch.

"They can be a bit much en masse," he joked. "I'm Sam, by the way."

"I'd know you anywhere, Sam," she exclaimed and threw her arms around him. "Elizabeth talks about you all the time. I just know we're going to be great friends."

"She's my heart," he stated, forever gaining a place in Charlie's. Elizabeth deserved nothing short of the very best after the tragedies she endured. Sam was it.

"Okay, you two, break it up. Peanut's hungry." Elizabeth had a hand on her rounded belly. Charlie averted her eyes. Smiling through her pain, she laced one arm through Sam's outstretched one and let him lead her to the house.

She turned her head, trying to take in of the natural wonder that surrounded them. "You guys picked a slice of heaven."

Elizabeth met her at the porch with a big hug before leading her inside. "Sam did a fantastic job before I got here. I'm just adding some touches."

"Don't let her modesty fool you, Charlie. She made this house into a home."

The love that flowed between the two warmed her heart. For a moment, she felt the briefest twinge. Something akin to envy. She tamped it down. "Well, kudos to both of you. This place is gorgeous." She handed the bag to her friend. "A little house warming present for you."

"You didn't have to do that," protested Elizabeth. "But I'm glad you did." She placed the bag on the breakfast bar and pulled out the paper. She pulled out a small clay bowl painted in earthen tones. "I love it," she cried before hugging Charlie again.

Sam laughed as tears flowed down his wife's face. "Hormones."

"I made the mistake of looking in that small craft store that's down the street from the inn. Wow! I could do some serious damage in there."

Elizabeth clapped her hands. "This & That; a favorite of mine."

"And we have the credit card bills to prove it," joked Sam.

Elizabeth swatted him. "Unfortunately, he's not kidding. I went to school with Lainie, the woman who owns it. She's an artist herself but also sells items from other local craftsmen. Besides the fact that everything is gorgeous, I love supporting local businesses."

"Oh good. Another reason to shop there. As if I needed one."

Elizabeth gestured to the kitchen table. "Since the sun will be setting soon, we decided to eat in here. You'll be surprised how the temperature drops after the sun goes down."

"This is perfect," Charlie murmured and took her seat.

Elizabeth sat across from her and made a face when Sam carried over a salad and placed it on the table. "He thinks I shouldn't lift anything."

"That's not true. I figure you're not exactly resting at work, so I like to spoil you at home." Sam joined them, a smile on his handsome face.

"Do you hear me complaining?" Elizabeth quipped. She squeezed his hand before placing a napkin on her lap.

Charlie took some salad and reached for the dressing. "So, Elizabeth, tell me about your boss. I'm excited about the interview tomorrow." She winked at Sam. "It helps to have a leg up."

Elizabeth laughed. "Not that you'll need it. The interview is a mere formality with your experience. Especially after today. Rescuing a local child from certain death goes a long way."

Charlie grimaced. "One has nothing to do with the other. And I was in the right place at the right time."

"Dr. Chamberlain is wonderful. He moved here from Boston a few years before I returned home. Eric leads by example. You couldn't ask for a better director."

"Sounds good," Charlie murmured between bites of her salad.

"Are you sure about relocating here, Charlie? I love Windsor Falls, but then it's my hometown since I was six. But it's not Chicago or Los Angeles. And I know it's not far from Charleston, and certainly closer than Chicago or Los Angeles, but wouldn't you rather take a position near your family? Not that I'm trying to talk you out of it, mind you. I was thrilled when you agreed to interview."

Charlie set down her fork. "I'm over big cities. I want to know my patients. And you've met my family, Elizabeth, so you get it. Windsor Falls is perfect. Close but not enough to encourage regular visits."

Sam laughed as he took a drink of his tea. "That bad?"

"Yes", she answered without hesitation. She wiped her mouth on her napkin. "Let me say this. I love my parents. But we get along better when I'm not local."

"Her parents are a challenge," offered Elizabeth.

Charlie laughed at Elizabeth's diplomacy. "That's putting it lightly."

Sam cleared their salad plates and came back with a large bowl of pasta. "Not allergic to shrimp I hope." He grinned. "A bit late to ask, though."

"Better than after I took a bite," answered Charlie. "But, no, I'm not allergic."

They passed the pasta bowl before conversation continued. "Charlie, when are you ever going to tell us about your adventures in Africa? I know from the news that you guys had some problems with local rebels."

Charlie's hand faltered ever so slightly as she raised her fork to her mouth. Progress considering where she had started. Several months after the incident, she was finally able to think about that time without wanting to curl up in a ball and cry.

"We faced stiff opposition from rival tribes." She stopped to take a breath, aware of the wobble in her voice. She cleared her throat. "It's not that I wasn't aware of the situation when I volunteered to go. The organization does an excellent job outlining the potential risks involved. But somehow, I thought we'd be safe. We didn't have an agenda. Other than to help people."

Elizabeth put down her fork. Rising gracefully despite her pregnancy, she walked around the table and took the seat next to Charlie. "I get the feeling there's more to the story."

Charlie tried to swallow the unshed tears that threatened to block her throat. She had never told the whole story to anyone. And though Elizabeth was her best friend, she wouldn't be doing so now either. Charlie didn't even allow herself to *think* about it most days. That was how she dealt with what happened to her. To her team. Although the physical scars were fading, the emotional ones remained the toughest to conquer. The loss she had suffered was the toughest blow of all. No, she wasn't ready to tell her story. She might never be.

She shook her head instead. "Another time. I'd much rather talk about this baby you're having." She smiled as though she meant the words. She didn't want to talk about the baby either, but it beat the alternative. Thankfully, Elizabeth was too awash in hormones to notice. She returned to her seat.

Sam moved his chair closer to his wife's and wrapped an arm around her shoulders. Charlie liked him that much more. Elizabeth's bright blue eyes shone with happiness. "At first, I felt overwhelmed." She turned her gaze to Sam, stroking his cheek. "After what happened last time, I was terrified. We didn't tell anyone until after the holidays when I really started to show. I, we, just wanted to be sure."

"That's understandable, Elizabeth. Who wouldn't be concerned after the loss you suffered? But you're healthy, right? Everything's fine with the baby?"

Her blissful smile told Charlie all she needed to know. "Yes." She made a funny face. "Of course, because of my history and 'advanced age', I'm considered high-risk. But I'm okay with that. It just means closer monitoring and more appointments. All good."

"I'm so glad." And she was. Really. If she wanted what Elizabeth had, that only made her human. She could deal. But not tonight. She stood. "I'm so glad to be here and to see your new home. But this day has taken its toll. I want to be sharp for my interview tomorrow."

Elizabeth stood, confusion drifting across her face. "Ok, sure. Didn't you want to stay for dessert at least? Coffee?"

"Thank you, no. Sleep is all I need." That wasn't far from the truth. Sleep had not been her friend since Africa. Nightmares were her constant companion. And though things were getting better in that area, she still had a long way to go. Charlie hugged Sam goodbye and Elizabeth walked her to the door. When they reached it, Elizabeth enfolded Charlie in her arms and held on tightly.

"You can tell me anything, Charlie," Elizabeth whispered in her ear.

She wasn't a crier, but tears sprang to her eyes now. Afraid to speak, she nodded. And hugged Elizabeth back. She left before she blubbered all over her friend.

On the drive back to the B&B, she thought about Elizabeth's parting words. She was the one person Charlie could tell. And the knot that she carried in her chest unfurled just the slightest. She wasn't ready to discuss it, but it helped to know she had someone with whom she could.

The next morning, Charlie awoke with the dawn. She felt optimistic. She'd slept better last night than she had since Africa. And today was a major step towards starting the next chapter in her life. To that end, she pulled on fresh running clothes and her sneakers.

Once outside, she stretched and set off. Despite the soaking bath, various muscles still ached. Through her recovery, she had worked her way up to a slow jog. Today, walking would be fine. The sun was rising, washing Windsor Falls in a rosy hue. She walked through the quiet streets, watching the town slowly came awake. There was a charm to Winsor Falls, with its center green and gazebo. Cute shops bordered the green.

She turned a corner, and a delicious aroma drew her to De Luca's Bakery. The sign said open, so Charlie walked in. *Yum!* Her mouth watered. *How to choose?* She heard the bell over the door jingle behind her as someone entered the bakery.

"I recommend everything," came a deep voice.

She spun around. Brendan, dressed for work and smelling of sin. The sight of him wasn't bad either. His hair, just this side of shaggy, begged her fingers to run through it. His blue eyes peered all the way into her soul. He seemed to study her. Try to figure her out. Her belly clenched, her palms dampened, and she resisted the urge to wipe them on her running shorts.

"Good to know." She flashed him her most winning smile. "Any chance you could narrow it down a bit?"

"He's right, it's all fabulous. I know because I made most of it." A woman burst through the swinging doors to the back room. "Hi, I'm Kat. My family owns the bakery. I don't know you, so you're either visiting or new in town."

The force of Kat's personality struck her. She couldn't help but smile in return. "I'm actually both. Maybe." She stopped and laughed at herself. "Let me try that again. I'm Charlie Avery, and I'm visiting. But, I am hoping to be your newest resident. I have an interview at the hospital today."

"Welcome, Charlie Avery. You'll love Windsor Falls. I know I do. And good luck today."

"That's not all she is, Kat. This is the woman who rescued Abby."

Like a whirlwind, Kat ran around the side of the counter. Before Charlie knew what hit her, Kat pulled her into a huge hug. "Why didn't you tell me who you were? You saved Abby. You're the town hero."

The skin of Charlie's face grew tight. *When would this ever die down?* "I'm happy I could help." She glanced at the display case. "May I have a cheese Danish please?"

"For you? Anything!"

Kat went back around and chose one of the delicacies for her. "It's on the house."

Brendan reached for his wallet at the same time. "Kat, if you don't mind, this is on me."

She didn't know who to address first. "Kat, I appreciate that. But it's not necessary." She avoided looking at Brendan until the last possible second, afraid she would fall into his clear, blue eyes. "Brendan, that's not necessary."

"It's the least I can do." He stepped closer, a five-dollar bill in his outstretched hand. If she wanted to, Charlie could reach out and touch the muscles in his upper arm. And she wanted to. Which is why she took a large step backwards under the guise of giving him some room. Men like Brendan were dangerous. They made you want things. Feel things. And she wasn't in a position to be wanting nor feeling.

Taking the pastry from Kat, she turned to leave. "I appreciate that, Brendan. Nice meeting you Kat. I'm sure I'll be seeing you." She all but bolted out the door in her haste to put distance between herself and Brendan.

*****

Kat laughed at the look on Brendan's face. "Not used to a beautiful woman wanting to flee from you?"

Lost in thoughts of Charlie and his gut-level reaction to her, he missed what Kat had said. "Sorry. I didn't hear you."

"Of course, you didn't. You were too busy watching Charlie leave. This ought to be fun." Glee rippled in her voice.

Annoyance flashed through him. He loved his hometown. And he liked Kat. Always had. But the everyone knowing your business part of Windsor Falls he could do without. He decided to play dumb. "What should be fun, Kat? Did I miss something?"

She cocked her head. Amusement lit up her chocolate brown eyes. "That's your story, huh? You have no idea about the attraction sparking between the two of you? Okay. Got it." She smirked at him. There was no other word for it. "Let me know how that works for you."

He grabbed the bagel he had come in for and left, not bothering to say goodbye. *Women!* There wasn't any attraction between them. The thought slowed his step for a second. Charlie was a beautiful woman. There was no denying that. Legs a mile long and eyes that a man could escape into. Who wouldn't find that attractive? Not that he was interested.

That last thought brought him to a halt, feet from his truck. He turned his head in the direction he figured she had taken back to the B&B. Small town life had its advantages. Everyone knew where the 'hero doctor' was staying. Tossing the bag with his bagel through the opened window of his pickup, he took off at a jog after her.

She was walking not running, but those thoroughbred legs of hers could move. Charlie was two blocks away when he finally caught up to her. Not thinking, he grabbed her arm. Brendan wasn't prepared for her reaction.

She whirled on him, hands up, a scream ripped from her throat. It was her eyes that got him though. They were saucers in her too pale face. Clearly, he should have called her name first or announced his presence, but this was over the top. She looked terrified.

"What is wrong with you?" She stepped back, wrapping her arms around her midsection. Her chest heaved. He felt like a jackass and wanted to help her somehow, but Brendan was afraid to touch her again.

"I'm sorry," he muttered. "I was trying to get your attention, not scare the life out of you."

"Do you always sneak up on unsuspecting women?" Her implication would have annoyed him. Except for the fear that shone in her eyes.

Brendan stepped back also, even though every instinct told him to enfold her in his arms. "No, I don't. And I didn't mean to scare you. I wanted to apologize for my behavior yesterday in the ER." He shook his head. "Now I owe you two apologies."

Something in his tone must have gotten through to her. Her expression softened, losing its guardedness. She faltered for a second, seemingly wanting to step closer to him yet unsure of her own actions. Finally, she laid a hand upon his bicep. "No, Brendan, I'm the one who should be sorry. I overreacted. You startled me."

He should respond. But for the life of him he had no idea what to say. He could only focus on the warmth that spread like a wildfire from her touch. He looked at his arm where her hand still lay and then up into her eyes. She must have felt it too, for she jerked her hand back as though burned. They stood there, staring at each other. Brendan's heart thumped wildly in his chest.

He finally found his voice and managed to string a few words together. "I should have never grabbed you like that. I'm sorry."

Her smile was thin and didn't quite reach her eyes. "Never mind. It's fine." She glanced away from him. "But I have to go. My interview is at nine, and I still have to shower and dress. Thank you again for the Danish. It was delicious." She turned and left, walking away at a fast clip.

Brendan stood there, rooted to the spot, and watched until she walked out of his view. Only then did he return to his truck. He waved to Kat in the bakery window, even though she was clearly gloating. He climbed into his truck, recalling the look of sheer terror in Charlie's eyes.

He had seen that look one other time. He'd been working with his crew when someone fired a nail gun. Just another day on the site, but his friend Jason froze. Beads of sweat formed on his forehead. His chest heaved with ragged breaths. Brendan peeled the hammer from his clammy hands. Brendan took one look at Jason's glassy eyes and sent the others to an early lunch.

Then he sat at his friend's side. It had taken almost an hour before Jason spoke. Told him about the three tours in Afghanistan. He'd only been home a few months and was still adjusting. Brendan didn't know at the time that Jason had PTSD.

That had been a few years ago, and Jason was doing better these days. They never discussed the incident, but Jason had taken a leave of absence right after it. When he returned a few weeks later, he assured Brendan that he was getting help and that he would be fine on the jobsite. In return, Brendan had assured Jason he would always have a job.

He didn't know anything about Charlie Avery. Elizabeth had mentioned her last year, but he hadn't really listened. He had always assumed Charlie was a he, just from the name, right up until the wedding last fall. 'He' turned out to be a 'she' who would have been the maid of honor except that she wasn't there. For the life of him, he couldn't remember why.

He wondered if Elizabeth knew about her friend's condition. But it wasn't his tale to tell. What happened to Charlie? Where had she been last Fall? He already didn't want to be thinking of her at all. He found her far too tempting. This kept her in his mind even more. Not what he needed.

Chapter Four

Dr. Eric Chamberlain had turned out to be everything that Elizabeth said. And more. The interview was more of a conversation. Charlie had been completely at ease, despite the rough start to the day. Something she had yet to even process. Africa had taught her that neat little trick. Compartmentalizing things in her brain.

Eric had not mentioned yesterday's incident other than to ask about her well-being. She was grateful for that. They discussed her experience, both in Chicago and Los Angeles. She was pleased to find Elizabeth had been right. Eric was easy going and personable.

He hadn't asked, so Charlie brought up Africa. Without going into detail, she discussed her work there. And that things ended badly. Eric now knew that she'd spent the past few months recovering in Charleston. She assured him that she was fit for duty. An hour later, Charlie had a job offer. She accepted on the spot.

Elizabeth was working day shift again, and Charlie had promised to stop by when she finished. After leaving Eric's office, she walked down the hall and into the heart of the ER. Elizabeth sat at a computer terminal, documenting someone's care. As if sensing her presence, she lifted her gaze and smiled at her old friend.

"Seems like you're stuck with me," Charlie said with an answering grin.

"Yay!" Elizabeth hauled herself up out of the chair. Not an easy feat for someone in their last trimester. She pulled Charlie into a hug. "I never doubted it. Or you."

Charlie hugged her back, thankful for this wonderful person in her life. And the new opportunity. She loved what she had seen of the town and was impressed with the friendliness of its people. She could be happy here. She *would* be happy here.

Elizabeth pulled back and smiled into Charlie's face. "I'm so thrilled! We're finally back together again. No more Skype. No more email. I'd offer to take you to a celebratory lunch, but I'll be swamped by then."

The department looked empty, with only one or two treatment rooms occupied. But she had been an ER doc long enough to know that could change in the blink of an eye. The same way your life could. "No worries. We have time."

"That we do, my friend. Tell me the details. When do you start? Where are you going to live?"

Charlie laughed at her friend's enthusiasm, even as it warmed her chilled heart. She had made a good choice. Being here, in this charming small town, was a fresh start for her. A place to put the past behind her. A place to heal. "I asked for a little time to get situated, which works since they have to credential me. As for the rest, I haven't a clue. I'm booked in at the B&B for another eleven days. That gives me time to find something more permanent."

Elizabeth shook her head. "You have to come stay with Sam and me. There's more than enough room."

She knew that Elizabeth meant what she said. It wasn't a hollow offer. But she couldn't take her up on it. "I appreciate that, but no thanks." At her friend's crestfallen look, she rushed on to explain. "You're so sweet to offer, but you're also still a newlywed. And I love the B&B. It's right in town, and I can walk anywhere. I'm going to start looking for something else. Rent for a while, until I can figure out what I want long term."

Elizabeth's face brightened. "I can still help you. Katie moved in with Flynn. You haven't met them yet, but you will at Sunday dinner. Anyway, Katie owns a lovely townhome that she's thinking about keeping as a rental property. It's only a block or two from the B&B, on the other side of the town square."

"Brilliant! I have to tell you, I really wasn't looking forward to living in an apartment again." She wrinkled her nose. "Not to sound like a diva, but a girl needs her space."

Elizabeth laughed. "You are the furthest thing from a diva I've ever met. I don't think you should worry about anyone mistaking you for one. And I know what you mean. After being in our new home, I can't imagine ever going back to a condo like I had in LA."

"Exactly. That sounds great. I look forward to meeting Katie, and the rest of the clan, on Sunday." She picked up her keys from the counter. "I'm going to head back to the B&B. I'd like to change before I break the news to Mom." She rolled her eyes.

"I don't envy you that. That woman scares me."

Charlie shook her head. "I'm still waiting for them to tell me that I'm adopted. I'll see you later." She turned and left the department.

Sliding on her sunglasses, Charlie left the medical center. She resisted jumping up and down with excitement. It was official. She had a new job and a new life. For the first time in longer than she could remember, she felt settled.

Chicago had been an amazing learning opportunity. Charlie was grateful for the experience. But it had never been home. She didn't like big, impersonal cities. And the weather alone was reason enough to leave. She loved growing up in Charleston, with its lovely architecture and Southern charm. But it also had her parents. Windsor Falls was charming and small enough to feel like she would belong.

She was still musing about the possibilities in her new hometown when she arrived back at the Blue Iris. She parked her car and headed inside, intent on changing from her stuffy suit to capris and flip flops. With the rest of the day ahead of her and no plans, Charlie couldn't wait to get outside and explore the town. Brendan Fitzgerald waiting for her in the lobby was the last think she expected.

Before she could react, Lorna leapt from behind the desk. "I told him that I couldn't release the identity of any of our guests," she huffed. Her small, wire-rimmed glasses had slid to the end of her nose, giving Lorna the look of an outraged librarian. "But he insisted on waiting for you." The look she shot Brendan was meant to chastise. He grinned instead.

Brendan unfurled himself from a deep wing-backed chair near the fireplace. He approached Charlie slowly, as if he didn't want to startle her again. "I explained to Lorna here that I already knew you were a guest. And that we know each other."

It might have been her imagination, but he seemed to purr the word 'know', giving it a whole other level of meaning. His face remained passive. No burning look of desire. No raised eyebrow. No crooked smile suggesting at anything more intimate. But tell that to her body. She felt a warm glow spread throughout her limbs. Brendan smiled at her, one dimple appearing at the right side of his mouth. The look was both boyish and hot at the same time. Enough so to make her wish for a glass of sweet tea. She needed to get a grip.

"What are you doing here?" Charlie forced herself not to wince at her own tone. If she wasn't careful, she would end up sounding like Lorna.

"How about lunch? It's the least I can do." He looked her up and down before gesturing to his work boots and clothes. "Obviously someplace casual."

This was a bad idea. But what the hell. She smiled and nodded, answering him before she could chicken out. "I need to change." She gestured to her suit, mirroring Brendan. "If you knew me at all, you'd understand that this is not my normal apparel. I'll be right back." She removed her heels and dashed up the stairs, her pulse bounding. And not from the physical exertion.

Letting herself into her room, she hesitated for a moment. What was she doing? Having lunch with Brendan was dangerous when being near him set her skin on fire. She didn't need more complications, and that might be Brendan's middle name. But the last few months of her life had taken their toll. She needed something fun and exciting. And it was just lunch. Not a marriage proposal.

Without giving herself time for more doubts, she shed her hated business suit. Pulling her hair out of its complicated bun, her professional demeanor melted away, making her feel younger and lighter. She grabbed a pair of capris and a short-sleeved peasant blouse to match. She stepped into a pair of espadrilles and slid her phone into her back pocket.

She headed back downstairs within five minutes. Brendan rose at the site of her. "Wow. That might be a record for a female to get changed," he joked. She laughed but didn't miss his gaze sweeping over her.

"Should I be insulted on behalf of women everywhere?"

He pulled open the front door, saluting Lorna on their way out. "That was meant to be a compliment. I have two sisters, so it's an observation based on years of experience."

She raised one perfect, blonde brow. "And that makes you an expert?"

He didn't rise to the challenge in her voice. Just grinned. "I know some things."

She turned to him, grabbing his arm. She chose to ignore the warmth under her hand. "Guess what!"

Brendan stopped, grinning at her. "Are you by any chance the newest ER doctor at the medical center?"

"Huh. How'd you know? Did Elizabeth call you? She's the only one I told."

He laughed and pointed to her face. "It might have been the grin from ear to ear. Congratulations. And welcome to Windsor Falls officially."

"Thank you." Charlie pulled her hand from his arm, missing the warmth already.

They walked in companionable silence for a bit. The scent of his skin was clean male, not overpriced cologne. She preferred that. Their arms swung at their sides. His passed closely to hers, making Charlie miss the feel of him.

"What would you like?"

She would have tripped over her own feet if not for his strong arms surrounding her. Her face flamed. "Like?" she squeaked.

"For lunch," he answered with a sly grin.

"Oh, anything is fine with me. I'm not shy about food. Ask Elizabeth."

He turned to her, his eyes hidden behind dark glasses. Even though she couldn't see them, she felt his gaze on her already overheated skin. "I love a woman who can eat. There's nothing more annoying than having a meal with someone who orders a salad every time. And then only picks at it."

"Sounds like that might describe someone you know. One of those pesky sisters again?"

The dimple she had come to enjoy disappeared. His face became a mask. "No."

The air between them chilled. "I wasn't trying to pry. If I said something I shouldn't have…"

The muscles in his jaw loosened. "No. I'm sorry. I was referring to my ex-wife, Jillian." He practically spat the word.

"Oh." She had wondered when Abby said they didn't have a mom. Charlie had thought their mother had died. Apparently not.

Brendan whipped the dark shades off his face and placed a hand on her arm. "I'm not one of those guys who goes on and on about his ex. I was married for about a minute. It was a bad match. But I got the girls out of it, so I don't regret it."

She returned his direct stare. "You don't get to be our age without the ghosts of relationships past. And you don't have to tell me about Jillian either."

Brendan ran a hand through his thick hair. Charlie watched, wishing it was her hand. His hair looked thick and soft to the touch. She had the oddest urge to find out. Instead, she put her hands in her pockets.

"You're right. I don't have to. It was years ago. Jillian and I had nothing in common. Her family had more money than God. Needless to say, they were less than impressed with me."

They continued walking, but the ease between them was ruined. After a few storefronts, he paused before the door to a small café. There were a few wrought iron tables in a courtyard at the side. "Inside or outside? Your choice."

His tone had evened out. The tenseness in his body gone. She smiled. "Outside if you don't mind. If Windsor Falls is anything like Charleston, then I won't be able to dine al fresco for very much longer."

"That's for sure." Brendan flagged a passing waitress who told them to sit anywhere. He led the way to a small table for two at the front. His hand was warm at the small of her back. She felt it all the way up and down her spine. "Is this okay."

"Perfect." She placed her purse on a chair. "I'm going to go in and freshen up. Could you order me an ice water with lime please?"

"Of course. Take your time."

She smiled and walked into the café, stopping to ask the same waitress for the location of the rest room.

*****

Brendan nodded to the waitress who approached the table. She handed him two menus, took their drink order and left. Since he came here often, Brendan didn't open his. Instead, he thought about Charlie. Her distress from this morning had evaporated. She hadn't made any reference to it, and it was beginning to feel like a dream.

Then there was her beauty. More than one man had given her a second, or third, look as they passed on the walk here. She hadn't seemed to notice. Jillian had been obsessed with her looks. She lived for the adoration and open stares of other men. Craved it. Jillian brought a whole new meaning to the word vain.

Not Charlie. She wore her beauty like an appendage; aware of its presence but not focused on it. Yet she was one of the most gorgeous woman he had ever seen. Tall and willowy, he wouldn't have to bend so far down to reach for a kiss. Not that he would be kissing her anytime soon. Or ever. She was Elizabeth's friend and now a full-time resident of Windsor Falls. Two strikes right there. She was off limits.

He sensed her before seeing her, a tingling at the back of his neck told him she had returned from the restroom. Brendan arose as she approached the table and pulled out her seat. But he did not touch her. No use in testing his resolve.

Her smile warmed his gut. And other areas lower. She was a ray of sunshine when she smiled. "Welcome back," he said. And immediately regretted it. He needed to keep this on a solid footing. Stick to the apology. And the thanks. Nothing personal could happen between them.

"Thanks." Charlie took the menu that he held out to her. She perused it for a moment before looking at him over the top of it. "What's good here?"

"Everything." He flashed her a smile. "I say that a lot but it's true. I know the owner. She's also the chef. I've never had a bad meal here."

"Damned with faint praise again, I see," exclaimed a woman in an apron who had appeared at their table.

Brendan stood and hugged her. "Claire, you know very well that I love everything you make."

"As well you should, since I'm brilliant in the kitchen." She turned to Charlie. "And who is this gorgeous creature? She's too beautiful for the likes of you, Brendan Fitzgerald."

"Claire Bonet, this is Charlie Avery. She's a friend of Elizabeth's and Windsor Fall's newest ER doctor. Charlie, Claire is the owner of the Sunshine Café. Claire and I went to school together."

Charlie extended her hand. "Lovely to meet you, Claire."

"Likewise, Charlie. Welcome to Windsor Falls. I'm sure you're going to love it here." She cocked her head a bit. "Is that a Low Country accent I detect?"

Charlie laughed. "Wow, you have a great ear. While I am Charleston born and bred, that hasn't been my home in many years."

Claire smiled, revealing even, white teeth. "I've always had a good ear for accents. Also, I was a bit of a vagabond prior to opening the Cafe."

"Claire is being modest. Something new for her. She graduated from the Culinary Institute of America before being a 'vagabond'. And by that, she means travelling the world to hone her craft."

Claire whacked him on the shoulder. "That much is true. I learned a lot from helpful people in many locations and brought their secrets back to my kitchen. But that's enough about me. What can I get for my new friend Charlie?"

"What do you recommend? I love to eat."

Claire rubbed her hands together. "Just what I want to hear. I've been working on an updated version of my gumbo. It's not on the menu yet, but I whipped up a batch this morning. How does that sound?"

Charlie patted her stomach. "That sounds heavenly."

"I'll have a bowl too, Claire," said Brendan.

"Of course, you will my friend. You'll eat whatever I bring you." She pointed a thumb at him. "Watch this one, Charlie. He's always been a bit of a problem. I'll be right back with some bread."

Charlie watched her move off before turning back to Brendan. "Wow, she's beautiful! She has the most perfect skin I've ever seen. I'd kill for that."

He could only stare at her. "You're kidding, right?" He had to remember to not let his jaw drop open. She thought someone else had the most beautiful skin ever? Hers was a true peaches and cream and flawless to his eye. Not that he was looking.

Charlie took a drink of her water. "Did you not see her skin? It's the perfect café au lait color. And those gorgeous braids."

He chose his words carefully. In his experience, questions like that could be a minefield. "I've known her all my life, so I know how gorgeous she is. Her father's family is from Louisiana, so Claire is half Creole."

"Ah. Is her mother Caucasian? That would explain the piercing blue eyes."

"She is. Her whole family still lives in town."

One corner of her mouth lifted, giving her a look of mischief. "So, what kind of trouble were you?"

To his chagrin, the back of his neck grew hot at her question. "Oh, you know, the usual boy stuff. Cutting up in class, etc." He took a sip of his drink. "Truth is, I had a bit of a crush on Claire for a few years in middle school. But she never had time for me."

"You have good taste."

She had no idea, he thought to himself. If Charlie had the slightest clue the direction his thoughts took, she wouldn't be smiling. "So, Abby is insisting that I bring you flowers, but I told her you're staying in the B&B and that lunch might be easier. She allowed that."

"I get the feeling Abby has quite a few opinions."

Brendan shook his head. "You have no idea. But seriously, lunch doesn't even begin to cover it. I can never thank you for saving Abby." He leaned forward while talking, placing his hands on either side of hers on the table. Still careful to not touch her. Being this close was dangerous enough.

"Abby alive and well in the world is thanks enough. She's a beautiful little girl. I'm thankful I was there to do something. Elizabeth can tell you what we see in our line of work every day. Sometimes the difference between life and death is pure, random luck."

Cold shuddered through him. She was right, which made him even more thankful. "I agree. Which leads me to my apology. I was so rude to you. That's not who I am." He would have said more, but she held up one slim hand.

"I know enough about you by now to know that's true. And you were being a scared Dad. That gets you some slack. If my child was injured and in the ER, I might have acted the very same way."

Brendan almost missed the fleeting wistfulness that crossed her face. It was brief but there nonetheless. He wondered at its meaning but didn't know her well enough to ask.

The waitress came then with two steaming bowls of gumbo. "Y'all must be royalty. She won't even let us taste it yet." She placed the bowls in front of each of them, along with a basket of corn bread. "Enjoy," she said and walked away.

Charlie leaned in and sniffed at the savory scent floating up from the bowls. "I'll warn you. I love to eat. I should be embarrassed by how much. But I'm not."

She brought a spoonful of the rich concoction to her mouth and blew on it. Watching her mouth pucker nearly sent him over the edge. He shifted to a more comfortable position in his seat and tried not to stare.

"Nothing wrong with enjoying your food."

"That's what I believe. I went out with a guy once who remarked about the amount of food I had eaten half way through the meal." She tossed her light blonde hair over one shoulder seemingly unperturbed by the comment.

"What could he have been thinking?"

She smiled. "That's what I wanted to know. But not enough to hang around. He seemed surprised when I left." She shrugged her shoulders.

He took a taste of his lunch and moaned. "Wow. Claire has outdone herself this time."

"Be sure to tell her, Brendan. You can't make remarks like 'I've never had a bad meal here.' You might get banned for life." She shuddered. "Then I'd have to come without you."

"I will. Since your food consumption is off the table, so to speak, what else can you tell me about yourself?" He wanted to ask her about what happened this morning. But although casual right now, he got the vibe she was a private person underneath the banter.

Charlie chewed and swallowed before answering. She reached for a piece of bread. "I'm quite boring. Born and raised in Charleston. I went to undergraduate at the University of South Carolina. Medical school at Tulane. I needed to get out of South Carolina. And then, off to Los Angeles for my residency. That was to piss off my mom, but the program was excellent. And I met Elizabeth, so well worth it."

"Sounds like you and your mother don't see eye to eye on things."

She put down the bread and leaned back in her chair. Storm clouds darkened her eyes. "I'm sorry. That's none of my business."

She waved a hand. "No worries. My mother and I, both of my parents really, have a difficult relationship. It's hard to hear, day in and day out, that you were never quite good enough."

She said it without any inflection, leading him to believe this was an old issue for her. He leaped to her defense. "You're a doctor. You spend your professional life caring for strangers. What's better than that?"

Charlie leaned forward and held out her hand, ticking off fingers as she spoke. "I'm not married. I'm too tall. I'm not a boy, much to my father's regret, but I'm not girly enough for my mother. I don't garden. Should I continue?"

She laughed, but he could tell in the lines of her face that the list had cost her something. "How about this? You're a doctor who saves lives. You're beautiful. You're fun to be with. You are kind and brave to people you don't even know. Don't those things matter?" So much for being objective.

Charlie's face suffused with color. She ducked her head before answering. "Of course, they do. To the right people. To me. I gave up caring about what they think a long time ago. Does it still hurt? Yes, of course it does. You never stop wanting your parents' approval. But I learned long ago that the things that interest my parents are all surface attributes. That couldn't matter to me less if I tried."

The passion in her voice made him like her even more. Against his better judgement, he took one of her hands in his. He rubbed a thumb over the back of it, both enjoying and fearing the warmth that spread up his arm. He didn't want to like her or be attracted to her, he reminded himself. He didn't need the complication of it. But her hand remained in his.

Charlie cleared her throat. "I'm going to need you to not fall in love with me."

She said it so seriously that, at first, he was struck by her words. But then he caught the gleam in her eye. And the slight quiver of her lips. And for a second, he felt disappointed.

He smiled at her and released her hand. "Well, that's a good thing to know up front. Here I was, all ready to fall in love with you."

"I know," she continued. "It happens a lot. Men can't help themselves. I'd hate to have to break your heart."

Her tongue was firmly planted in cheek. He ate more of his lunch. After wiping his mouth on the yellow, linen napkin, he spoke. "I have to say the same to you. Women are always begging me to marry them. But my heart is already taken. By two little girls."

She laughed, a silvery, tinkling noise that sent shivers across him. "And who could blame you? They are a delight. You're a lucky man, Brendan Fitzgerald."

"That I am. And I never forget it."

She finished her gumbo, swiping the last bits of liquid with her bread. "I told you I like to eat."

She wasn't apologizing for her appetite. He found it very refreshing. "I'm glad you enjoyed it. We have our fair share of excellent local restaurants."

"Well that's good news. I can get your heart started again, but cooking? Not so much. Just add that to the lengthy list of sins in my mother's eyes. Although, it's something I always wanted to learn. Maybe once I get settled in, I can take a class. I like to learn new things."

"Where are you going to live? Can't stay at The Blue Iris forever."

She shook her head. "I stopped in to see Elizabeth after my interview. She mentioned that your sister, Katie, might be looking to rent out her townhouse. That would work for the short term. I want to buy a house of my own. Something with a yard. I lived in a condo in Los Angeles and Chicago. That made me appreciate the idea of a yard."

"If you decide to build, Aidan can design your house and Fitzgerald Construction can build it," he quipped.

"I'll keep that in mind."

The waitress came and cleared their plates, leaving the bill. He grabbed it before she could think of doing so. "This is on me. Like I said, it's the least I could do."

"Then thank you very much. But this is the last time, Brendan Fitzgerald." Charlie leaned back in her chair, closed her eyes, tipping her face to the sun. He couldn't help but admire the long, slender column of her neck. He wanted to put his lips on it. Maybe nibble a bit. Instead he pulled his wallet from the pocket of his jeans to distract himself from such thoughts.

The waitress came back around, and he handed her the bill with some money. "Keep the change," he told her and she thanked him and told them to come again.

Brendan stood and came around the table to Charlie's chair, holding it for her as she stood.

When they were back on the sidewalk, he headed towards her B&B. She stopped him. "I'm going to do some window shopping. Thank you again for lunch. It was wonderful."

He slid his sunglasses into place from the top of his head. "I'm so glad you liked it, and you're welcome." He stood there, unsure of his next move. This wasn't a date, so kissing her wasn't expected. Thankfully. That might kill him. And yet the impulse to lean in, close the distance between them, rocked him. He pulled his keys from his pocket to occupy his hands. "I'm sure I'll be seeing you around."

"I'm sure you will. It's a pretty small town from what I've seen so far."

Neither moved away. They stood there, staring at each other, both frozen in place. Finally, feeling like a teenager again, Brendan broke eye contact. Muttering "See you" under his breath, he turned and walked away.

When he rounded the corner, Brendan shook his head. That had ended weirdly, kind of the adult version of 'no, you hang up first.' He lengthened his stride and headed back to the B&B to get his truck. At the last moment, he had wanted to kiss her. Just lean in and place his lips against hers. But he knew instinctively that a kiss wouldn't be enough.

Chapter Five

Charlie turned into the first store she came upon, a bookstore called Between the Covers. She loved to read, and even though she had an e-reader, she still loved the feel of an actual book in her hands. She read all kinds of books but preferred fiction. These days, Charlie read romance novels. After all, her personal life was devoid of romance and probably would remain so. And who didn't like a guaranteed happy ending?

"Hello. May I help you?"

She turned to see a woman maybe a few years older than herself, standing just a few feet away. She had a smile on her face and a name tag that read 'Jamie.'

"Hi. I need something to read. Guess I came to the right place." Could she be anymore lame? Brendan had scrambled her brain for sure. And he wasn't even here anymore.

"Since I only sell books, you did. May I help you find something?"

"Uh, romance. That's what I've been reading lately. To make up for the lack of it in my life."

Jamie stared at her for a long moment, during which Charlie curse her usual bluntness. Then Jamie burst out laughing.

Jamie led her to the right section. "I like your honesty. Too many women still hide their romance novels. Like it's crack or something." She stuck out her hand. "I'm Jamie, by the way."

"I'm Charlie and new to Windsor Falls." She shook Jamie's hand. "Nice to meet you. I'll be in here a lot."

Jamie clapped her hands. "Funny and buys books. I like you already." She pulled a flyer from a holder on the wall next to her. "Here's a list of upcoming events at Between the Covers. Maybe you can make one."

She glanced at the sheet, delighted to see reading groups and local author events. "Great! I'd love to meet some people."

"Well, Charlie new to Windsor Falls, you're in the right place." She gestured to the section, larger than Charlie had expected. "As you can see, you're not the only one lacking a romantic life. Let me know if you need anything else."

Jamie left her to peruse, and she turned to the shelves. There were so many to choose from. She ran a finger along the spines, searching out some of her favorite authors. Charlie had done a lot of reading at her parents' home. God knows she had the time. Other than physical therapy, there hadn't been a lot to do. Unless you counted accompanying her mother to her various charity luncheons. Charlie did not.

She selected the latest offerings from two of her favorite authors. She glanced around the store as she did. Between the Covers was a gem. The walls were painted in relaxing hues of blue and green. There were several overstuffed chairs that encouraged you to stay and read awhile. There was even a cheerful children's section for young readers. It made her think of Brendan's daughters and wonder if they liked to read.

She wandered to the register and placed her purchases on the counter. A loud thump and a mumbled string of curses came from below. A moment later, Jamie popped up, rubbing her head. When she spotted Charlie, her face reddened. "Oops, sorry. I had no idea you were there."

Charlie laughed. "That's okay. Interesting choice of swear words. Although, I'm not sure that last one is anatomically possible."

Jamie blinked at her from behind her glasses before laughing. "You're right. But I like the way it rolls off the tongue." She picked up the books and scanned each before putting them in a bag.

Charlie handed over her credit card. "I'm so glad I found this place. And I love the décor. I'll definitely be back."

"I'm so glad." She handed her a receipt to sign. "Oh, I put a reminder for the next book club meeting in your bag. You should check us out. It's always the second Wednesday of the month, which is next week. The meetings are held here. The group is small so far, but I think you might enjoy it. In fact, one of the books you just bought is the one we're reading currently." She named the first book Charlie had chosen.

"Sounds great. Thanks for inviting me. My schedule is up in the air, but I'll start reading that one in case I can make it." She picked up her bag. "It was nice meeting you, Jamie."

"Right back at ya," Jamie called.

She continued down the street, window shopping along the way. She came upon a building that looked like it held professional offices. One caught her eye. Dr. Tom Lowery, licensed psychologist. Before she could talk herself out of it, she entered the building and took the steps to the third floor. Her heart beat like a humming bird's wings in her chest when she reached his office. It wasn't from taking the steps. She grasped the bag containing her new books in both hands, her knuckles white with the effort. Her palms were slick against the plastic.

The door opened, revealing an older man. He had small, wire-rimmed glasses and thinning white hair. A kindly smile wreathed his face. "Oh, I was heading out to grab some lunch. May I help you?"

Words wouldn't come out past the lump in her throat. She shook her head and turned to leave.

"I could stand to lose a few pounds anyway," Dr. Lowery called. He held open his door, and she walked into the office. He led the way into the inner office.

Taking a seat, he gestured to the other furniture, a love seat and a full-sized couch. "Sit wherever you like."

She did so without thought, choosing the love seat. "My name is Charlie Avery. I need help. I'm sorry for showing up like this."

"Okay, Charlie, that's a good place to start. And don't be sorry." He picked up a legal pad and pen from the table next to him. "Do you mind if I take notes?"

"No." She took a deep breath, trying to organize her thoughts so that they didn't all come out in one big clump. "I'm a physician. I was just hired full time at the medical center."

"Well, Dr. Avery, you know that anything discussed here is confidential. I was on staff there but retired last year. This practice is part time for me; a way to stay sharp and out of my wife's hair at the same time."

She smiled, feeling more relaxed than she thought she would. "I had a few sessions last month in Charleston. That's where I'm from. We, the therapist and I, didn't connect. Or at least I didn't. It didn't help, so I stopped going. Then I moved here."

He nodded his head. "Wise decision. Psychologists are like everyone else, Charlie, good, bad, and ugly. I'm actually brilliant," They both laughed at his joke. "Some not so much. To get something out of this, we need to build a rapport. More than anything, you must trust me. Sounds like that didn't happen last time for you. Maybe you could start by telling me what brings you here."

She swallowed hard. She liked him instantly and felt more comfortable with him already than in several weeks with her past therapist. But this was still a painful process. She had survived the past few months by not talking about what had happened to her. Despite knowing that wasn't healthy.

"I have PTSD. I thought it was behind me. For the most part." She closed her eyes for a moment. "But this morning, someone grabbed me by the arm to get my attention, and I overreacted. I yelled at him, when all he did was touch me"

Dr. Lowery put the pad and pen back on the table and leaned forward, grasping his hands between his knees. "He didn't just touch you. He frightened you. And you know that part of PTSD is the hypervigilance and exaggerated startle response. I have treated individuals with PTSD in the past. In my experience, Cognitive Processing Therapy, or CPT, works best. And that's either with or without medications. We can also discuss other therapies such as Eye Movement Desensitization and Reprocessing. Are you familiar with either of those?"

"Only from what I've read on-line. I had some physical recovery to do. After the incident." A harsh laugh escaped her. "That's how I refer to it, 'the incident'. Somehow that makes it better. Takes away the trauma."

"We do what we can to survive. From what I can see, you're holding it together well. But you can do better than that. And I'm here to help you."

The two talked, with Charlie telling him the bare facts of what had happened in Africa. She was shocked to see almost an hour had passed when he glanced at his watch. "I have another patient soon, so I'm going to stop here. Would you like to set up an appointment?"

She would and she did. She left his office promising to come back next week and feeling lighter than she had in quite a while. But she was also exhausted. A nap in her comfy bed at The Blue Iris seemed like a great idea.

She slipped in the front door without any notice and escaped to her room. Once inside, she turned down the air conditioning to freezing. She stripped to her underwear before sliding under the covers. She hoped to fall right to sleep, but images of Brendan came to mind. With his daughter in the ER. Sitting across from her at lunch today. The way the cotton of his Fitzgerald Construction shirt had stretched across the muscles of his chest. Her fingers had begged to touch him.

She blew out a breath and rolled over onto her side. She winced at the muscles in her abdomen protesting. Months later, she still felt the occasional twinge. A souvenir from the emergency surgery that saved her life. Knowing they were only internal adhesions didn't make them hurt any less. But that pain lessened with time.

Charlie flipped the pillow to find the cool side and laid her face against it. Part of therapy would be discussing, in detail, what had happened to them over there. What had happened to her. What she had lost. How her life had been changed in the blink of an eye. How her plans, the ones that involved marriage and children, had disappeared in a puff of smoke. This was exactly the reason she had joked with Brendan today about not falling in love with her. She might look put together on the outside. But on the inside, she was still a mess. Terrible dreams often interrupted her sleep. She never knew what might send her into a full-blown panic attack. So, tempting as thoughts of Brendan might be, that's all they could be. Thoughts. Fantasies. Desires. She was better off not getting involved with anyone right now. Maybe never. With that depressing thought echoing in her head, she fell into a deep sleep.

*****

Brendan walked into his parents' home, herding the girls with him. "Now remember ladies, Abby needs to be careful with her cast and not go banging it on stuff. Got it?" Kerry and Abby yelled 'yes, Daddy' in tandem before running to the basement door and going down the steps. Their cousin Liam, Donovan's son, was probably down there playing video games already.

He continued into the kitchen. "Something smells amazing." He stopped in the doorway, watching the scene in front of him. It never got old. His mother, Maggie, stirring something in a pot on the stove while humming an old Irish tune. His sisters, Riley and Katie, carried plates and silverware into the dining room. Brendan walked up to his mother and gave her a resounding kiss on her upturned cheek.

"There's my favorite son. How are you today, Brendan?"

He laughed before replying. It was common knowledge that Maggie always called whichever of her children she was alone with her 'favorite.' They never took offense. Maggie had a heart the size of Ireland itself. She had more than enough love for all her children. And their respective spouses and offspring.

"I'm great, Mom. But look at you. Color in your cheeks and looking like a thirty-year-old."

Maggie's cheeks turned a pretty pink at the compliment. "Oh, go on with you. No, really. Go on. Tell me more." She winked and turned back to the stove. "Where are my angels?"

"Down in the basement with Liam. What's for dinner? Could that be your world-famous pot roast I smell?"

"Someone's been kissing the Blarney Stone I see. You know very well it's pot roast. And it's not world famous." She winked at him. "Just in Windsor Falls."

Brendan heard the front door open. "That'll be Elizabeth and Sam. See if they need any help," his mother ordered.

Brendan left the kitchen, stifling a chuckle, and headed for the front door. Elizabeth was one of the most capable people he knew. But Maggie, and the rest of the family, had been treating her like spun glass because of her pregnancy. He was still musing about that when awareness prickled his skin. He stopped in his tracks at the sight of Charlie standing in the living room. He hadn't known she would be here, and the unexpected sight of her was a punch to the gut. Even though he hadn't seen her since their lunch a few days ago, thoughts of her had kept him company. Day and night.

"Hi, Brendan," she called with the voice that echoed in his dreams.

"I didn't expect to see you here." The words had no more left his mouth, and he wanted to kick himself. Her shoulders slumped. Her smile faltered. *Good going.*

"You're here!" Maggie all but knocked Brendan out of the way to get to Charlie. The sight of his short, round mother hugging the tall, slim Charlie might have been comical if it didn't strike him right in his chest.

Maggie let Charlie go and backed up a step or two, but her enthusiasm continued in full force. "I'm so very glad to meet you, Charlie. What you did for this family. How you saved my…" She broke off as the sobs overtook her, shaking her sturdy frame.

Like most men, a woman crying made him want to run. Brendan stood there, wondering how to make her stop, when Elizabeth stepped in. She must have seen the deer-in-headlights look on her friend's face. She took Maggie by the shoulders and spoke softly to her. Brendan couldn't make out the words, just the soothing tone.

After a few moments, his mother dried her eyes on her apron and offered Charlie a watery smile. "Don't mind me. The thought of losing that precious girl is too much to bear. You're an angel sent straight from Heaven."

"I don't know about that, Mrs. Fitzgerald. I happened to be in the right place at exactly the right time. And I'm so very thankful that I was. And for the invitation to dinner. I hear you make a mean pot roast."

And the tiniest chink fell away from the armor around Brendan's heart. In that very moment, watching Charlie interact with his Mom, the regard he already had for her grew a bit.

"You'll call me Maggie, young lady. 'Mrs. Fitzgerald' always makes me look around for my Joe's dear mother, God rest her soul. Now, I hope you brought an appetite. Dinner's ready in two shakes of a lamb's tail." His mother bustled back into the kitchen.

Brendan stepped closer to Charlie, who looked a bit dazed. "And that whirlwind was my mother, Maggie Fitzgerald. She's serious about your calling her Maggie too. What I meant to say earlier was welcome. I was surprised to see you today."

"Elizabeth told me that your mom wouldn't take no for an answer. And you have no idea how refreshing your mother is."

She was so earnest in her comment, that he had to ask. "I take it she's a bit different from yours then."

That light, silvery laugh that he was coming to love trickled out of her. "You have no idea." She shook her head. "They're night and day. Be thankful you'll never have the 'pleasure' of meeting mine." She smiled and followed Elizabeth into the kitchen.

"Interesting."

Brendan turned to Sam with a puzzled look on his face. "Okay, I'll bite. What's interesting?"

"Oh, the stream of emotions that flashed across your face when you first saw Charlie. Interesting." He smiled smugly, like he knew a secret that Brendan didn't.

And then the lightbulb clicked on. "Oh, no. Just because you're all wide-eyed and newly married, don't go wishing that on me." He shook his head in disgust. "Hell, Sam, what happened to you?"

"I'm crazy in love with a baby on the way. That's what happened to me, Brendan. But that has nothing to do with what I'm talking about."

"Enlighten me. And when you're done, maybe we could braid each other's hair," he added with a touch of sarcasm.

Sam smirked. "I don't think either one of us has long enough hair. Your face, when Charlie walked through the door. That's what I'm talking about. Recognition. Lust. Regret. Disbelief. You name it."

Brendan snorted, telling Sam just what he thought of his theory. "You got all that in a flash? Been sniffing fumes at the store by any chance?"

Sam chuckled. "Scoff all you want, buddy, but you didn't see your face. I did. What's up with you and Charlie?"

"Dinner's served. Let's go everyone," came his mother's voice from the dining room. Saved by the bell. Brendan had no ability to answer Sam's question, even if he wanted to. Which he didn't. There was nothing between he and Charlie, other than a mutual friend and the fact that Charlie had saved his daughter's life. He tried to ignore the pang that thought invoked.

"I'll go get the kids from the basement." He could have sworn he heard Sam cluck like a chicken, but he kept going. He dragged his daughters and his nephew away from the video game, herding them upstairs for dinner. The girls were running ahead of him. Abby shrieked Charlie's name. By the time he caught up, Abby launched herself into Charlie's arms. Brendan watched, a lump in his throat, as the tall, blonde woman bent down and scooped Abby into her arms. It was hard to tell who was happier to see the other.

Abby held her arm aloft, showing Charlie the green she had chosen. Their blonde heads were bent together. Any bystander might have thought they were mother and daughter. His father, Joe, joined the melee, hugging a surprised Charlie. She'd better get used to it if she was going to spend any time with his family. The Fitzgeralds were huggers.

"Daddy!"

He looked down to find Kerry tugging the hem of his shirt. "Sorry, honey. What's up?"

"We want to sit with Charlie, Daddy. Abby and I don't want to sit in the kitchen at the kid's table like we usually do. Can we, Daddy? Please?"

He looked to his mom to fix this last-minute seating crisis. Then Charlie jumped in. "What if I join you in the kitchen? Would that be alright?"

His mother objected. "Oh, that's so sweet of you, Charlie. But we were looking forward to getting to know you better."

His suspicions were confirmed by the slightly glassy look to her eyes. "Charlie, that's a great idea. In fact, why don't the four of us dine in the kitchen? I can help Abby cut her meat since she's down to one good hand." He turned to his nephew. "Liam, would you do me a favor and take my spot at the adult's table?"

Liam, who forever lamented the fact that he *still* had to sit at the kiddie table, jumped at the idea. "I am almost a teenager, you know." He even puffed out his thin chest. The adults roared with laughter at his antics.

"Besides, Mom, it's not like Charlie's going to run away after dinner."

"Of course, dear. Charlie, you're welcome to sit anywhere you like. Now let's eat before dinner gets cold."

His daughters led a relieved looking Charlie into the kitchen, each of them holding one of her hands. The sight warmed his heart. All three sat practically on top of each other, leaving him the entire opposite side of the table to himself. This would be better for her. He had a feeling Charlie hadn't been up to the Fitzgerald Inquisition. No normal person would be.

He reached into the cabinet and grabbed two regular dinner plates, handing one to her. "I'm not sure that Doc Mc Stuffins is exactly your speed," referring to the child-sized plates on the table."

She accepted the plate. "I don't know, Brendan. She's female and a doctor. We have a lot in common." She grinned at the girls who were hooting with laughter. Then she tilted her head as though putting a lot of thought into this. "On the other hand, this plate is bigger, so I can get more food. I like to eat, and I heard your grandmother makes the best pot roast ever. And there's all that yummy broccoli." She rubbed her stomach for emphasis.

Kerry's eyes were huge in her face. "You like broccoli?"

"I do. It's like eating little trees. And it's good for you too."

Abby piped up immediately to not be left out of the conversation. "Daddy, may I have some trees too?"

Saver of small children and able to get his daughters to eat vegetables. Was there no limit to her magic? "One order of trees with a side of pot roast coming up."

"Me too," yelled Kerry, not to be outdone.

"Girls, why don't you grab your plates and come with me. Charlie can get her food while we do." There was a moment of chaos when both girls jumped up from their seats and grabbed their plates. Abby frowned, struggling to balance it with her cast. Of course, his leftie had broken her left wrist.

"Abby, you didn't tell me you were a southpaw. Me too. What are the odds? Since we're the same, how about I carry your plate for you? You can point to what you want, and I'll load it up for you."

The little girl scrunched up her face. "Southpaw? What's that, Charlie?"

She laughed. "Southpaw is a nickname for someone who's left-handed. It's cool. Only one in ten people are left handed. Did you now that?"

"I want to be a southpaw too," piped Kerry, not to be outdone by her twin.

They had reached the dining room. "How about I take your plate since you're helping Abby?"

The smile she bestowed on him did something funny to his heart. She grinned, and her warm, whiskey-colored eyes sparkled. He could get used to seeing that face on a regular basis.

"Is there something on my face?"

Brendan realized he'd been staring. He had to get a grip. Soon. "Uh, sorry. Lost in thought for a moment." Of course, conversation had ceased and his entire family was staring at him. There'd be no end to the questions…

"Okay." She handed her plate to him. "Thank you for getting my food. I'll take some of everything. Remember, I love to eat."

She turned to Abby. "Now, young lady, what may I get for you?" She did a deep curtsey, which had both of his girls giggling.

"I want everything you're having, Charlie. Especially the trees."

She eyed the little girl. "Are you sure you can keep up with me? I'm a world champion eater. Ask your Dad. He seemed kind of surprised at the amount of food I ate."

"When did you eat with Daddy?"

"Yeah, Brendan," drawled his younger brother Aidan. "When did you eat with the pretty, new doctor?"

Charlie's head whipped up. Her eyes grew wide, and a pretty blush stained her skin. Brendan didn't know women blushed anymore. His ex-wife hadn't. Dr. Avery was a puzzle.

Sending Aidan a look that translated into 'you're dead', he spoke up to let her off the hook. "I took Charlie to lunch at The Sunshine Café this week, if you must know. It was the least I could do after what she did for Abby."

"Uncle Aidan, Charlie's a hero. She saved my life you know."

Aidan wore an amused look on his face. "I know, Abby. We're all very thankful to Charlie." He shot Brendan a look. "Some of us more than others."

She nodded to the girls. "Uncle Aidan's jealous. I ate the most delicious gumbo ever created."

"Oh, gumbo! That Claire is amazing. I'll have to go try that," his mother commented.

Brendan laughed at the jibe. He liked it that she could hold her own with his family. "Now, if you're done with the interrogation, I'm sure Charlie would like to eat." He nodded in his mother's direction. "It all smells great, Mom."

The four of them filled their plates and headed back into the kitchen. He noted with satisfaction that Abby's plate had everything that Charlie's did, just in smaller portions.

When they were seated at the kitchen table, Charlie opened her napkin and placed it on her lap. Kerry and Abby followed suit. Brendan was amused at how enthralled they were with her. But he was also concerned. After all, she had just entered their lives. Or was there a deeper meaning?

Chapter Six

Lunch passed without incident. Charlie had been more than a little relieved to sit in the kitchen with Brendan and his daughters. Overwhelmed by the sheer size of his family and their interest in her caused a case of the jitters she had not anticipated. She understood their curiosity, but center stage wasn't for her. The fact that Brendan noticed made her pulse quicken and heat pool low in her belly.

"Wow, ladies. You cleaned your plates. Even the 'trees'. Fantastic job!"

Kerry looked at Charlie, her expression quizzical. "'Clean our plates?' We didn't do that yet. Besides, the boys do that." There was a smugness to her voice.

Charlie barked out a laugh before she could stop herself. She caught Brendan's eye. "I like that idea."

He smiled back at her, his dimple flashing. "What Kerry means is that whoever cooks gets out of dish duty. It usually ends up that the women cook and the guys do the dishes. But not when it's grilling season. Then, it's reversed."

"Was that a challenge? Are you saying that women can't grill?" The gleam in her eye should have been a warning for him.

"No challenge. In the Fitzgerald clan, the women *don't* grill. So, then it's their turn to do the dishes."

"You do know that this is a new century, right?"

"Daddy, women can do anything they want to do."

Charlie bit her lip to stop from laughing. "Yes, Brendan. What she said."

Both girls giggled. Brendan had the grace to look sheepish. He even hunched down to be on their level. "Let me explain. Yes, women are completely equal to men; superior in some ways. Any smart man will tell you that." He winked at Charlie. "But in this family, it just happens that the women never grill. So, then it's their turn to do the dishes. Understood?"

Two heads nodded. Both girls carried their plates to the sink. Charlie grabbed hers and walked towards the sink. She passed him, whispering near his ear. "Nice save, Dad." She brushed against Brendan. And felt it all the way to her toes. She kept moving, more to put some distance between them than anything else. She heard him take the girls from the room and breathed a sigh of relief.

She rinsed her plate and placed it in the dishwasher. Maggie walked into the kitchen. "Oh, my dear, no. I don't expect you to do dishes. You're our guest."

Charlie smiled and shook her head. "But I didn't cook, and it's unlikely that I will be anytime soon. Although I may have to grill something to prove a point."

"Ah. You've been talking to Brendan about this."

"I have. And I have to say I was somewhat disappointed in him." A mischievous glint appeared in her eye. "But I set him straight."

Silence reigned, and she feared she had taken a step too far. But then Maggie threw back her head and laughed. Maggie finally stopped laughing, breathless and wiping her eyes. "You're exactly what he needs. This is going to be interesting."

"What?" She cringed at the strident note in her voice but couldn't do anything about that. "Brendan and I, uh, well there isn't any 'Brendan and I'. We don't even know each other very well. And I'm not interested in a relationship."

Maggie closed the distance between them and placed a hand on Charlie's shoulder. "That's what makes it interesting, dear. Neither is he."

"But you're not listening. I'm *not* looking for anything. With anyone. It's nothing against your son of course."

"Of course not, dear. And Brendan would say the same about you. He's not ready. He's not looking either." Maggie waved her hand in a gesture that told what she thought of that. "But sometimes, things happen. Opportunities come along.

Doesn't matter that you weren't looking. Life is short, my dear."

She was aware of that. Now more than ever. She looked at Maggie. "Yes, it is. That's why I'm here, Maggie. To start my life. Or rather, to start it over again. I needed a change."

She cleared her throat against the tightness forming there. Why was she having this conversation with Maggie? A woman she barely knew. "I don't know how much you know about me, Maggie. I was in Africa for a while, doing some work with a relief organization." She stopped again, unsure how to continue. "It didn't go so well. I've been in Charleston for the past few months, getting back on my feet. Windsor Falls is a new chance for me to get my life together. I can't take on anything else right now. It might sound self-centered, but I'm focusing on me. At least for now."

Maggie did something then that wasn't in Charlie's experience with mothers. She hugged her. Walked right up to Charlie and hugged her. And not because Charlie had saved her beloved grandchild. Just because. She wrapped her arms around her and held on tight.

She closed her eyes and soaked in the warmth of Maggie's arms around her. All she had ever gotten from her own mother was judgement. And disappointment. She honestly couldn't remember her mother ever putting her arms around her for no reason. Silent tears slid down her cheeks.

"You're not alone here, Charlie. We're all here for you. Whatever you need. All you have to do is ask."

She looked into Maggie's face. The tears were flowing freely now. "You can't know how much that means to me."

"Maybe not, dear girl. But I know how important having the support of family is." She sniffed. "That's enough of that. Let's go join the rest of them. You can tell us about yourself. Whatever you're comfortable telling."

"May I use your powder room first? I'd just like to freshen up a bit."

Maggie pointed down the hall off the kitchen. Charlie followed her directions to the powder room but stopped short, fascinated by all the family pictures gracing the walls. There were pictures of all the Fitzgerald siblings, from birth through early adulthood. Photos of Brendan drew her eye. From an apple-cheeked toddler to a gangly pre-teen, she could see the promise of the man he was today.

There was one picture, taken around age twenty. He was sitting in the grass, his arm thrown around the neck of a very old dog. Both were grinning into the camera. There was something different about this Brendan. A lack of concern. The Brendan in the picture looked like he didn't have a care in the world. She traced the smile on his face with one finger, wondering what had happened to the younger Brendan. Life happened, she reckoned. He grew up. Became a single father. Even with the help of his family, that couldn't be an easy road for him.

"That's Skip, the best dog ever."

She hadn't heard him approach, lost in her thoughts. He stood so close, his breath stirred the hair at the nape of her neck. And did other things to her. Her heart thumped in her chest. A wild animal trying to escape. She continued to look at the picture.

"I'm sure he was. How old was he in this picture?" She was surprised she could even speak. Liquid heat coursed through her veins.

"Fifteen. Skip passed away a few weeks after that was taken. We had been together most of my life. I loved that dog. The girls have been begging me for a dog for years. I don't know why I've resisted. They should have a Skip of their own."

"I always wanted a dog." Wistfulness colored her tone. "My mother always said they were too much work. What she meant was that she couldn't have a dog messing up her perfect house or flower beds." She rolled her eyes. "I vowed I would get one when I became an adult. But then there were years of schooling, followed by crazy hours and living in cities. The time was never right." She turned to Brendan and smiled at him. "But now, I'm settling down here. I can get a dog of my own."

"I like seeing you happy." That was the only warning she got. He closed the tiny space between them and captured her lips with his own. She stood still for a moment, sensations coursing through her. This wasn't what she wanted. A relationship with Brendan, or anyone. But her lips hadn't gotten that message.

She kissed him back, leaning into him. Her hands came up from her sides and rested on his shoulders.

After a moment of pure bliss, he broke the contact of their lips. He rested his forehead against hers. "I've been wanting to do that for a while now."

"What took you so long?" Was that breathy voice hers? That wasn't what she meant to say at all. She meant to tell him this couldn't happen again.

He broke their contact, stepping back a pace. He lifted one hand and pushed her hair back from her face. A look of regret flashed across his face. "I shouldn't have done that. But I won't say that I'm sorry."

"I should hope not. That was amazing." She ducked her head for a moment. "But you're right about it not happening again. It's for the best. I'm not in the right place to have a relationship."

"Me neither," he returned, scrubbing a hand down his face. The muscles of his shoulders tensed. "Being a single dad is the greatest job I've ever had." A smile, like the one in the picture, lit his face. "Those girls are everything to me. Which is why I'm so careful. I don't do relationships. I don't want them to get attached to someone and then have that person walk away." The smile vanished as his voice roughened. "They've already lost enough."

Charlie's heart seized at the pain in his voice. She didn't know the story behind his being a single father, but it had to be agonizing. She raised a hand to his face, wanting to smooth the hurt and regret she saw there. He turned his face into her cupped hand.

"Oh, excuse me," came a female voice from behind them. The two sprang apart.

A lovely woman with flaming red hair stood there. Grinning. "You must be Katie," Charlie said. Even to her own ears her voice sounded a bit unsteady. She took a breath and extended her hand. "It's so nice to meet you."

Still grinning, Katie ignored the outstretched hand and hugged Charlie. "Likewise. Sorry we weren't introduced earlier. Family dinners are always a bit much until everyone is fed. Elizabeth told us so much about you that I feel I know you already." She smirked at Brendan. "Although, I guess some of us know you a bit better already."

He growled out her name. "Was there something you wanted?" His younger sister's green eyes danced with delight, not the least bit intimidated by him. Charlie liked her already.

"Don't mind my big brother, Charlie. He gets like this sometimes. Such a stick in the mud. But, I love him. That's beside the point. I was looking for you. Elizabeth tells me you're looking for a place to live. I happen to have one of those."

"That would be great. She mentioned you might be looking to rent out your townhome. It would only be for a few months most likely. I'll be looking to buy something once I get settled."

"Perfect," Katie exclaimed. "Between school, work, and planning a wedding, I don't have time to deal with the house right now. And I haven't lived there in months. Haven't even had time to figure out what to do with the furniture. Flynn already has most things we need."

"You are so making this too easy for me. I came here with clothing only. I have some books and personal stuff at my parents' home in Charleston, but I don't need those right away."

"I'm so happy. You're a huge help, Charlie."

Charlie smiled back. "I was the one about to be homeless. I'd say you're saving me, Katie."

"Do you have time tomorrow to look? See if it's what you need."

"I lived in a tent in war-torn Africa, Katie. I'm sure your townhome will be fine. But I can come by anytime tomorrow. The hospital is working on my credentials, so I have some free time until then."

"Great! How about in the morning? I'm still working per diem and picked up a shift tomorrow night."

"That's perfect." Charlie rattled off her cell number. "Text me with the address."

Katie's fingers flew over her phone. "Got it. I'll send you a text in a moment. You two go back to whatever it is you weren't doing."

Charlie turned to Brendan, amusement in her eyes. "I like her. She's funny."

"Oh yeah," he agreed. "Unless you're related to her. Then it can get a bit old."

"Nah, I would have killed for a sibling. And you have quite a few. Lucky." Wistfulness laced her voice again.

"I'd be happy to lend you one. Or four." Brendan cleared his throat. "About earlier, Charlie. I meant what I said. I can't do this. At least not until the girls are grown."

"I get it, Brendan. It's fine. But I have a feeling we're going to be running into each other quite a bit. Just remember; no falling in love with me." With a laugh, she was gone.

Charlie walked into the kitchen and found Maggie slicing a cake. A pie cooled on the counter. She groaned even though her mouth watered. "Are you trying to kill me, Maggie? Cake and pie? How can I choose?"

"Well, you don't have to my dear. That's why I cut the pieces small. Be a love and grab some dessert dishes from that cabinet please." She waved the knife vaguely over Charlie's head.

Charlie looked in three cabinets before she found the requested dishes. They were a different pattern then the dinner dishes, less formal with riotous flowers in a rainbow of hues. "These are lovely, Maggie."

She looked over her shoulder and nodded. "Yes, they are. I've always loved those."

"If you don't mind me saying, these suit you better."

Maggie laughed. "Very astute of you, Charlie. The good china belonged to Joe's grandmother. They're old and very beautiful; not quite my style. These are more me."

"Do you want them in the dining room?"

"No need, dear. If you could just stick your head into the other room and yell dessert, they'll come running. Just back up when you do." Maggie laughed at her own joke.

Charlie smiled and shook her head before walking into the living room. The word dessert wasn't even completely out of her mouth when members of the Fitzgerald family stampeded into the room. Maggie had been right to warn her.

Elizabeth got up, helped by her very attentive husband. She waddled over to Charlie. "Let's have ours out on the deck. I feel like I haven't even had a chance to see you since you arrived." She turned to Sam and kissed his cheek. "Would you mind bringing some out for us, honey?"

"You don't have to do that, Sam," Charlie retorted. "I can grab some dessert." But he waved her off and headed for the kitchen.

Elizabeth chuckled. "Nice try. But Sam is intent on spoiling me. And I am letting him. You may as well reap the benefit. Let's go."

She led the way out a side door from the living room. Once on the deck, Elizabeth lowered herself into a chair and propped her feet on another. "Ah," she sighed. "That's the life. I knew the days of swollen ankles were coming. I never turn down the chance to prop them up."

Sam came out through the kitchen door holding two dessert plates. "Here you go ladies. Anything else I can get for you?"

"No, Sam. Thank you so much for this." Elizabeth pulled him down for a brief but hot kiss.

"Sorry. Taking advantage of the hormones."

Sam smiled and backed away. "I'll leave you to whatever it is women talk about when they're alone." He turned and walked back into the house.

Charlie couldn't help but notice the love radiating from Elizabeth's eyes. Her old friend's happiness moved her. "Wedded bliss agrees with you. As does pregnancy. I'm so thrilled for you, Elizabeth."

Her friend picked up a fork and took a bite of the chocolate cake. "Mmmm," she murmured. "I've been dreaming about that all week. Couldn't wait. Sam insists that I eat healthy stuff most of the time." She put down her fork and sighed. "And I know he's right. But why can't healthy stuff taste like this?"

Charlie laughed. "I know, right? I've been trying to eat healthier, especially in the past few months. Not an easy task at my parents'. Their cook's idea of healthy is southern comfort food. Delicious but not in the last bit healthy."

"You never did tell me why you stayed there so long after returning from Africa. Is everyone okay? I thought one of your parents might have been ill."

Charlie finished her bite of cake, chewing and swallowing before answering. It gave her a chance to think about how she would answer Elizabeth. "They're fine thanks. Now that Daddy is retired, he's taken up golf full time. Better than spending time with my mother of course." She shook her head. "Other than 'Averys don't divorce', I can't imagine how they're still married."

"Are you sure you weren't adopted?"

Unfortunately, Charlie had taken a large bite of chocolate cake. She managed to swallow most of it but not without sputtering and choking on the last bit. Elizabeth tried hard to not laugh. "Sorry about that. Bad timing. But it's the truth."

When she could breathe again, she agreed. "Preaching to the choir, sister. You have no idea what growing up with them was like. My still being single can't come as a shock."

"Hmmm, that's true I guess. They weren't a very good example. You and Brendan seemed cozy."

Luckily, the fork was only half way to her mouth this time. She lowered it to the plate. "What?" She kept both her voice and expression neutral. Elizabeth would be hard to fool.

"Oh, I don't know. Maybe it was having lunch the other day and then eating with him and my nieces in the kitchen today."

"Oh."

"Then of course there's the sexual tension that radiates off the two of you in waves."

Charlie squirmed in her chair. "He seems nice."

Elizabeth put down her plate and leaned forward as far as her pregnant belly would allow. "Nice? Yes, he's a nice person. But that's not the first word I would think of to describe Brendan Fitzgerald. Hard working. Devoted father. Yummy. Those are more suitable."

Yummy, indeed. Her lips tingled at the memory of Brendan's kiss. "Hush, Elizabeth! What's wrong with you? The Fitzgeralds don't strike me as the type to keep secrets."

Elizabeth's blue eyes danced with merriment. "I notice you're not denying it. Was it 'yummy' that got your attention?"

Charlie put down her plate. She had already eaten too much anyway. "Alright. Yes, yummy works. But that's in theory of course."

"Of course, it is." Elizabeth didn't even try to restrain her delight.

Charlie fixed her with a stare she used sometimes on difficult patients. It had no effect. She sighed and leaned in. "Okay, I find him attractive. Like drop my panties at the sight of him attractive. But, I'm not going to act on that. Ever."

"Why ever not? You're both single, good looking, healthy."

She wasn't sure about that last one. At least not yet. "You're missing the point, Elizabeth. I just got here. And he's a Fitzgerald for goodness sake."

"What does that mean? You make sound like he's royalty or something."

"What it means is that he's family to you. And as your best friend, I'm sure I'll be seeing a lot of them now. I don't want to muddy the waters, so to speak."

Instead of saying anything, Elizabeth leaned a bit closer to Charlie. And clucked. Like a chicken.

Charlie stared at her in disbelief. "Did you call me a chicken?"

"Implied more than actually called you one. But the intention was the same."

"I've been an ER doctor in two of the toughest hospitals in the country. Not to mention my time in Africa. And you're calling me a chicken?" Disbelief, and outrage, raised her voice several octaves.

Elizabeth's face lost all traces of humor. She Charlie's hand. "When it comes to a personal life, yes. I know how tough and brave you are. I watched the news daily when you were in Africa. I can't imagine it was a picnic. But you don't let people, and by that I mean men, close to you. Name one guy you were involved with in LA."

"I could say the same of you, Elizabeth."

"Exactly. I was closed off and afraid after losing Connor. For ten long years, I threw myself into my training and my work. It took coming home, back to Windsor Falls and facing my past, to move forward. With Sam." She laid a tender hand on her belly. "And I'm so thankful that I did."

Charlie sat back in her chair and averted her eyes. Elizabeth knew her too well. She couldn't lie to her, even if she wanted to. Her chest tightened. Her voice was barely a whisper when she finally spoke. "How did you do that, Elizabeth? How did you ever move past your fear? I'm frozen."

Elizabeth blew out a breath on a noise that was half laugh, half sob. "Not very well. I stayed away for so long, even though Windsor Falls was always my home, out of fear. I was afraid of everything, loving, losing again. I loved L.A. for that. Apart from you, I was anonymous. Jeremy never even knew my story."

"Wow. I guess I never realized." She smiled at her friend. "Thank you for trusting me with that. I'm not sure I ever told you how much it meant for you to confide such a tragedy in me."

Elizabeth squeezed her hand. "And I never thanked you for listening. You were the first person I could be myself with. Not hold back an entire part of my life from. I only hope someday I can return the favor."

Tears stung her eyes. She didn't know how to respond. The incident that had changed her life forever had been over in a matter of hours. Yet months later, she was still trying to get her life back together.

"I'm not there yet, Elizabeth. But I'm trying to be." Even though she wanted to, Charlie couldn't bring herself to tell Elizabeth about it. Partly because the horror was still fresh in her mind and retelling it took too much out of her. But also because of Elizabeth herself. She wanted to protect her friend from the dark reality of what had happened to her.

"I know, Charlie. It's fine. Know that I am here for you. For whatever you might need."

Both women stood, Charlie a bit quicker. Elizabeth laughed and placed a hand on her belly. "Don't get me wrong. I love being pregnant. Especially after everything I've been through. But I cannot wait to see my shoes again."

Charlie hugged her. "You are such a good friend, Elizabeth. I'm so thankful to be here and for this clean start."

"Right back at you!"

They walked into the house. She turned to her friend. "Do you think Maggie would mind if I ducked out? It's been a long week, and I'd like to get to bed early tonight."

"I know for a fact that Maggie wouldn't mind at all," joked the woman herself. She came into the kitchen with some dessert plates in her hand. She shooed them both away when the women tried to help her. "Go on with you now. Charlie, it was a pleasure to meet you. I expect we'll be seeing a lot of each other."

"Thank you, Maggie. I enjoyed meeting you and your family. It helps to have new friends when you start over someplace."

"Well anytime you're feeling down or missing a home cooked meal, you come on over." Maggie hugged Charlie one last time and then turned to the sink.

"I'll walk you out," Elizabeth said. Charlie grabbed her purse from the back of a kitchen chair and followed Elizabeth. On the porch, she hugged her friend. "One day soon," she whispered in Elizabeth's ear before stepping off the porch and walking to her car.

*****

Brendan stood in the dining room window and watched Charlie leave. Why he had kissed her? Probably because he had to. The impulse had been there, and he followed it. But life as a single father left little room for impulsivity. Especially when it came to women and relationships.

She was a striking woman, but it went beyond that. She was also bright, funny, and warm. Any man would be drawn to her. But there was also a darkness, a sadness, about her that called to him. He had noticed it when she thought others weren't looking. Her smile faded. Or her eyes clouded when she was lost in thought. It made Brendan want to take away the sadness. Bring back the joy to her life.

And that was exactly why Charlie was all wrong for him. He had to remember his priorities; Kerry and Abby. His chest rose and fell as he sighed. His girls were fine. Because he worked hard to make sure they were. He needed to protect them. But on some level, he wanted what his parents had. Love. Respect. A partnership.

Jillian Harris had been everything but those. Her father had taken one look at Brendan and deemed him not good enough; which was all Jillian needed to hear. Always at odds with her protective daddy, Brendan was the perfect revenge. Their marriage had been as brief as their whirlwind courtship.

Brendan turned from the window. Thoughts of Jillian were never productive. She meant nothing to him now, even though he thought he had loved her then. She was the mother of his children, but that was pure biology. Jillian had walked out of the hospital hours after giving birth and never looked back. The cruel, abrupt end to their marriage had cured him of that bit of fancy. Yet he didn't regret it. How could he when he had his girls?

Glancing around the entry to the living room, he smiled as he watched his family. His siblings took turns with colorful markers, adding their own brand to Abby's cast. Both of his girls were talking a mile a minute and laughing as much. No, he wouldn't change a thing. And he wouldn't do anything to jeopardize their little family.

Chapter Seven

Charlie walked through the center of town, jingling keys to her new house in one hand. She'd met with Brendan's sister and loved the townhome. Even better, Katie still had many of her possessions there. Since she didn't have anything in Windsor Falls other than clothing, this worked out perfectly.

The sun warmed her skin, making her smile. She strolled along, her speed designed more for sightseeing than fitness. People passing by waved to her, most calling out a greeting. She had missed the South. She loved Los Angeles and liked Chicago, but her heart was here. The friendliness of people warmed her heart. She wasn't naïve. North Carolina had the same problems faced by the big cities: poverty, gangs, drugs, etc. But these issues were in your face when you worked in a busy, inner-city trauma center.

Here, she could make a difference in a way that she had never been able to in the cities. Certainly, not in Africa. Here, she could deal with these issues in smaller numbers and on a more personal level. Her Grandmother Ruth had known what she was doing when she left her estate to Charlie.

Her father's mother had been her ally growing up. Grandma Ruth was a true Southern matriarch and the only person who intimidated Charlie's father. When it came time to go to college, her parents thought they knew what was best for their only child. She would go to the right school before marrying the right man. Someone they picked for her, of course. But Grandma Ruth, still kicking at a spry ninety at the time, called a halt to that. Charlie enrolled at the University of South Carolina, majoring in biology.

Grandma Ruth died during her sophomore year. To honor her memory, Charlie continued her education, fulfilling her dream to be a doctor. If she further damaged her already tenuous relationship with her parents, she never lost sleep over it. They made their choice when they tried to force her into their mold so many years ago.

Over the years, she only touched that money to work with several charities she supported. Smart investing had allowed her to do so without even dipping very far into the principal amount. But, now that she was settling here, building a life in Windsor Falls, she wished to be more involved. She wanted to roll up her sleeves and participate, not just write a check.

Her stomach rumbled, reminding her to eat. She looked around for something different to try for lunch and spied several food trucks open for business. What a perfect option for a sunny day. She could choose something for lunch and then wander over to one of the park benches in the town's square.

She was trying to decide between Greek and Mexican food when she heard, "You can't go wrong either way", behind her. She didn't have to turn around to know Brendan stood there. His deep voice sent a warm sensation across her skin.

Still looking at the overhead menus, she replied. "It smells delicious."

"Can I buy you lunch once you decide?"

At last, she turned to face him. "I thought we decided to avoid situations like this." Her gentle tone softened her words.

"I said no kissing. I didn't say anything about not having lunch together." He leaned in closer, until he almost touched her but not quite. His nearness messed with her. "And right now, being here with you, I'm trying to remember why we decided kissing would be such a bad idea."

She took a deep breath to steady herself. But, that was a mistake. The scent of him filled her senses. "You're a tricky man, Brendan Fitzgerald. I'm not sure what to think of you."

His dimple flashed. "I could say the same." He spread his hands. "I'm not trying to play games with you. I still don't think a relationship between us is a good idea. For either of us. But then I'm near you, and I struggle to remember that."

"Wow. Just wow. I appreciate your honesty. Even if it does mess with my head. Greek, it is."

He laughed. "Well that was a one eighty."

She laughed too, more at herself than his comment. "Relationships are hard. Food is easy. I know what I want. And today, I want a gyro. Veal or lamb is fine. And thank you. Although, there isn't any debt."

His dimple disappeared. "That will never be repaid, and this has nothing to do with Abby." Leaving her more confused than ever, he walked up to place their orders.

She picked a bench that was partially shaded and sat in the sun. Because she wore sunglasses, she took the time to watch him. Wow again. He was handsome and had a body to die for. Yet he lacked the arrogance that sometimes accompanied those two things. His dark hair was shone in the sunshine. She itched to run her fingers through it to feel the texture. Would it be soft or course?

He was wearing what she had come to think of as his work uniform: form fitting jeans and a green Fitzgerald Construction tee shirt. The shirt molded to his chest and upper arms, leaving her in no doubt of his build. His skin was tanned, probably a permanent state from being outdoors so much.

The young man in the food truck handed Brendan some change, and he started towards her. She kept herself from checking for drool. He was a fine specimen for sure.

"Do you want some help with that?" He balanced their food and two large cups.

He shook his head and approached the bench. "I'm fine, thanks." He handed her a foil wrapped sandwich and a bag of chips before placing his on the bench. Then he handed over a cup. "Whew. Managed to not drop anything."

She laughed and picked up her sandwich. "That smells amazing." She took a large bite. "Mmmm."

"Guess you like it." He stared at her mouth.

Feeling a bit self-conscious, she raised a brow. "Is there something on my face?" She looked around for a napkin.

He pulled one from his pocket and handed it to her. "You have a little something right here." He pointed to the right side of his mouth. Before she could react, he reached out with one finger and wiped away the sauce. Watching her the whole time, Brendan placed the finger in his mouth and licked it clean. "Delicious," he said in a deeper timbre.

Her insides quivered. Especially the lower ones. "You're killing me," she scolded half-heartedly.

"Good. Now you know how I feel." He unwrapped his gyro and took a big bite.

Charlie watched in fascination at the working of his jaw muscles. They ate in silence for a few moments, each lost in the deliciousness of the gyros and their own thoughts. With her back to the gazebo, she had a splendid view of the south and east side of the town square. Each was filled with adorable shops. The more she saw of Windsor Falls, the more excited she became about her new life here.

When she finished eating, Charlie balled up the wrapper and walked to the nearest garbage can. She returned to the bench. He had chosen the shady section of the bench and had pushed his sunglasses to the top of his head. His deep blue eyes drew her. There was a kindness in them that she found comforting.

"Elizabeth always spoke highly of you. Like a brother. You were good to her when Connor died. I remember that. It can't have been an easy time for you."

If her words surprised him, he didn't show it. He finished the last bite of his sandwich and chewed for a moment before swallowing. When he finished, he turned to face her on the bench. "It wasn't." His eyes clouded with grief. "It was the worst time of my life. But somehow it was harder on Elizabeth. She lost the love of her life, and their unborn baby, in a matter of days."

He closed his eyes for a moment. Charlie's heart ached. She placed a hand on his arm for comfort. But that was the last thing she felt. His skin was warmed by the sun and lightly sprinkled with dark hair. Underneath, the muscled contracted at her touch, sending waves of sensation through her.

"I'm sorry for bringing it up Brendan."

He opened his eyes and looked at her. Down to her very soul. "Please don't be. That was a lovely compliment. Elizabeth and I share a bond. One formed long before Connor's death. She was a good friend back in the day. And I was there for her when she needed a male's perspective. Someone other than Connor's that is." He grinned, brightening his whole face. "I even had a crush on her for about a second."

"Really? She never told me that."

"She didn't know. It was brief and pointless. In fact, I always assumed she knew. But a few months ago it came up in conversation. She was as shocked as you are."

"I can imagine. And how do you feel about her marrying Sam?"

Brendan didn't even hesitate. "Sam's great, and he's loved her since they were kids. Seems our Elizabeth caught more than one young male's fancy back in the day. But seriously, I love Sam like another brother. They're good for each other. And I'm going to be an uncle again."

"Yes, you are. Elizabeth looks amazing. She glows when she talks about Sam and their baby to be." Her heart clenched. But she pushed it aside. "Do you ever want to have more children, Brendan?"

She could have bitten her tongue when the words left her mouth. She held up a hand. "Please don't answer that. I'm not sure what's wrong with me today." She needed to stop talking.

But he wasn't offended or even annoyed. "That's a normal question. Why wouldn't I answer that? I'd love to have one or two more. Not that the girls don't keep me busy enough. But, I won't. I never planned on being a single dad in the first place. And I'm never getting married again."

Charlie's phone beeped then, breaking the spell. She pulled it from her back pocket and silenced it. She glanced at Brendan. "Sorry. That's the reminder I set." She stood. "I have to go. Thanks again for lunch, Brendan. I really enjoyed it."

She turned to walk away, but he caught her by the arm. "Are you okay? Was it something I said?" Concern tinged his voice.

She shook her head. "Oh, no. I have an appointment in fifteen minutes. I have to go."

He jogged to keep up with her. "Well can I at least give you a ride somewhere?"

Charlie stopped in the middle of the sidewalk to battle with herself. She had a second meeting with Dr. Lowery today. She wasn't ashamed of it, but did he need to know? Of course, he witnessed her meltdown last week. Chewing on her lower lip, she tried to decide whether to tell him.

"I didn't mean to pry. It's none of my business."

The slight hurt to his tone was her deciding factor. She stopped him with a hand on his arm. "It's okay." She took a deep, steadying breath. "I have an appointment with a therapist."

His expression softened. He nodded but didn't say anything.

"Last week, when you startled me on the sidewalk, you probably realized I have an issue. Things in Africa didn't end so well. And I have Post Traumatic Stress Disorder or PTSD." Her breath hitched. "I'm learning to live with it."

"I'm glad you're getting help. I don't understand, or even know, what you went through, Charlie. But I'm here if you ever need someone."

Hot tears burned her eyes at his kindness. She glanced at her phone again. "I really have to go now."

She turned and almost ran away from him. Charlie appreciated his understanding. But did she want the hot guy thinking of her as a basket case?

*****

Brendan watched Charlie go, torn between giving her some space and going after her. He was glad she was getting help and not giving into the stigma that surrounded mental health treatment. He could only imagine what had happened to her in Africa.

On the other hand, the urge to follow her, protect her, overwhelmed him. That thought stopped him in his tracks. When had he become her self-appointed protector? Guardian? She would want to punch him; women were funny that way. His life was filled with tough, independent women. What could he possibly be thinking? He didn't know her well. And, more importantly, he was *not* getting involved with her. In any way.

Having assured himself of that fact, he headed for his truck. These days, he acted more in a supervisory capacity for the family firm. His job was to manage various projects underway. Make sure things ran smoothly. But he also liked to keep his hand in the physical side of it. It wasn't uncommon to find Brendan swinging a hammer right alongside his crew.

A hammer might help to ease the frustration he felt. The frustration a certain blonde had caused. Brendan drove to the edge of town where Fitzgerald Construction was building a new development. The future home of Blue Ridge Acres sat in what used to be an empty field.

His father chose home construction a long time ago. He wanted to build someone's dream home, rather than an office complex or fast food joint. Brendan agreed, and Blue Ridge Acres was his dream. Each home site set on a decent size plot. And was affordable. While Fitzgerald Construction had been involved in the construction of homes worth over a million dollars, these were meant for families starting out. For families that could not have afforded to own a home otherwise. He got a lot of personal satisfaction from these types of homes.

Arriving at the site, he sat in his truck for a moment and allowed himself to think about Charlie. She touched him. She intrigued him. She got under his skin. She got under the armor he had built around his heart since Jillian. So, what was he supposed to do about that? Would it be the worst thing in the world if he asked her out on a proper date? He hadn't had one of those in quite a while.

But she wasn't some woman he met in a bar. Or at the park. She was Elizabeth's best friend. She was a fixture in his life now. His girls knew her. And liked her. Both Abby and Kerry had talked about nothing else Sunday night. 'Wasn't Charlie pretty, Daddy?' 'Do you think Charlie would want to come over for a play date, Daddy?' His favorite had been, 'I bet Charlie likes dogs'.

That one had gotten to him. Almost since they were old enough to talk, the girl had longed for a dog. Begged. He couldn't say why he had resisted so long, other than all the responsibilities in his life. But it was time. Past time. They were old enough to take on some of the care of a dog. At least supervised. He had always had a dog growing up. Sometimes more than one. Skip had been his favorite.

Decision made, he thought about how psyched the girls would be. Then he thought of a brilliant plan, and a smile spread across his face.

Chapter Eight

Charlie left Dr. Lowery's office with a lighter step and heart. She knew that what had happened in Africa would never leave her. But she was one step closer to dealing with it. She had talked with him today about why she hadn't told anyone yet the details of that terrible time. She still wasn't sure.

Even after staying at her childhood home for several months, her parents didn't know the full story. Or extent of her injuries. She had only told them the bare minimum to explain her prolonged stay there. Charlie had known instinctively that they wouldn't want to know.

Looking both ways, she crossed the street and started back towards the B&B. She was building a life. She'd be moving into Katie's house on Monday. She had gotten a call from the medical center this morning. The necessary information and documents for her temporary privileges were in place. She started orientation to the department next week.

Yes, everything was falling into place. The nightmares and restless sleep had diminished since she arrived in Windsor Falls. And other than last week, she hadn't freaked out in broad daylight either. There was a peacefulness to this small town that rejuvenated her soul. And the mountains! Elizabeth had spoken about the Blue Ridge Mountains with reverence in her voice. Now she understood.

Last week, on impulse, she had jumped in her car and driven along the Blue Ridge Parkway. Since she had never been on it before, Charlie felt compelled to stop at almost every pull off. Each time, she would get out and take in the view. And it had never failed to inspire her. Beyond the physical beauty of the scenes, the mountains had a timeless strength about them. They had stood there, enduring all kinds of weather and man-made disasters, for who knew how long. And they would still be standing long after she was gone.

The next piece of her recovery would come when she could talk Africa. Elizabeth needed to know. She hated to keep something of this magnitude from her. Telling Dr. Lowery was one thing. The idea of telling the whole story, even to her best friend, chilled her. Despite temperatures in the seventies. A fine line of sweat formed down the middle of her spine. Her vision began to gray at the edges. Her heart, beating away madly in her chest, felt like it would explode with the effort. Every breath was rapid and painful.

Knowing a full-blown panic attack was coming on, she walked to a bench. Lowering herself to the seat, she closed her eyes and concentrated on her breathing. Deep breath in for a full count of four. Hold it for another eight. Blow it out for four. Picture her 'happy place'.

That had seemed absurd to her at first. How could imagining someplace in her mind help? But she continued to breathe deeply, and think about a deserted beach. The panic slowly lessened its icy grip on her. Charlie could feel the warm, wooden slats of the bench beneath her. Smell the beguiling flowers in the window box of a nearby store.

Her heart rate dropped from the one twenties, and she opened her eyes. She was in a safe place. And no one around her gave her any funny looks. That was a plus. Charlie had some rough moments since Africa. In Nigeria, she woke up screaming in terror from nightmares that had been based in reality. They had patched her up and sent her to an army hospital in Germany. The hospital staff had been better equipped to deal with her emotional trauma, having dealt with thousands of soldiers.

In the hospital, she started to learn to take back the control she had lost in Africa. Control of her own life. She was grateful to the nurses and doctors who had helped her to heal. By the time she had reached Charleston, she felt closer to her old self.

But there was still work to be done. The fact that she was recovering from a panic attack in the middle of Windsor Falls proved that. Baby steps she told herself. She was better today than she had been three weeks ago. While she'd like to be free of the 'attacks', at least she had been able to handle this one. Even cut it off before if became full blown. Yep, baby steps.

Charlie rose from the bench; reasonably sure she could do so without falling. Gave her shaky legs time to adjust. She grabbed her purse and headed towards the B&B. She looked around as she made her way back. The world had gone along without her. Birds were chirping. People went about their business. There was a normalcy in it that comforted her.

She reached the driveway when her phone chirped announcing a text. She stopped to read it, shading her eyes from the brilliant sun.

"Hey! It's Brendan. Fitzgerald. Wanted to see how you were. Elizabeth gave me your number. Hope you don't mind."

Charlie moved into the shade of a Magnolia tree to better see the screen. She read the text again. And then one more time. It was cute that he felt it necessary to mention his last name. Like there were a hundred Brendan's in her life. And he used actual grammar and whole words. Another point in his favor. She continued to stare at the phone. For someone who spent their life making decisions in a snap, she couldn't seem to decide what to do about his text. Answer it? What would she say? Ignore it? Not an option. Grandma Ruth would roll over in her grave.

Then she realized her silliness. It was a text. Not a lifelong commitment. The phone had locked itself, so she swiped her finger along the screen. And then chewed on her nail as she considered her reply.

Fine, thanks. You?

She slid her phone into her back pocket and walked up the driveway. Then her phone chimed again. A nervous giggle escaped her. She decided to wait until the privacy of her room to read the next text. So, of course, Lorna stopped her in the entryway.

"Hi, Dr. Avery. Isn't it a gorgeous day? Were you in town? Can I get you anything?"

It would be rude to respond with 'shut up and let me read my text from the hot man', so she murmured a 'no thanks'. And took the stairs two at a time.

Once in the safety of her room, she locked the door and stretched out on the bed. She pulled out her phone. She held her breath and opened his text.

Good to know. I have a favor to ask. Would it be alright if I called you?

She nodded. And then remembered he couldn't see her. What was it about him that reduced her to puddle of idiocy?

Sure.

She screeched when the phone rang in the next second. "Hey, Brendan. That was fast."

"How'd you know it was me?" he joked. The rich, deep timbre of his voice set loose the butterflies in her stomach.

"Psychic I guess."

"Now that you have my number, you should save it in your contacts."

"We'll see." Her heart pounded in her chest. Was she flirting with Brendan? Where was her good sense when she needed it?

A hearty, male laugh sounded over the line. "Are you flirting with me, Dr. Avery?"

She pressed the mute button and gasped. Could he read minds as well? She needed to be more careful with this man. She barely knew him, and her heart already fluttered whenever she was around him.

She undid the mute button. "Hardly," she said in her best Avery disdain. "But I don't put just anyone in my contacts. They have to be worthy."

"Well then, I guess I'll have to prove myself worthy. There was an actual reason for my call. I've decided to get the girls a dog."

"That's wonderful. Are they thrilled? I imagine there was a lot of shrieking involved."

"I haven't told them yet, and that's the reason for my call. I'm planning to surprise them on Saturday by taking them to the local rescue." He hesitated, and she could hear him breathing. "And I would like you to come with us."

Charlie stopped breathing. "Oh. Brendan, are you sure?" Why would he want her involved in a family event like that? They barely knew each other.

His voice was strong and sure when he answered. "Absolutely. You are a constant topic of conversation around here. Both girls are dying to see you again. But especially Abby. She thinks you two have a special bond."

"I'd like to think we do, Brendan. Your daughters are very sweet, and I'd love to go." She would? She would. But Charlie was a little afraid of what that meant.

"Great. I'll call you Friday with the time."

"Great! I look forward to it." And she did, despite the warning voice in the back of her head. She liked him. And his girls. She wanted to develop ties here in Windsor Falls, her new home. But she was concerned also. She felt a connection to Brendan, even after a few days. That scared her. She wasn't ready for any type of commitment. Especially with a man who made it plain he would never marry again.

"And Charlie? I'm so glad you had that appointment today. And if you need someone to talk to, or be there, call me. Anytime."

Charlie gripped the phone tighter, wishing she could be closer to him. "That means a lot to me. More than you could ever know." She cleared her throat of the unshed tears lodged there. "I'll see you Saturday."

Charlie hit end on her cell and flopped back on the bed. She hoped she knew what she was doing. Agreeing to spend time with Brendan Fitzgerald and his precious daughters. But she had a feeling it was already too late for caution.

*****

Brendan tossed his phone onto the passenger seat of his truck. Glancing in the rear-view mirror, he laughed at the goofy smile on his face. *"Get a grip, Fitzgerald"* he told his reflection. But his reflection didn't pay him any attention. He was in too good of a mood. It was a beautiful day. His girls were healthy. And he had made a date with a stunning woman. What else could he ask for?

Maybe this wasn't the best idea. Maybe he had been right to be cautious when he first met Charlie. But then he remembered the taste of her lips under his. The feel of her body against him. The smell of her hair. And above and beyond that, he liked her. And respected her. She was smart and funny. He knew from how she had treated Abby that Charlie was kind and compassionate also, not to mention brave.

And he wasn't asking for her hand in marriage. She was going with them to pick out a dog. This would be okay he decided. They would be friends. His daughters would gain another positive, female role model. It was all good. And the silly smile spread back into place.

*****

The rest of the week flew by. Orientation started next week. She could also move into her new home then. The Blue Iris was lovely. But she looked forward to the privacy of her own place.

She had spent the week exploring her new home town and hanging out with Elizabeth. She had been out to their home for dinner twice this week. Sam was amazing with the grill, she had been happy to learn. Even showed her a thing or two. This was the first real time spent with Elizabeth since they were both residents in Los Angeles. She loved not having to depend on Skype and phone calls anymore.

She still hadn't told Elizabeth about Africa, but she would. When she was ready. Dr. Lowery had been adamant that the timeline is her own. She had met with him again on Wednesday, and they decided to continue twice a week when her schedule allowed.

Brendan remained the only fly in the ointment, so to speak. Charlie hadn't had any nightmares this week, though images of him interrupted her sleep. If only she could run. That would tire her out. She spent more time thinking of him than she should. Especially since she shouldn't be thinking of him at all. He was a friend and that's all. But while her mind understood that, her body shouted something altogether different.

Their kiss may have been brief but intense. When she laid in bed at night, trying to sleep, she swore she could still taste him on her lips. Fanciful she knew, but lying in the dark it was real to her. As was the feel of his broad chest and muscular arms. And that was only from one kiss!

And now it was Friday and she counted down the hours until she saw him again tomorrow. She had never been *that* girl. The one that pined by the phone, waiting for some guy to call. Yet that's what this felt like now.

She was just bored, she told herself. After all, she could only do so much window shopping. Although grateful to Katie, Charlie longed for her own home. She'd never owned her own home, and the apartments she had lived in were impersonal at best. She couldn't wait for that day. She wanted lots of windows and natural light so that it never felt dark or chilled.

She had grown up in a beautiful house filled with beautiful things, but it had never felt like home. Her mother was forever reminding Charlie to not touch anything. Anna Mae's prized possessions were everywhere, but they were to be admired not played with. She wanted a home that was lived in. Comfortable. Where you could touch things. And that was exactly what she would have.

She was walking back to the Blue Iris, the setting sun torching the sky, when her phone chirped. Charlie glanced at her phone and saw a text from Brendan. Excitement curled her toes. Soon her toes weren't the only parts of her body that curled.

"Is nine too early tomorrow? The rescue doesn't open until ten, but I thought we could grab breakfast first."

Now wasn't soon enough, she thought. Charlie's fingers flew over the tiny keyboard in response. *"Nine is perfect. You know how I love to eat. Are you sure you want to feed me again?"*

She could see that he was already typing. Charlie held her breath in anticipation. She didn't have to wait long. A smiling emoji appeared on her phone, followed by *"I'm willing to take my chances. Besides, my girls will eat healthy stuff if you're there. Pick you up at nine, sharp."*

Glee raced through her veins. She did a little happy dance before continuing back to the B&B. She replied with a thumb's up emoji before sliding her phone back into her pocket. Now she only had to get through this evening and sleep well.

*****

Brendan knocked on his friend Quinn's front door before entering. Knocking was only a formality. "Hello," he called out to the empty foyer.

"Be right down," came from the direction of upstairs, so he continued inside. Quinn Adams was a local firefighter whom Brendan had met through Sam. They were all part of a bi-weekly poker game that rotated between their homes. The group was ever changing and included his brothers, Sam, Quinn and two of his fellow firefighters, AJ and Jack. Flynn, his soon-to-be brother-in-law, was their newest member. Not everyone made it every time, but there was always a lot of fun to be had on poker night.

Quinn came running down the stairs, his hair still wet from the shower. "Hey, man," he said, clapping Brendan on the back. He and Brendan had become good friends over the past few years.

Brendan looked around at the barren house. "I like what you've done with the place."

Quinn laughed and crossed to the fridge to grab a couple of beers. "I've only been here for two months. You should have seen it before. And I don't have a ton of free time between the station and my painting business."

"Such a slacker," quipped Brendan. This was the latest of the homes that Quinn bought and 'flipped.' "I like this one."

Quinn flipped him the bird and laughed. "Yeah, that's me. Slacker. I schedule sleep these days."

"So, when do you date?"

"Date? What's that?" He handed Brendan a cold bottle from a local micro-brewery. "You must have me confused with Jack."

"I wouldn't call what he does 'dating'. More like a hit and run." Jack was notorious in their circle for his three-date limit. He didn't want any woman to get the wrong idea.

Quinn nodded. "Jack is Jack. He likes the ladies. And they like him. What about you, Brendan? It's been a long time since I've heard you mention anyone." Quinn cocked his head. "Actually, I can't remember the last time."

"There's a reason for that. I don't date."

"At all? What do you do about, uh, you know?"

"Sex? Are you asking me about my sex life, Quinn?"

A brief knock sounded on the front door, followed by the sound of several guys piling into the house. Brendan turned to see his brother Donovan and soon-to-be brother in law, Flynn. "Dr. Reynolds, I hope you brought your money tonight. I'm feeling lucky." He rubbed his hands together, making them all laugh.

"You may be lucky, but I'm skilled at poker. We'll see who walks away with the pot tonight."

Brendan pulled out a chair from the table. They were all about the trash talk. Money had very little to do with it. Brendan enjoyed his time with these guys and considered them his good friends. They were all seated, and Donovan was shuffling, when Sam came in at a run.

"Sorry, sorry!" he called and took the remaining chair next to Quinn. "Elizabeth walked in the door as I was leaving. Her shift that was supposed to be eight hours but ended up being closer to ten."

Quinn held up a hand to stop him. "Okay. We don't need the details."

Sam grinned and shook his head. "Get your mind out of the gutter, Quinn. My pregnant wife came home dripping with exhaustion. I made sure she had something to eat and a hot bath before I left."

"That's even worse," Brendan piped up. "You are so whipped, man." Chaos ensued when the others joined in on that sentiment.

Sam helped himself to a beer and some chips. "Say what you want, gentleman. But I am a happy man with a beautiful woman in his bed every night and a baby on the way. How many of you can say the same?"

There was some grumbling but mostly silence until Donovan spoke up. "I can. Except for the baby part." He looked around at the others. "Y'all have no idea what you're missing."

Brendan knew his brother and friend were right. He'd cut out his tongue before telling them. He'd never live it down. "If you ladies are through, let's play some poker."

"Now, that's what I'm talking about," yelled Quinn, and the game began. They played a few hands with conversation centered on how the Braves were looking this year. The pizza delivery man came, and Quinn got up to pay. Whoever hosted provided the food.

They all took a break to grab some food and another beer before settling back down at the table. Flynn gestured to Sam. "Hey, I finally met Charlie today. Although, between Katie and Elizabeth, I feel like I already know her."

Brendan listened without comment. There was no need for any of them to know about his growing attraction to her. He'd never hear the end of it. They were worse than women that way.

Sam picked up his cards and groaned, throwing three down. "You're right about Charlie. She's great. We've had her over for dinner a few nights this week. Charlie's very low key, and she and Elizabeth laugh for hours. And of course, she saved Abby, so what's not to like?"

"Yes, she did," Brendan replied. "I can never her thank her enough or that."

"Although lunch at the Sunshine Café was a nice touch," quipped Donovan.

"A cut above lunch from the food truck," agreed Quinn. "Although, Spiro's gyros are to die for."

Brendan should have known better. No one could keep a secret in a small town. He was doomed. The best defense was a strong offense. "Both lunches were good. The food truck thing was a coincidence though. We were both there at the same time." He had been calm and objective. No way the vultures could read into that.

"Kind of like serendipity. Wouldn't you agree, Flynn?" This from Donovan, his older, pain in the ass brother.

Not to be outdone, Flynn grinned at Brendan and then addressed Donovan. "Good word, Donovan. Might I even take it further and say it was fate?"

"Okay, we get it. You know that I like her. Well, who wouldn't? She's beautiful and smart. Doesn't mean I'm going to do anything about it."

"Never took you for an idiot." Sam grinned and accepted new cards from Donovan.

"I'm not a fool. Nor am I going to start something with her just because she's beautiful." Although he wanted to. "I have the girls to think about. They come first." His tone was curter than he would have liked, but thoughts of her had been plaguing him all week.

Donovan put down his cards and turned to Brendan. "Of course, the girls come first. That's the way it should be, Brendan. Always. You're a great father to them. No one would say otherwise. But you get to have a life outside of being their dad."

Brendan looked over his cards, blowing out his disgust. "I'll take three also. I know you mean well. I'm careful, I guess, when it comes to the girls. They've never met any woman I've been involved with. But they already know Charlie. It's complicated."

Donovan picked up the deck and dealt Brendan three new cards. "It is, and you're right to be cautious. Any plans?"

Brendan perused his new cards and hid a smile. Lady Luck was finally remembering him. "As a matter of fact, yes. Tomorrow she's coming to the animal rescue with us. I'm finally getting the girls a dog. And they've been asking to see Charlie again anyway. Two birds. One stone." He pulled a five-dollar bill from the small pile of money before him. "I raise you ten."

Donovan laughed out loud and threw a five on the pile. "Abby and Kerry finally wore you down, huh? Kind of surprised it took them this long."

"I'm not sure why I waited. I loved having dogs when we were growing up. I'm looking forward to it."

The rest of the guys folded, leaving only Brendan and Donovan still in the game. Brendan gave his brother a dead stare, daring him to call his bluff. All he had was a pair of aces. He watched Donovan, waiting for his 'tell'. His older brother had no idea he always cleared his throat when he was bluffing.

Donovan stared at his hand and then the pile of money. He cleared his throat. Reaching his hand towards the pile he dropped a ten. "Raise you ten. Sucker."

Brendan dropped a bill on the growing pile. "I call. What do you have?"

Donovan grinned at Brendan. "Only a pair of kings. But then I didn't ask for three cards. How about you?"

Brendan dropped his eyes and let the corners of his mouth drop. "Yeah, I did need three…to get these." He laid down his cards with a flourish, showing the pair of aces.

The others erupted in laughter. Donovan muttered 'Son of a bitch!' Brendan raked in the pile of cash. He might be unlucky in love, but he was ahead at cards tonight.

Chapter Nine

Charlie blew out a breath of disgust and reached for the pair of capris. She was not a woman who thought twice about her clothing. The growing pile on the bed might disagree. Breakfast and a trip to the animal shelter didn't require haute couture. Not that she owned any. But she was going with Brendan. She wanted to look decent. Okay, she wanted to look hot. She immediately pulled on a tee-shirt and pair of tan capris. She braided her long, blonde hair.

Peering into the mirror, she was pleased with the final production. Her skin glowed with the light tan she had acquired since moving to Windsor Falls. Not waking in the grip of a nightmare didn't hurt. The dark circles that had been under her eyes for too long were now history. Although she wasn't cleared for running yet, the daily walks through town had helped. All in all, Charlie was beginning to look, and more importantly feel, like herself again.

She picked up her phone, glancing at the time, and rushed out the door. Brendan would be here any minute to get her. Couldn't keep him and the girls waiting. She smiled as she thought of his daughters. Kerry and Abby were delightful. She couldn't wait to see them again. It had nothing to do with their smoking hot father. At least that's the lie she told herself.

Charlie glanced out the window on the Inn's stairway. Her breath caught at the sight of Brendan's truck pulling into the driveway. She skipped the rest of the way down the stairs, her heart lighter than it had been in months.

He was already out of the truck when she reached the driveway. She waved to his daughters who could hardly contain themselves. "Hello, ladies. What are you doing here?" Kerry and Abby both spoke at once, making it impossible for her to understand either of them.

Brendan laughed and held up a hand. "I think they're excited to see you, Charlie."

Deep dimples bracketed his smile. Charlie felt an answering tug low in her belly. Brendan Fitzgerald was a dangerous man. Combined with his adorable daughters, he was downright lethal. How would she ever resist?

Pushing aside those thoughts, Charlie leaned in the window of the back seat. "Who's hungry?" She smiled at the chorus of 'I am!' that answered her. "Good, because I'm hungry enough to eat all your breakfasts."

"You wouldn't, um, eat my breakfast," protested Kerry.

"She's kidding, Kerry," assured Abby. Her green cast was still bright but now covered in colorful writing.

Brendan came around the front of his truck and held the door for her. This brought him way too close for comfort. His warm body next to hers made Charlie long for things she couldn't have. She jumped up in the truck before he could help her. The last thing she needed was his hands on her. She winced at the discomfort her actions caused. She wasn't quite ready for that.

After fastening her seatbelt, Charlie turned to the little girls in the back. "I am hungry. I like to eat. Ask your Dad." She heard a chuckle from the driver's seat.

"That's true, girls. Charlie loves to eat!"

The look of approval, and something else, almost stopped her in her tracks. "But I promise to not eat your breakfasts as well." Giggling came from the backseat. She turned back and faced him. "So, where are we going? Your restaurant choices have been perfect so far."

Brendan slid shades over his eyes, shielding them from the brilliant morning sun. He grinned at her. "I'm not sure that a food truck counts as a restaurant. Besides, you were already there. I didn't choose it."

"Well, that may be true, but you did recommend the gyro, which was amazing!"

"I'm taking you to Bob's. Don't want to ruin my perfect batting record now." A chorus of shrieks and claps came from the back seat.

She laughed at the girls' enthusiasm. "Bob's? Sounds like a winner." She twisted to see the girls again. "What's so great about Bob's?"

Kerry held her hands apart about a foot. "The pancakes are this big, Charlie."

"And they have chocolate chips in them," chimed Abby.

"My goodness! That big? I'm not sure even I can eat that big of a pancake." Her laughter mingled with the girls'.

Brendan stopped at a red light and turned to face her. "That may be a bit of an exaggeration. Though not by much. And you don't have to get them with chocolate chips. The slight grimace he made told her how he felt about them.

"Daddy! Charlie might like them. Besides, you always say we should try new things."

A dull red crept up his neck, making Charlie laugh. "Busted, Dad. Besides, I happen to love a good chocolate chip pancake." She patted her stomach. "Yum. I'm getting hungrier thinking about those."

"Luckily for you then, we're here." Brandan pulled into a parking lot across the street from the medical center.

Charlie looked out the window. They were parked in front of a small, square building painted yellow with a sign proclaiming 'Bob's'. She hadn't noticed it during her other trips to the hospital. Brendan opened her door, and this time she took his proffered hand. Warm tingles exploded where their hands touched. She risked a quick glance at him. Heat sizzled from his gaze.

He turned to the back door to help his daughters. Kerry and Abby were both already out of their booster seats and jumping out of the truck. Each took one of Charlie's hands to lead her into the diner. Brendan chuckled and walked a bit faster to open the door for them.

Delicious smells tickled her nose when she stepped inside. Her stomach growled in appreciation, sending the girls into fits of laughter. "I warned you guys. I hope your Dad brought enough money," she joked.

"You can always do the dishes."

"Ah, my princesses are back!"

Charlie started at the deep voice to her left. A huge man with skin the color of night stood there smiling. The girls squealed with delight and launched themselves at his legs. She watched the big man hugged each girl. Bob made the appropriate noises over Abby's cast.

When they let go of him, the man clapped Brendan on the back with enough force to stagger a smaller man. "Brendan, my friend, how are you?"

"Doing great. You?" He turned towards Charlie. "Let me introduce Windsor Fall's newest resident."

Bob stopped him with a raised hand. "This would be the lovely Dr. Charlotte Avery, the medical center's newest ER doc." His huge hand enveloped hers. "I'm so very pleased to meet you, Dr. Avery. Welcome to Windsor Falls, my dear."

"News travels fast." She shook the other man's hand. "Please, call me Charlie. I've heard all about your world-famous chocolate chip pancakes, Bob. I can't wait to try them."

Bob grinned at the two little girls. "I guess someone has been singing my praises. Thank you, princesses." He grabbed a couple of menus. "This way, my friends."

The four followed Bob to a booth in the corner. Charlie and Brendan slid in across from each other while both girls flanked Charlie. Bob handed menus to Charlie and Brendan before placing paper kids' ones in front of the girls.

"Mr. Bob, you have to put extra chocolate chips in Charlie's." Abby glanced at Charlie. "She saved me from the car."

Bob's large, dark face split in a wide grin, exposing a shiny, gold tooth. "Did she now? I guess the grapevine forgot that little bit of information."

Charlie tried hard to not squirm in her seat. "It was nothing. I did what anyone would do in the situation."

Bob grinned down at her. "I don't know about that. I do know that your pancakes are on the house. Anyone who would risk their life to save my princess deserves at least that. I'll be back in a moment to take your orders."

She watched the big man walked away with more grace than she would have imagined. "This has to stop. I can buy my own meals." She shook her head.

Brendan opened his menu. "Get used to it. It's a small town. People remember things like that."

"Are you gonna have the chocolate chip pancakes, Charlie? For real?" Kerry's voice held a bit of skepticism.

"For real. I'm looking forward to them as a matter of fact." She rubbed her belly to drive the point home.

He shuddered. "Not sure I've ever seen anyone over eighteen eat them. Hope you know what you're doing."

Bob's return saved Charlie from answering. "Have we made a decision yet, folks? You could pretty much close your eyes and point. There's nothing on that menu that will disappoint you." His big belly shook as he laughed at his own joke. She liked him even more.

"Well I don't know about anyone else, but I'll have the chocolate chip pancakes, please. May I also have a fruit cup on the side?" She handed her menu back to him.

Both girls rushed to chime in their order. "Us too," they said as one. "And the fruit thing. Charlie has good taste in food. We even ate trees with her," bragged Abby.

"Trees, huh? Okay then. And you, Brendan? Still not a fan?"

Brendan shifted in his chair. "I'm sure they're fabulous. Not my thing. I'll have scrambled eggs and bacon with rye toast please. And OJ for everyone." He glanced at Charlie and she nodded in agreement.

She smothered a laugh in her napkin. "By trees, they mean broccoli."

"Yeah, the fluffy end looks like a tree," added Kerry.

"That they do, "Bob responded. "I'll have your food our in a few moments." Bob turned and walked away.

"So, I hear you have a new home."

"I do, indeed. Katie is finishing up her move this week-end. So, I'm free to move in on Monday. It won't take me long. All I brought with me was what I have at the Inn."

"Where's all your stuff, Charlie?" Kerry's face showed her curiosity. "I have way more than that, and I'm only six."

She leaned over and tousled Kerry's long, blonde hair. "The rest of my stuff is in Charleston with my parents. I've moved around a lot in the last few years, so I haven't got much stuff."

Kerry wrinkled her nose. "Don't you have any stuffed animals with you? You could have one of mine."

"Or mine," piped up her twin.

"That's very sweet of you, girls. I'll be okay. I'm going to be living in your Aunt Katie's house for a bit. Until I find my own home. Then I'll buy more stuff."

"Aunt Katie is going to marry Dr. Flynn," announced Kerry.

"Then he'll be our Uncle Flynn," added her twin.

"I heard about that. They both work at the Medical Center. I'll be starting there on Monday."

"We started a new school last year. It was scary. Are you scared, Charlie?"

Charlie grinned at Abby. "No, I'm not scared. I'm excited. Think of all the new people I'll meet. And I'm back with my best friend, your Aunt Elizabeth. What could be better than that? Besides, I've missed working, so I'm glad to get back to it." Charlie could have bitten her tongue. That was more information than she needed to give.

Brendan raised an eyebrow but didn't comment. Curiosity burned in his gaze. The girls didn't hold back. "Why haven't you been working, Charlie? You sure took good care of me." Abby raised her casted arm and waved it like a flag. "You knew right away I broked my arm."

"Broke," corrected her father. "And we don't ask questions like that. It's not polite."

Charlie grew warm at his concern. "It's not a big deal. I took some time off and stayed with my parents in Charleston. I needed a break and had to figure out what I wanted to do next. And here I am."

"We're so glad. Aren't we, Daddy?" Kerry took it upon herself to answer for her twin. Something Charlie had noticed they both did a lot.

"Of course, we are honey."

The deep timbre of his voice made her want things she had no business wanting. Like that man in her bed. "Well, I'm glad to hear it. Windsor Falls is my new home. And I'm very excited about that."

"Here we are, folks." Bob stopped at their table with an impressive number of dishes in his hands. He handed out their breakfasts. Charlie noticed Kerry and Abby were both given a fruit cup identical to hers, but smaller in size. Both gazed at the assorted melons and berries with something akin to skepticism.

"Yum, kiwi, my favorite." Charlie plucked a wedge of it off the top with her fork and popped it into her mouth. She hid a smile watching the girls did the same. The shock on their faces was priceless.

"It's not bad," they exclaimed in unison.

"In one week, you've gotten my daughters to eat both broccoli and kiwi. Are you a magician? Or a sorceress?"

She finished chewing and swallowing a bite of cantaloupe before answering. "Nope. Just a fresh fruit and vegetable lover. Maybe they've caught on."

He shook his head but watched them both eat the sweet melon. "Well, whatever it is, I'm pleased. They never want to try new things."

Conversation lagged as the four dug into their breakfasts. Nothing remained on anyone's plate when they'd finished. Even the fruit cups were empty. Charlie tried to get the bill from Bob when he brought it, but Brendan grabbed the slip. Before she could even make a token protest, he strode to the front to pay. She sighed and turned her attentions to the girls and their sticky hands and faces. When they were cleaned up, the three joined Brendan.

"Bye now, folks. Come again. And Charlie, don't you be a stranger."

"Starting next week, I'll be across the street several days a week. I'm sure I'll be seeing you."

They all said goodbyes to Bob and left the restaurant. Brendan opened the doors to his truck and helped all three ladies into it. Charlie wondered at the spark she felt. The briefest placement of his hand on hers was enough to send her up in flames. How was she going to do this? She only hoped that her new life would keep her busy. And out of Brendan Fitzgerald's path.

*****

Brendan slid behind the wheel and tried to not look at her. Because that was the least of what he wanted to do to her with her. But those were dangerous thoughts. So, he busied himself with making sure everyone buckled in. He started his truck. With deliberate casualness, he turned to the passenger seat. "Do you have a little time? I thought you could come with us for a bit."

A huge smile spread across her face. "Sure. I'm not doing much today. What did you have in mind?"

He backed out of the parking space. "Oh, just an errand."

A sigh came from the back seat. One filled with poorly concealed impatience. As only a six-year-old could make. "Daddy, errands are boring. Charlie won't like us if you bore her."

Both adults smothered a chuckle. Charlie glanced at the girls in the rear-view mirror. "What does your father do on these errands?"

Another sigh. "He goes to the grocery store or the post office." Kerry made the two sound like death itself. "Why can't we go to the park?"

Charlie met his eye and winked. "Well, maybe he had something else in mind."

"I was thinking of getting the oil changed in my truck, girls. Won't that be fun?"

"Daddy," cried Kerry. "That's not any fun at all."

The debate about what was fun, and what wasn't, continued for several miles. Neither little girl noticed they had pulled into the county animal shelter until the din of many, canine voices reached them. Brendan turned around to see the realization dawn on their small faces.

Abby spoke in a small voice. "What are we doing here, Daddy? This is where they keep the doggies and kitties who need a home." Her voice shook with emotion.

"Well, I think this is a good time for us to get a dog. But if you don't want to…"

The happy shrieks of the girls filled the cabin of his truck. Both had undone their harnesses and were jumping up and down in the back seat. She couldn't hear exactly what they were saying. They both yelled at the same time. And spoke at a hundred miles per hour.

He turned to Charlie. "I think they're excited."

She cocked her head and looked at the girls. "How can you be sure? They don't seem very excited to me."

Kerry and Abby looked at the adults, then each other, before bursting into tears. "We've wanted a dog forever!" Not to be outdone, Abby added, "Daddy always said no."

Brendan winced. "What I said was when the girls were older." He didn't want Charlie thinking he was a bad father.

"Your Dad was right, girls. Owning a dog is a big job. It's not for, say, someone who's five. You must walk the dog and feed him. And make sure he gets brushed and stays healthy. Does that sound like things six-year-olds can do?"

His heart swelled as his girls shrieked "Yes" from the backseat. She was wonderful with the girls. He opened his door. "Well, I guess we should go in and see if they have a dog who's been waiting for two little girls."

He smiled at Charlie in gratitude. She had gone above and beyond. Kerry and Abby scrambled out of his truck. Both grabbed a little hand as they entered the shelter.

Once inside, a volunteer approached them. His name tag read Henry. "How can I help this lovely family today?" Brendan felt Charlie stiffen at the man's mistake, but he didn't bother to correct Henry.

"We're looking for a dog. Do you think you might have one who's looking to live with a couple of little girls?"

Henry peered over his glasses at Kerry and Abby. "Would you two be the young ladies in question?"

"We are," they squealed in unison.

"Very good. And what type of dog would you be looking for today?"

The girls looked at each other and nodded. "One that needs a home, Mr. Henry," piped up Abby.

Brendan's heart squeezed in his chest. That simple statement almost brought him to his knees. He cleared his throat. "I'm not sure we had any type of dog in mind. Maybe we could look around?"

Henry smiled. "That's a great plan. See who picks you, I always say. Come this way." He led them into an inner room, which was long and flanked on both sides by kennel runs. The noise level raised to a deafening pitch with their arrival. Dogs of all shapes and sizes clamored for attention.

Charlie clapped her hands. "I know where I'm coming when I get settled in my own home."

Henry stepped up. "Why don't the ladies look around a bit while I take you to fill out the application, sir?"

Brendan looked at Charlie, but she was already waving him away. "We've got this."

"Okay, Henry, I'm all yours."

*****

Charlie watched him walk away with Henry. She tried to not sigh aloud. The rear view caught her breath. That man had quite the butt on him. She felt a tug on her shirt and turned back to the girls. "Now, where should we start?"

Kerry and Abby both grabbed a hand and led her to the row of kennel runs. Each contained a dog of various size and pedigree, or lack thereof. There were large dogs and small dogs. Furry and short haired. At the girls' prompting, she read the short bio that adorned the gate of each run. It gave the bare facts; age, gender, name, breed.

"How are you guys ever going to choose?"

"We'll know," piped the twins in unison. Their unique ability to read each other's minds still caught her off guard.

They inspected each run in the first row when Brendan caught up with them. "All finished with the paperwork. Any contenders?"

Charlie left their side to join him in the middle of the room. "Only everyone," she joked. "But oddly enough they haven't looked twice at any."

"That's good, I guess. I had nightmares of leaving here with a dozen dogs." He pointed to the end of the row, where both girls were seated in front of a run, hands folded in their laps. "I wonder who's in there."

Brendan scooped her elbow with his hand, guiding her towards the girls. She tried to not think about the warmth of his skin or the subtle scent of him. She failed on both accounts. You're here for the girls, she reminded herself. Not to crush on their dad.

"I see they've found our veterans," observed Henry.

"Veterans?" inquired Charlie.

Henry shook his head. "That's what we call the ones who have been here for a while. As you know, we're a no kill shelter. That means they stay until they're adopted. Fred and Ginger have been here close to a year now." His face softened. "It's a sad tale. An elderly woman, who was very ill the last few years of her life, owned them. She couldn't take care of them. Or herself really. A neighbor brought them to us when the old lady died. No family to take care of them. Said she'd tried to talk the woman into surrendering them earlier. But the owner feared the pair would be separated. Few folks come in prepared to adopt two and older dogs at that."

Charlie leaned forward to see the card. "Fred is a male Basset Hound. Ginger is a female Italian Greyhound. Looks like they're both seven years old."

She squatted down next to the girls. Kerry turned her face upwards to her. "They want to stay together, Charlie. Like me and Abby. I think they're twins too."

Brendan chuckled at his daughter's comment. "They are very cute, girls, but I thought you wanted a puppy or a younger dog. I don't think Fred is up for playing with a couple of busy little girls. We should look at the other dogs, honey."

Abby laced the fingers of her good hand into the wire gate. "It's okay, Fred. You're sad." Her twin nodded in unison. "You miss your owner. But Kerry and I would take very good care of you. We promise." Her voice trembled at the end.

No one spoke as they all focused on the pair of dogs. Then, Fred's tale began to sweep the elevated bed he was lying on. Back and forth, slowly, almost as if he had forgotten how to wag his tail. Ginger jumped up and barked, once, before prancing towards the gate. Halfway there, she paused and looked back at Fred over her tiny shoulder. She ran back and licked his face before coming to the gate.

"She likes us," breathed Kerry.

Ginger sat in front of the girls and cocked her head. Her liquid brown eyes shown with intelligence. If Charlie didn't know better, she would have sworn the dog smiled at them. Her thin, whip like tail brushed the ground.

Fred sat up and stepped down off the elevated bed. The Basset stretched down to the ground in a funny bow. He lumbered across the run and stopped behind Ginger.

"Fred has a bit of arthritis in his legs, nothing out of the ordinary for a dog in his middle years. And nothing that regular exercise wouldn't make better. Chasing after a couple of young girls might go a long way towards his rehab."

"I know we only came for one, Daddy," started Abby.

"But you heard Mr. Henry. They have to stay together," finished Kerry.

Both stared at him with solemn eyes. Charlie had a feeling they would be leaving with two dogs today. She couldn't imagine how he could ever say no to them. Great. Another reason to like him.

"Fair enough. It only seems right that my twins would want 'twins' of their own."

Whatever else he said was lost in the happy screams of both girls. Fred and Ginger must have picked up on the vibe. They lended their voices to the chorus. Fred's deep baying bounced off the walls of the run, while Ginger yipped and danced around him.

Chapter Ten

On Wednesday evening, minutes shy of seven, Charlie pulled open the front door of Between the Covers. She carried this month's book club choice; only half read but better than nothing she figured. She sat in hospital orientation for three, long days. At least that was over. This was the third hospital she worked for, and orientation never changed. She could have been back in Los Angeles or Chicago. It was all about patient confidentiality and ethics. Which was fine, except she could teach those by now. Funny how orientation in Africa had been so very different. More life and death stuff.

"You made it," exclaimed Jamie, the store owner. She hugged a startled Charlie before dragging her further into the store. "Come meet the others."

Charlie smiled at the group of a dozen women sitting in an informal circle. Their ages ranged from barely an adult to seventy plus. Each held a copy of the book in her hands. Jamie made a round of introductions that she knew she would never remember.

"Hi, everyone. I'm Charlie. And I'm a book-a-holic," she joked by way of introduction.

Laughter greeted her in response. A woman in her late twenties waved her over. "Hi, Charlie, I'm Paige. Come sit here." She pointed to one of two empty chairs next on either side of her. "My friend Amy is joining us. She'll be late, as usual."

Charlie smiled in thanks. "I'd love to." She chose the chair to the left of Paige and sat.

The bells over the front door jingled, followed by a hurried, "I'm here, I'm here."

A lovely, blonde woman, similar in age to Paige, joined the group. After a round of greetings, she sat on the other side of her friend. Leaning around Paige, she stuck her hand out to Charlie. "Hi! I'm Amy. I don't believe we've met."

Charlie shook the outstretched hand. "Hello. I'm Charlie, and I'm new to Windsor Falls. Pleased to meet you."

"Right back at you. Most of us are born and bred, so if you need anything, let us know." Amy placed her book on the seat and headed to the refreshment table.

"That's very kind of you. I've been busy settling in, so I didn't finish the book." She grinned. "I did read half and loved every word."

"That's okay," Jamie answered. "While we do talk about the book each month, this group is very informal. It's more about getting out of the house and socializing. Right ladies?"

"And dishing about the latest gossip," quipped the oldest member of the group.

"And talking about men," came another reply. A round of laughter followed each comment.

Jamie pointed to the small table against the wall. "Not to mention the wine and snacks."

"We love it when Kat comes," commented a woman in her forties. "Not that I need any more of her delicacies." Several women laughed at that and nodded in agreement.

"Y'all know there aren't any calories at book club."

Charlie recognized the voice and turned her head to spot Kat from the bakery. She was arranging pastries on a plate. She waved. "Hi, Kat. I didn't see you when I first came in."

"Hey, Charlie. Nice to see you again. I thought I'd wait until the roar died down. We don't get a new member every month."

"Well, I'm thrilled to be here. I only knew one person when I moved here. And with my erratic work hours, making friends won't be easy."

"Hey, congratulations by the way." Kat addressed the group. "Charlie is Windsor Fall's newest ER doctor. Fresh from the wilds of Charleston."

Another round of cheers and comments ensued. After a few moments, she raised her hand. "Thank you so much. I'm excited to be here. I love what I've seen of Windsor Falls so far."

Jamie held up a hand. "Now that everyone knows each other, let's get started. Amy, since you're there, can you grab a glass of wine for Charlie, please."

"Uh, no thank you. Just water please." She felt the odd stares from several women and tried to shrug them off. She had stopped drinking alcohol all together when it had become a bit too easy to lose herself in a glass, or several, at her parents' home. She didn't feel the need to tempt herself by having a glass now.

Amy handed her a bottled water and retook her seat. "Thanks," murmured Charlie. She took a long sip to quench her thirst.

A lively discussion ensued. She found herself holding her sides as she laughed at several points. She grinned and she looked around the group. These were lively, funny women. Just what the doctor ordered. For herself.

The group took a break to get snacks. She stood to stretch when Paige tapped her on the arm. "Okay, tell us everything we need to know about you in thirsty seconds or less." She laughed at Charlie's expression. "Think of it this way. Otherwise, we'll only know what the gossip mill tells us. You don't want that." Amy nodded in agreement.

"Fair enough. Start your timer. You already know my name. I'm thirty-seven, single, from Charleston by way of USC for undergraduate, Tulane for medical school, Los Angeles for residency, Chicago, Africa and now here. I don't drink as you found out. I like to run and can eat pretty much anything I want without gaining an ounce. Don't hate me for those. I love my family but more now that I'm away from them again. I'm a dog person without every owning one." She glanced at her watch. "I think time's up."

Paige and Amy looked at each other. A silent communication passed between them. The type that can only happen between lifelong friends. They turned to Charlie, grinning from ear to ear. "You'll do," Paige quipped.

"Despite the eating without gaining thing. Not sure I can forgive that," added Amy. "Although I do love to run. I can show you some of my favorite spots."

Charlie felt an instant connection to these two women. "I'll take you up on that, Amy. Once I'm back in shape."

Paige scoffed. She looked Charlie up and down. "If that's 'out of shape', then there's no hope for me."

"I know it may not look that way, but I got, uh, very sick when I was in Africa." The water she drank threatened to come back up. "I'm doing much better but not quite a hundred percent yet. These days, I'm only up to a slow jog. More of a fast walk."

"That's more my speed. Amy can get her miles in, while you and I stroll, Charlie."

Relief flooded through her. "It's a date."

"Did she mention Brendan Fitzgerald yet?" Charlie turned to see Kat standing behind her. She was once again back in the center of attention with all three women staring at her in anticipation.

"Uh, Brendan? Well, Elizabeth, his former sister-in-law, is my best friend. We did our residency together, in Los Angeles." She broke off knowing anything she said would only make it worse.

Kat slapped her arm. "Sorry. Couldn't resist. But your face was priceless." With minimal detail, she told the other two women about Abby and the almost car accident. "But our Charlie doesn't wish to be thought of as a hero. Even though she is. So, we're not to mention it again."

Something in her face must have backed up Kat's words. The other two women kept their comments to a minimum. Paige grinned. "I did hear about the trip to the shelter. Henry's an old friend of the family. In his defense, everyone had pretty much given up on Fred and Ginger being adopted together. That was a remarkable thing you did."

Charlie shook her head. "Can't take credit for that one, Paige. That was all Brendan. I went along for the ride. Those little girls fell in love. Quick and hard. Poor man never saw it coming. Before anyone knew it, we were headed out with two dogs. Not sure who was happier, Kerry and Abby or Fred and Ginger." She grinned. "Well, I may not drink wine, but I refuse to say no to those pastries." The other women agreed and joined her at the table.

*****

Brendan sat on his back deck, beer in hand. He watched the girls chase Fred and Ginger across the yard. Or maybe the dogs chased them. Hard to tell. Ginger moved at the speed of light, darting in and around the girls' legs. No one caught her unless she wanted them to. Fred had the occasional burst of speed, more like a few feet of trotting, before he collapsed in an undignified heap. Usually square on his back with all four feet in the air.

The past few days had brought with them a few adjustments and a large bill at Sam's store. Who knew two dogs could need so much? But the sounds of his girls laughing without a care in the world was well worth any dent to his credit card.

After the first night, it had been smooth sailing. Fred's mournful baying awoke him at one and then three in the morning. Sure that his new roommates needed to go out, he dragged himself out of bed. Twice. In the middle of the damned night. Both times the dogs were thrilled to see him. Almost waking the neighborhood in their enthusiasm.

On the second trip back in the house, he forgot to lock the new kitchen gate. By the time he realized this, both dogs were gone. He caught a quick peek of the very tip of Fred's tail rounding the corner. Only the sound of nails clicking on the hardwood stairs gave him a clue as to their location.

At this age, the girls still preferred to share a room. And they still insisted on the door being open at night. And a nightlight. Sure enough, peeking in, he found his new dogs. Fred lay below Kerry's outstretched hand, snuffling it as though to make sure she was okay. Ginger, the far more agile of the two, had hopped up onto Abby's bed. Her long, rather Aquiline muzzle, lay on the bed next to his daughter's cast. She swiped her pink tongue over the exposed fingers once before closing her eyes on a doggy sigh.

Brendan stood there, wishing he had his phone to take a picture. Being a smart man, he knew when he was beaten. "All right you guys. You win. This round. But no funny business from either of you. Understand?" And he shook his head at his ridiculousness before going back to his own bed.

Sleep was usually his friend. He worked hard during the day and then chased after the girls during the evening. Except for the first few months with the girls, he fell asleep with ease. Not tonight. As soon as his head hit the pillow, images of Charlie danced behind his eyes. Her long, blonde hair. Her whiskey-colored eyes. Her hand in his as he helped her out of his truck.

It was the last image that robbed him of sleep. He growled and rolled over on his side. He had no business thinking about her at all. Let alone at three in the morning. But any man with a pair of eyes that worked would have *those* thoughts of Charlie. She took away his breath.

More than her physical beauty, it was how she treated his girls and how she made him feel that kept him up tonight. He didn't need this complication. His plan was simple. Raise the girls to the best of his ability. Make sure they were happy and well adjusted. Despite not having a mom. No room for Charlie. Or any other woman.

But she was far from any other woman. There had been women, of course. He hadn't lived like a monk. But they weren't his priority. Kerry and Abby were. Never had a woman captured his imagination. Ruined his sleep. Brendan flipped over to his back again. Wisps of moonlight flickered across the ceiling while the fan blew air across his body. Perfect sleeping conditions. Just not for him.

Even if he considered trying a long-term relationship, Charlie wasn't the ideal candidate. Not that he was considering it. She was Elizabeth's best friend and had fit right in with his family. When something went wrong, and it always did, where would that leave them?

And then there was the real reason. The fact that she and Jillian could be sisters. No wonder the shelter manager had thought they were a family. Brendan's heart clenched a bit whenever he saw her with his girls. With their fair skin and hair a hundred shades of blonde, Kerry and Abby looked more like Charlie than him.

Charlie and Jillian might look alike, but they were polar-opposites in personality. At least from what he had seen of Charlie so far. And he had been watching. And waiting. Waiting for her *true* self to surface. It was unfair of him to judge her this way, but he could not help it.

Brendan had a terrible track record with women. He thought he knew Jillian. He thought she had more underneath the glossy surface. He thought that, even when their brief marriage was headed down the tubes. Right up until the moment he found the appointment card for the abortion she scheduled.

Even now, more than six years later, his stomach heaved at the memory. Jillian wasn't even going to tell him. She made an appointment. Like the many she made every week: pedicure, seamstress, highlights. Abortion. That's how simple it was for her. Any last shred of feelings he had for her died that day.

Jumping from his bed, he stalked into the shower. He stood under the punishing, cold spray. A nice long run would have been better, he thought as the icy water pummeled his shoulders. But he couldn't leave the girls alone in the middle of the night.

Several excruciating minutes later, he got out again and dried himself with a towel. Climbing into bed once again, Brendan laid down his head and willed himself to sleep. It worked within minutes this time. But dreams of Charlie made it an uneasy slumber.

*****

Sweat trickled down the sides of Charlie's face. She grunted and slid the chest tube into place. She watched her patient's chest rise symmetrically for the first time. "There. That should help his breathing. Let's get an x-ray done to ensure placement." She snapped off her blood-soaked gloves, tossing them into the nearest garbage can.

Charlie leaned over the young man on the ER table. Ted Sanders, twenty-five and a motorcycle enthusiast, lay unconscious on the table. Better for him, she thought. He dumped his bike. Hitting the ground forty-five miles an hour came at a cost. Ted paid the price.

"Need a hand," Elizabeth offered, waddling into the room.

"We're good for the moment. Waiting on the surgeon."

"That'd be me," answered a tall blonde man dressed in green scrubs. "What do you have?"

"Hey, Dan. I'd like you to meet Charlie Avery, our newest ER doc. Charlie, this is Dan Martin, my favorite surgeon."

Dan wagged his eyebrows. "All the happily married, pregnant women say that to me. Nice to meet you, Charlie. Welcome to Memorial." The surgeon gestured towards the stretcher. "I gather this is my motorcyclist?"

"Thanks, Dan. Ted here failed to negotiate a turn in the rain. Bike skidded out from underneath him. He took the brunt on his right side. Open femur fracture, flailed ribs. I put in chest tube. He's already had two hundred milliliters blood out, but he's breathing a bit easier. Saturation is back in the nineties. Hasn't regained consciousness though."

"Great, Charlie, I'll take it from here. Let me know if you want to grab a coffee sometime."

She held back a laugh and waved. She stripped off her bloodied, protective gear. They exited the trauma bay. When the doors swung closed behind them, she turned to Elizabeth. "Was he serious?"

"Yep, that's Dan. Nice guy but a bit of a flirt." She arched an eyebrow at her friend. "But then, you're single. Why not?"

Charlie rotated her head on her neck. The popping noise drew a sigh from her. "No thanks. Surgeons aren't my style. But that went well in there. Good to be back in the saddle, so to speak."

"You did great, not that I had any doubts."

She smiled in thanks. "Didn't realize how much I missed it. Not bad for my first full day back." She had finished her orientation. The hospital granted her temporary privileges while she awaited her North Carolina license. She was tired, but a good tired. One that came from a hard day's work.

"Well, we're done now. I see the cavalry coming." She gestured to the oncoming night doctor. "Why don't you come home with me for dinner?"

Charlie barely heard the last part through Elizabeth's poorly smothered yawn. "You don't look up for company. Another time. I'm looking forward to stretching out in Katie's fabulous garden tub." She rubbed her lower back. "This was my first whole shift in quite a while. My muscles will remind me in the morning." She hugged her friend. "You go home and let that fabulous man spoil you a bit. You deserve it."

"I will. Night, Charlie."

She waved and headed for the locker room. Looking at the blood stains on her scrubs, she opted for a quick shower before changing into jeans and a tee shirt. She smothered her own yawn. She wasn't kidding when she mentioned the jacuzzi tub. The two had a date for exactly how long it took her to drive home.

Daylight hung on for a few more minutes, but long shadows bathed the parking lot. Charlie got in her car and headed home. Thoughts of Brendan, and his daughters, crowded her brain. For someone she wasn't going to get involved with, he sure crossed her mind a lot. She wondered how life faired with two new dogs. She felt more than a bit responsible for that. She could stop by. Make sure everyone was okay. Only because of the dogs, she assured herself. Yeah right. She was still thinking about Brendan when she pulled into the driveway of the townhouse. So the site of him seated on her porch stairs surely must be a hallucination.

Chapter Eleven

Brendan grasped the bunch of brightly colored Gerbera Daisies a bit too tightly. He watched Charlie exit her car. Loosening his grip to avoid damaging them, he stood and waited for her approach. She wore a stethoscope around her neck and fatigue etched into the lines of her face. He wondered if today had been her first real shift in the ER.

"You're probably wondering what I'm doing here," he offered.

She waited to answer until she reached him. "I should be. But I'm just happy to see you." So much for playing it cool. She gestured to the flowers dangling from his hand. "If those are for me, then I'm even happier."

"They aren't for Ginger."

Charlie laughed and grabbed them from his outstretched hand. "Now all I need is food. You didn't happen to bring some of that, did you? This week has been hectic at best, and I didn't make it to the grocery store yet."

Brendan whipped his phone from his back pocket. "Sorry no, but I have Thai, Cuban, Italian and pizza that will make you cry on speed dial. Which will it be?" He held his breath while she considered it. What had started as a simple impulse had morphed into dinner. He, who didn't date, had no idea what he was doing, but he also didn't care.

Charlie unlocked the front door before turning her dazzling smile on him. "You pick. You haven't been wrong yet."

Something warm unfurled in his chest. "Cuban it is, then. I get enough pizza between the girls and poker nights. Any requests?" At the shake of her head, he dialed and ordered.

When he finished, he slid the phone back into his pocket and looked around. "Looks a bit different."

"Katie took everything that she was moving to Flynn's. Several more boxes went for donation this morning. Not sure what she's doing with the rest. She kindly left me some kitchen stuff, although I'm hopeless in that room. Said I could use it until I find a place of my own." She moved to the fridge and grabbed a Pepsi for herself and a beer for him.

"When do your cooking lessons start?"

Puzzlement colored Charlie's face. "Oh, right. I did mention wanting to take cooking lessons one day. Good memory. Maybe when I have some time to breathe." She held out her arms. "This is great for now, and I am appreciative to Katie, but I'd like my own place in the not too far future. So, tell me about these poker nights."

He named the participants. "Everyone has weird schedules and busy lives, so the cast of characters changes every time. It's more about fun and trash talk than actually winning money."

"Hmm," she murmured. "No women?"

Brendan swallowed his first sip of beer, which now threatened to come out his nose. "Uh, no. Not by design. The group has grown and changed over the past few years. First Sam was added when Fitzgerald Construction built his home. Then he brought Quinn, Jack, and AJ, firefighter friends of his. Flynn is our latest new member." He gave her a direct stare. "Did you want to play?"

She looked up at him from under her lashes. "No thanks. I have my book club. Just curious."

"Book club, huh? Sounds wild."

"Oh, you'd be surprised, Brendan. We talked about men. And sex." She cocked her head and smiled. "Your name came up."

Brendan set his beer down with a thump, thankful he wasn't drinking this time. "Really?" Curiosity ate at him, but he refused to give into it.

"Yes. There was talk of our lunches and your new dogs. This is, after all, a very small town."

"Some days smaller than others," he muttered under his breath. "I'm sorry if they bothered you. I'm sure you didn't move here expecting to be embroiled in local gossip."

"I've never worried what others thought, or said, about me. Learned that lesson at my parents' knees."

Her voice held a note of sadness. Or maybe resignation. "You told me that they don't 'approve' of your choices. Still find that hard to believe." He sat on Katie's overstuffed couch and patted the seat next to him. "Care to tell me about it?"

She slid onto the sofa, pulling her legs up underneath her. "There's nothing else to tell, Brendan. I wasn't the child that either wanted." Her smile grew a bit sharper. "But then, they weren't exactly the parents I would have chosen." She shook her head and took a sip of her drink. "First world problems. I had a roof over my head and food in my stomach. Way more than can be said for the children I cared for in Africa."

Brendan's heart ached at the loss that colored her voice. "You could tell me about that. Help me to understand, even a little. If you wanted."

She raised her gaze to his, her eyes searching his for something. Understanding? Compassion? He didn't know which, but she began to speak. So low he could barely hear her. "I thought I was prepared for what I would see. Knew what I was getting myself into." A harsh laugh escaped her. "But you cannot understand that level of poverty until you see it. It's hard to complain about my parents, and their lack of support, when these people don't even have clean drinking water, Brendan. The conditions were horrific. Too many mouths to feed and no sustainable food. No access to medical care." She broke off on a rough sigh that was just shy of a sob.

She remained quiet for so long, he thought she'd finished. Never comfortable with a woman's silence, he was about to say something, anything, when she spoke.

"The kids were the hardest. But then they always are. Babies so thin and sickly that they don't even complain."

He placed a hand on her arm to comfort her. Or him. Brendan wasn't sure. But the small human contact made him feel better. She smiled at him, though it didn't quite reach her eyes. "Bet you're glad you stopped by, huh? Regular party girl."

He leaned in and brushed a stray hair from her face. "Not looking for a party girl." He was so close to her that he could see her pulse beat wildly in her neck. He longed to cover it with his mouth.

Her eyes widened. Her pupils dilated. "What *are* you looking for, Brendan?"

"I'm not looking for anything. Or anyone." Her breath quickened, warming his skin. "Yet I keep finding you." Brendan closed the tiny gap between them, placing his mouth on hers. He didn't think. Only felt. And tasted. Chocolate and her. Brendan wrapped her in his arms.

Charlie moaned deep in her throat and pressed against him. Her arms left her side and wrapped around his neck. There wasn't an inch between them anywhere. The kiss that had started out so simple now raged out of control, taking on a force of its own. He slanted his head and traced the outline of her lips with his tongue. Her fingers played in the hair at his nape, pressing him even closer.

Brendan knew he only had to press her backwards into the soft couch cushions. Which is why he pulled back instead. And dropped his arms from around her. Because all he could think about, in this moment, was the opposite. Hurt and confusion chased through her eyes.

He scrubbed a hand down his face and counted to ten in his head. It worked with the girls. Sometimes. "I don't need or want a woman in my life, Charlie. Yet, here you are. What I want, right now, is to take you in my arms, to your bed, and make love to you until morning." The words all came out in one, long sentence. "So, I let you go. Because I don't think either of us is ready for this."

She sat back on the couch, a safe distance away from him, he noticed. "You're right, of course." She blew out a heavy breath, stirring her blond bangs. "Doesn't mean I have to like it. I like you, Brendan. More than I've liked anyone in a long time."

Something warm and light stirred in his chest. Hope? Brendan tamped down the feeling. He had no right thinking that way. "The unspoken 'but' is deafening, Charlie."

She ducked her head. But not before he saw the dull red creep across her high cheek bones. She nodded once before lifting it again. "I'm the last person who should be starting anything. With anyone. I've been in town about a second." She gestured with her arm. "I don't even have a permanent address yet. I started a new job. I need to focus on that." She added in a small voice, "Then there's the other thing."

He grasped her hand. "The PTSD."

She nodded.

"How's that going? I've wanted to ask. Wanted you to know that I care. But, I uh."

"You didn't know how to ask? Or if you should?" She patted *his* hand now. "It's okay to talk about it. That means you care. It's a part of who I am, but it does not define me. My sessions with Dr. Lowery are going well. I actually look forward to them." She laughed at his puzzled expression. "His office is a safe place. I go there knowing I can speak about anything. No judgement."

He held his hand up in protest. "I don't judge you. Would never judge you."

"I'm not saying this right. It's different in that office. I go there, say what I need to say, and leave it there. It's a neutral zone. Dr. Lowery isn't part of my real life, out here in the world."

"Okay." He didn't necessarily understand, but if it helped her, then he was all for it. "I'm happy that you're feeling better. You look better." He stopped before he could put his foot any deeper into his mouth.

She laughed. "I know what you mean. I feel better. Less jumpy. Less brittle. I've been walking every day and taking time for myself. I love being back at work. Feeling useful again. My sleep is mostly better also."

"Mostly?" His sleep had been spotty lately. New for him. And she was to blame. Not that he'd tell her that.

Charlie leaned into him. "You're the reason I'm not sleeping. I close my eyes at night, and there you are."

Her words struck him right in the chest. "Huh. Always that honest, are you?" Most women, Jillian sprang to mind, would play games. Not Charlie.

"Yep." She waved a hand between them. "That kiss didn't come out of nowhere. There's a thing, something powerful, between us. You know it. I know it. I keep busy during the day, but at night." She paused, smiling at him. "But at night, when I crawl in to bed exhausted, my mind starts racing with thoughts of you. Of us. Is that too much information for you? Should I have kept quiet?"

"No. But I also have the girls to think about. They never meet any of the women I get involved with. Not that there have been a lot. But they already know you, and you're Elizabeth's best friend. It's not like you're going to disappear."

"Windsor Falls is my home now. I'm not going anywhere. And I adore Kerry and Abby. The last thing I want to do is hurt them."

"I know that, Charlie. But where does that leave us?" *Us?* There wasn't any us. What was he thinking?

The doorbell rang, giving Brendan the reprieve he needed. "That'll be dinner. I'll get the door." He pulled his wallet from his back pocket, thankful for the few moments to clear his head. He wasn't getting involved with her. At least not any further than he already was.

He paid the delivery guy and carried the food inside. He found her in the kitchen, grabbing plates and silverware. "I thought we'd eat in the kitchen, if you don't mind."

"Not at all." He walked to the table and placed the food in the middle of it. There seemed like a lot of food for the two of them. "I hope you're hungry."

She pointed to the table. "Everyone in Windsor Falls could be hungry, and there'd still be enough food."

He noticed that she had grabbed his beer and her soda from the living room. Thoughtful. What he'd come to expect of her. "Well, I wasn't sure what you liked. Besides, leftovers are always good."

"You're right about that." She rung her hands and shifter her weight from side to side. Brendan could understand that feeling. He was feeling a bit lost himself.

"If you've never had Cuban food, this will be a great introduction. To start, we have Platanos Maduros or baked sweet plantains and Beef Empanadas. Then, there's the choice of Ropa Vieja, a shredded beef and rice on a tortilla, or Arroz con Pollo, a chicken and rice dish. I like them all, so you choose first." He opened each container. His stomach growled in appreciation of the savory smells that wafted through the air.

Her light laugh danced across his skin. "Would it be okay if we shared it? You made it sound so good, and it all smells delicious."

"That's a great idea." The tightening in his gut had nothing to do with the food and everything to do with the woman sitting next to him. Over the mouth-watering smells of the food, Brendan could smell her. Something floral and all woman.

They spent the next few minutes dishing up a little of this and a bit of that until both had filled their plates. he pointed his fork at hers. "Are you sure you can eat all that?"

She placed a napkin on her lap. Her light laugh surrounded him. "Worry about your own plate. I spent over eight hours on my feet and can't remember when I last ate. So, this might be round one. Did you remember to get a dessert?"

Against his better judgement, he leaned in and sampled her lips. He only lingered for a moment, a heartbeat, before pulling back. "I can't imagine anything sweeter than that."

"You don't play fair."

"Who says I'm playing at all?" All logic, along with his carefully laid plans, flew out the window in her presence. "What if you and I were to have a relationship, Charlie?" He had spoken the r-word without dropping over dead.

Her fork fell, banging against the plate. "You don't do relationships. And I'm not in the right place to start one. We both know that."

"Agreed. And yet here we are, again. I don't know what I'm saying, other than I want to spend time with you. Get to know you better. I don't usually involve my girls, but they're already involved. They like you." He placed one hand over hers, smoothing out the death grip she held on her drink. "So do I."

"You're right, Brendan. This thing between us isn't going away. I've tried to not think about you. Or the girls. I've tried to do the right thing. But I like you too."

He blew out a big breath. "So, we agree." When she nodded, he continued. "I don't want to make a big deal of this. Or set a lot of ground rules. But I do have to consider the girls. I'm their only parent. I am the example they see." He twisted his napkin in his lap. Why was this so difficult?

She smiled and placed her hands over his. "No sleepovers at your house then. Is that what you were trying so very hard not to say?"

He laughed out loud. "Yes, that's it exactly. It's not that I don't want to have sex with you. You must know that. I can't, won't, do it with them in the house."

Charlie smiled. The kind that had been leading men astray for centuries. "Good thing I don't have any roommates then, isn't it?"

He stood and pulled her up with him. "I'm not hungry anymore. At least not for food." The last he all but growled against her lips.

She sighed and kissed him deeply. Then she stepped away from him, leading him to the stairs.

*****

They almost didn't make it up the stairs. Charlie stopped several times to taste him. She couldn't believe this was happening. Despite all their protestations, and good reasons for those, Brendan was here. In her house. In her arms. And none of those reasons mattered anymore.

"You're wearing too many clothes," he groaned as his hands crept under the hem of her shirt. He lifted it up and off her. His fingers trailing across her abdomen were the first cold splash of reality. He still didn't know what had happened to her. How would she explain the scarring on her lower abdomen?

Rational thought fled when those wandering fingers found her breasts. Even through the cup of her bra, her flesh puckered at his touch. They had reached her room. She was thankful for the darkness that had descended outside. No need for him to see the what had happened to her. Not yet.

Her fingers mirrored his, creeping under his shirt. But she settled on the waist of his jeans, teasing the firm flesh with a whisper of touch. She fingered the belt. He kissed her to the depth of her soul. Lost in sensation with his tongue teasing hers, her hands stalled out where they were.

"Where are the lights? I want to see all of you."

"And I want to *feel* you," she replied. She pushed him onto the bed and poured herself on top of him, covering him like a blanket. "We fit. I knew we would."

Brendan grabbed her and rolled until she lay under him. "We're going to fit even better soon."

The tender way he brushed hair from her face was almost her undoing. He was a sensitive man. One that might break her heart in the end. She squirmed under him. "Now who has too many clothes on?"

He obliged her by pulling off his shirt and tossing it on the floor. "Better?"

She ran her tongue along the ridge of his shoulder. "Hmmm I think you forgot some." Charlie bit down, not quite gently. She moved her hands to between them and started working on his belt. Brendan propped himself up on his elbows to help her. She undid the belt and top button before sliding one hand down the front of his jeans.

A low moan ripped from his throat. "You like that I guess," she murmured. She cupped the length of him, teasing his head with her thumb. "Think how good it'll feel when you're naked."

"Christ, Charlie, are you trying to end this before it even begins?"

She kissed him with everything she had, pouring months of loneliness into it. He pulsed in her hand, bulging against the constraints of his cotton briefs. She gave herself over to the sensations swirling around her. His tongue met hers in a timeless dance. Each stroke brought her higher. Her hips moved beneath his on the bed.

He tore his mouth from hers, gulping in air. He jumped off the bed, pulling down his jeans as he went. "I need to feel you on me. Nothing in the way." He pulled a condom from his wallet and placed it on the nightstand. He turned back to her with a grin. "Your turn."

Charlie lifted her hips from the bed. He grabbed the waist of her jeans. She sighed as he stripped them down her legs, but her eyes remained serious. She worried her bottom lip with her teeth.

He sat on the edge of the bed. He picked up her hand. "Charlie, what's wrong?"

Tears sprang to the edges of her eyes. She dashed at them. "I'm so sorry. It's been a long time for me."

"Scoot over." When she moved further to the middle of the bed, he scooped her into his arms.

She closed her eyes, willing away the damned tears. Her voice was thick with them when she spoke. "I'm such an idiot."

"There's no hurry, Charlie. We don't have to do this right now."

"But I want to do this right now. I've wanted to do this since I saw you in the ER."

He turned his head to look at her. "Even though I acted like an out of control idiot?"

Moonlight streamed in from the partially opened curtains. Charlie could make out the expression on his face. "You were a freaked-out Dad. I knew that. Maybe a few minutes after that."

"Oh, like when I burst into the exam room and caught you half naked." He shook his head. "It's a wonder you even still speak to me."

She laughed, holding her lower abdomen. "This is exactly what I needed." She placed a light kiss on his cheek. The whiskers tickled a bit. "It has been awhile, and the past few months have been a strain. To say the least." She placed her lips against his.

He leaned up on one elbow and put more pressure into the kiss. All fears flew out of her mind. She kissed him back, matching each stroke of his tongue. She sighed as he moved his mouth down along the sensitive line of her jaw and then lower still. Her nipples tightened into tiny buds when he blew across them.

"Two can play at that game," she warned. Charlie cupped him again, this time without the barrier of his underwear between them. He was steel wrapped in velvet in her hand. His eyes closed. She ran her fingers down the length of him. She circled back to tease the very responsive head. "Lie back. Let me take care of you," she murmured, giving him the tiniest shove.

He landed on his back, legs parted, eyes closed. Satisfaction shown from the half smile on his face. Charlie took a moment to enjoy the view. His body was muscled in all the right places. The way she liked it. A light coating of dark hair covered his chest. It tapered down his abdomen, like a map pointing to buried treasure. She raked her nails ever so gently across his abs, winning a sharp intake of breath for her effort.

"You *are* trying to kill me," he muttered. His eyes remained closed.

"Would it be the worst way to go?" Before he could answer, Charlie wrapped her hand around him again. She spread the tiny drop of moisture on his head. Encouraged by the noises he made, she slid her hand down his length and cupped his balls. She leaned in and swirled her tongue around the quivering tip.

"Christ, Charlie," he groaned from deep in his chest.

Before she realized his intent, he reversed their positions. "I wasn't finished," she protested.

"I almost was," Brendan responded. "There's plenty of time for that later. I need to be inside of you."

His words went straight to her center, making Charlie want to curl her toes. Before she could come up with a witty reply, his finger slid through her damp curls. "Open your eyes. I want to watch you."

She did as he asked, soft, brown eyes staring up into blue ones. Brendan slid one, thick finger inside of her, and her hips moved to their own rhythm. His lips travelled along her collarbone, sliding downward until they found her nipple. Charlie dug her heels into the mattress to keep from flying apart. The sensations surrounded her, driving her upwards. She almost lost in when he inserted another finger.

"Please, Brendan," she begged. Her hips bucked off the bed to further encourage his hand. "I need you."

Brendan drew back his head and blew lightly across the already sensitized nipple. He chuckled deep in his throat. "What do you need, Charlie? Tell me exactly what you need." His gaze never left hers.

She couldn't remember ever feeling this kind of connection. It warmed and scared her at the same time. But her body's needs were greater. "I need to feel you inside of me."

He didn't break their gaze as he reached for the condom on the nightstand.

The sound of the foil packet tearing mingled with their rapid breaths. She took it out of his hands and rolled the condom down the length of him, teasing him along the way. His eyes darkened to navy.

His hand once again found her center. He slid a finger in and out of the moisture. "I think you're ready."

"More than," she breathed.

Brendan positioned himself over Charlie and nudged the tip of his penis into her. She smiled and raised her hips to meet him. "Please."

He slid home at her plea, pushing himself all the way in until he filled her. "That's it."

Before she could savor the moment, he pulled almost all the way our and then plunged back in. Charlie wrapped her legs around him, locking her ankles on his lower back. Locking him inside her.

He smiled down into her face. "I've dreamed of this. Being inside of you. But the dreams pale in comparison." He lowered his head to the other breast, teasing the puckered nipple with his tongue.

Charlie gasped. Her abdominal muscles protested with a twinge, but the sensations below them more than made up for it. He moved his hips faster in response, driving in and out of her. She answered with her nails digging into his back.

"Yes," she cried. Tension rose in her body. She was so close to the edge, dangling by her fingertips, when he surged into her one final time. Bright lights exploded behind her eyes. Charlie flew apart into thousands of pieces. Moments later, he stiffened with release before slumping onto the bed beside her. Their sounds of their rough breathing filled the room.

Brendan kissed her shoulder and got out of bed. Charlie watched him head into the bathroom. She slid under the covers, pulling the sheet to her breasts, suddenly shy alone in the bed. She couldn't stop the smile spreading across her face, even if she wanted to. He never strayed far from her thoughts, and she had imagined them in exactly this position. But she never thought it would happen. It had happened all right. Despite their reservations. Despite the good reasons why it shouldn't. Her smile dimmed. Those reservations and reasons were still there. Nothing had changed. She pulled the covers over her head.

Chapter Twelve

Brendan splashed cool water on his face, stalling his return to the bedroom. How had this happened? He shook his head. He knew how of course. Why he had let it happen was a better, far more dangerous question. Nothing had changed. Knowing he couldn't put it off any longer, Brendan hit the light and returned to the bedroom. In the dim light coming from the hallway and windows, he could make out Charlie's shape under the sheet. Her whole body was covered. Not a good sign.

He slid in next to her. "I doubt you're asleep that fast," he murmured to her smooth back.

"Maybe I am," came her muffled reply. "Maybe I'm one of those lucky people who falls asleep the moment their head hits the pillow."

Despite the situation, he chuckled. "No way." He placed one hand in the middle of her back and rubbed in circles. "Tell me what's wrong."

Charlie sighed before rolling over to face him. She tucked the sheet around her like armor. Another bad sign.

"I've already seen you naked. Remember?" she had never struck him as the shy type, even when he had burst in on her half naked in the ER. He wondered what had changed.

"I'd have to have suffered a stroke to forget."

She inched closer and laid her head on his shoulder. He wrapped an arm around her, pleased to have her back against him. Already, he stirred at her nearness. But this was not the time for round two.

"That's a good thing, right. You not forgetting so soon?" *Yikes.* He sounded like an insecure sixteen-year-old. They were both happy at the end of round one. He didn't need reassurances.

She swatted his chest. "Fishing?"

He puffed his chest up a bit. "No need." If only he felt as confident.

She traced a finger through the hair on his chest. Brendan tried to stay focused. But he knew how talented those fingers were. "Do you regret this, then?" He mentally crossed his fingers.

"No," she replied in a less than sure voice. "Maybe." She sighed and raked a hand through her tangled hair. "The timing isn't the best, Brendan. I've been in Windsor Falls about a second. Plus, I'm a bit messy. And you have the girls to think about."

"All true, except the messy part." He smoothed a hand over her arm when she would have protested. "There are issues in both of our lives, and yet here we are. Can you honestly say we made a mistake?"

She eased up on one elbow and looked down at him. Her beautiful smile started small and then spread across her face. "No, Brendan, I can't." She leaned in and placed a gentle kiss upon his lips before lying against him once again.

Brendan turned onto his side to face her. Even after a long day of work, with her hair tangled around her, the site of her stole his breath. He combed the fingers of one hand through her long, blonde hair. "I'm glad you feel that way. I have no idea what I'm doing. And you're right, I have the girls to think about. But you make me happy."

"Good. Because you make me happy too."

Her hand slide down his chest and over his abdomen. His body tightened. He looked at his watch and sighed. "Leaving is the last thing I want right now. But, I have to get the girls from my mother."

Charlie placed her hands on either side of his face and kissed him. One he felt all the way to his toes. She broke off after a moment. "Something for you to remember me by."

He grabbed her and rolled her under him. He pressed his naked body along the length of hers before scorching her mouth with his own. He only stopped when oxygen became necessary. "I'm not likely to forget," he joked before getting out of bed in search of his clothes.

When he turned around wearing only his underwear, he found Charlie watching him. He raised an eyebrow. "Like what you see?"

She laughed. "You know I do."

"If I didn't have to go get the girls, you'd be in big trouble right now." He shook a finger at her for effect. It didn't have the one he intended.

Charlie laughed so hard she had to hold her abdomen. With a smirk, she asked, "Oh?"

He grabbed his jeans and pulled them on before she lured him back into her bed. Propped up against the pillows with her golden hair spread out around her, she was a siren. He pulled his shirt on over his head. "You'll have to wait until next time to see."

The corner of her mouth quivered. "There's going to be a next time, then?"

He leaned over her and brushed a strand of hair behind her ear. "I have no idea where this is going, but I'm looking forward to finding out." He kissed her before picking up his boots and leaving the room.

*****

Charlie lay back against the pillows and listened as he left the house. She could hear his whistling until he shut the front door behind him. She shook her head at the craziness of the situation. Their timing sucked. But they were both happy, so she refused to think about it.

She traced the scar on her abdomen with a finger. It was a harsh reminder of everything she had endured in Africa. And of her future. Someday, soon, she needed to tell him about it. But not today. And not this week. She would revel in the unexpected joy of hot sex with Brendan and worry about it another day. Scarlett O'Hara had nothing on Charlie Avery.

The ringing of her phone shattered the peace of the moment. The ring tone, one especially dark and foreboding, warned it was her mother. Charlie considered letting it go to voicemail. But that would only be putting off the inevitable. She had learned it was better to deal with her mother.

"Hello, Mother," she answered.

"When are you going to come to your senses and come home, Charlotte?"

Her mother never was one for beating around the bush. Or taking her daughter's wishes seriously. She bit back a sigh and settled for rolling her eyes. "I've already told you and Father, I am home. I live in Windsor Falls now."

"Well that's ridiculous, Charlotte Grace. You finally come back to the South but insist on living hours from your family. What will people think?"

And there in lie the issue, she mused. It never mattered what she might think. Or feel. Only others. She took a deep breath before answering. Keeping her sanity depended on holding her temper and getting off quickly. "Mother, I don't care what people might think. I'm happy here. I have a job I love, and the town is gorgeous. Everyone has been so friendly and welcoming." Unlike her own family she decided against adding. Not once had they made the effort to make her feel wanted or comfortable.

"Surely you don't plan on staying there. You'll come to your senses and move back to Charleston. It's your home."

"Mother, I haven't considered Charleston my home since I left for college at eighteen. You must have noticed by now. I have no intention of living in Charleston again."

"But what about the house? When your father and I die, it will go to you. An Avery has lived in this house for generations. You have an obligation, Charlotte."

She gripped the phone until her knuckles whitened. Talking to her mother was pointless at best and painful at worst. She took another cleansing breath. Her stomach knotted. The Avery house was a museum to be admired and envied. It was never a home.

"Mother, we've had this discussion too many times to count. I will not be living in that house. Ever. Any one of my many cousins would love it."

"Of course, they would, Charlotte. But I want you to have it. Your father is the eldest, making you the rightful heir." Her mother's voice rose to an unpleasant pitch.

"Well, I don't want it. Never did. Never will. I'm not going to change my mind, Mother."

A strangled noise sounded at the other end, followed by the clatter of the phone being grabbed. Her father's aristocratic voice boomed over the distance.

"What's all this nonsense, Charlie? You're giving your mother a migraine. And you know how impossible she is when that happens. One day, you'll get this foolishness out of your system and come home where you belong."

She ground her molars, hoping she'd have any left when this conversation ended. It didn't go unnoticed that her father's concern was for himself. "Father, I have been very clear. I am not moving back to Charleston. I am not planning to live in the house. What don't you understand?"

"Young lady, you will not talk to me in that manner."

"I only talk to you in that manner when you do not listen to me. I am not moving back to Charleston. I have a job I love here in Windsor Falls. I'm making friends. Soon, I'll be looking for a home of my own. Neither you nor Mother are dying anytime soon, but feel free to make whatever plans you wish for the house. I have to go now."

Charlie hit end on her cell, missing the days of being able to slam the receiver. Probably better this way. Her parents reduced her to a child with only a few words. The years of never being understood, or good enough, came flooding back. Hot tears rolled down her face. She brushed them away. They weren't worth crying over.

Angry with herself for caring, she got out of bed and headed for the shower. She had already washed away the day's work, but a long, hot shower would do wonders for her stress. Charlie winced as she rolled her shoulders. That's what she got for talking with her mother. Her stomach grumbled. Brendan made her forget about dinner. They'd eaten only a few bites. She'd see to that after her shower.

Charlie shampooed her hair and then grabbed her hanging sponge. Certain long-unused muscles were beginning to ache. That brought a smile to her face. They shared an amazing chemistry. Something she learned the very first time he touched her. But a hand on her arm was nothing compared to what had exploded between them.

Charlie finished up, skipping putting conditioner in her hair. She stepped out, wrapping one thick, yellow towel around her head and another around her body. She closed the bathroom door and stepped in front of the body length mirror attached to it. With a trembling hand, she wiped away the condensation. She parted the towel wrapped around her torso. There were a series of scars, not just one.

Meeting her gaze in the foggy mirror, troubled eyes stared back at her. The scars one couldn't see took the heaviest toll. The loss that no one could observe. She struggled with that. She wrapped her arms around her abdomen. Hot tears coursed down her face. Her appetite vanished.

She shook her head, trying to clear her mood. Most days she focused on being alive. Having running water and easy access to medical care. Having a great new job in a safe, small town. Her parents' relentless campaign to shape her into something she would never be annoyed her. But that was a first world problem. It served her well to remember that.

That's enough pity for one day. Charlie shrugged off any lingering, gloomy thoughts. She finished drying off and slipped into an old, ragged tee from medical school. She had washed the shirt so many times, she could barely read the word Tulane. But it was soft and reminded Charlie of all she had accomplished.

She maneuvered her wet hair into one thick braid and placed a towel across the pillow. She yawned hugely and slipped into bed. She thought of Brendan, and her mouth widened in a smile. She had no idea where they were headed, but she couldn't wait to find out.

*****

Little girl shrieks greeted Brendan as he walked in the front door of his parents' home. He glanced around, marveling at how little had changed. They had bought new furniture over the years, but the general feeling of family, warmth, and happiness remained unchanged.

"Daddy," cried Kerry, throwing herself against his legs. "Nana made us s'getti for dinner. It was yummy!" She rubbed her belly.

"I can see," he replied, wiping a dab of sauce from the corner of her mouth. "I love your Grandmother's spaghetti, honey. She used to make it for me when I needed cheering up."

"Really? Cool."

Brendan laughed at his daughter's enthusiasm. "Yes, it is. Now where's your sister? We need to get moving."

"Here I am, Daddy," called Abby, skipping into the room. She wore an identical sauce stain on her face. She looked around the room. "Where's Dr. Charlie?"

"I imagine she's asleep by now, honey. She had a very busy first day at work."

Abby's face clouded. "But I thought we were going to see her tonight. I wanted to show her the tricks that we've teached Fred & Ginger."

"Me too," cried Kerry. I teached them too." Her mouth curved downward and tears threatened to spill from her wide, green eyes.

"Now, girls, your poor Dad is barely in the door. What's all this noise about?"

He smiled in gratitude at his Mom. "Charlie will see Fred & Ginger soon, girls. In fact, why don't we invite her for a bar-b-q this week-end? Then she can spend some time with us at the house."

"Yes, yes, yes," both girls shrieked. They danced around him, tears and pouts forgotten.

"It's a plan. I'll call Charlie tomorrow to make sure she's available. Let's get going now, ladies. It's past your bedtime."

A series of groans and protests followed, but the girls were both yawning. Brendan swallowed hard as he watched them say goodbye to his mother. He was so grateful for his family. He couldn't imagine raising the girls without their help.

He gave his Mom a big hug and kiss on the cheek. "I'd be lost without you."

She hugged him back before backing up a step and looking up at him. "No, Brendan, you wouldn't. You're doing an amazing job with those girls. You'd be fine."

He let out a shaky laugh. "We both know that's not true. Yes, I would do what I had to do to raise them, but having you here makes it so much easier. And better."

"Well, that much is true," Maggie joked. Her eyes grew serious and she lowered her voice. "The girls are wonderful young ladies, with no thanks to their mother." She practically spit out the last word.

Brendan glanced around to make sure the girls hadn't heard before nodding. "Do you ever think they'd be better off with a mother." At her horrified look, he hurried on to explain. "Not Jillian. But a mother. Someone to help me raise them. Give them a woman's perspective." He shook his head. "I don't know. I worry about them growing older. They're going to need a woman when they're teenagers."

Maggie shook her finger at him, as she had so many times during his childhood. "Brendan Patrick, don't be an idiot. If you find someone to love, then yes. But not if you're talking about marrying someone to give the girls a mother. That's the most foolish thing I've heard you say yet."

He held up his hands in defeat. "All right. Message received loud and clear."

"But if you were to fall in love with someone wonderful, like Charlie for instance, then I'd say go for it."

"No one was talking about Charlie, Mom."

"Oh? Weren't we? My mistake."

He barked out a laugh. Brendan couldn't remember the last time his mother had been wrong. Or at least admitted to it. She knew exactly what she was suggesting.

He wasn't ready to think that way yet. It was way too early in their relationship. Or whatever they were doing. He had a lot to think about.

"Let's go, girls. It's getting late."

That resulted in another round of hugs and goodbyes to their grandmother. Finally, they were in the car and on the way home. The motion of the car lulled his girls into sleep before they were half way home. He pulled into his driveway and turned off the motor. He swiveled in his seat and watched them sleep. Their stillness amazed him. They were whirling dynamos when awake.

The girls were growing up fine without their mother. But they were already six. Those first years had flown by in the blink of an eye. Would they resent not having a mother when they were older? He knew that wasn't a reason to marry. His mother had been quick to point that out. And he had resisted the idea this long. Then Charlie barreled into his life.

And it wasn't just the electrifying sex they shared. He liked her. Enjoyed spending time together. Their very different career paths never seemed to be an issue. She was easy to talk with and didn't take herself too seriously. She possessed a warmth and inner beauty that Jillian never had. He could never see his ex-wife helping others in Africa.

Glancing at his phone, he wondered if she was still awake. He decided to chance it. He dashed off a text.

"Hey, it's me. The girls would like to invite you to a bar-b-q at our house t his week-end."

He felt like he was back in high school, not that they texted then, as he awaited her reply. It took less than a minute.

"The girls, huh?"

He leaned forward and bounced his head against the steering wheel. He knew he had said the wrong thing. Even before he hit send. What was wrong with him?

"My bad. I get credit for the idea. They agreed. Are you working?"

"Off and I'd love to come. Can't wait to see Fred and Ginger. Plus, Kerry and Abby."

Everyone but him, he mused. He liked this lighter side of her.

"What about me?"

He held his breath. The little bubbles told him she was responding.

"I suppose… What time and day? What can I bring?"

"How about Saturday? 3? Just yourself."

"I was raised better than that. I'll think of something. Don't worry. It won't be something I made."

His hearty laugh woke the girls. He slid his phone in his pocket and opened his door. "Kerry, Abby we're home. Time to wake up."

Kerry stretched and squeezed her eyes shut against the truck's interior light. Abby bounded out of the truck into Brendan's arms, always the first of the twins to wake. "Daddy, I had the best dream! Charlie moved in with us and became our Mommy. Isn't that great?"

He wasn't sure whether her words or utter happiness snagged his heart. The girls never talked about wanting a mother. Or the fact that they missed having one. Ever. But the pure joy in her voice pierced his heart. This was exactly why he had never introduced any of the women he dated to his girls. He didn't want anyone getting any ideas.

"Daddy? Did you hear me? Wasn't that a cool dream?"

He could have kicked himself at the subdued tone of Kerry's voice. "I heard you, baby. Sorry. Daddy was thinking of something else for a moment." He smiled to ease her concern.

"Oh," Abby piped up. "You mean you were wood gathering. That's what Nanna calls it."

Brendan laughed, grateful for the lightened moment. *"Wool* gathering, you mean. And you're right." He grabbed one hand of each girl. "Now, let's go in and get the bath done. It's been a long day."

Chapter Thirteen

The next few days flew for Charlie. She worked days in the ED, getting to know the routine and her new coworkers. Without exception, everyone welcomed her. But working again with Elizabeth took the cake. She hadn't realized how much she missed seeing her old friend until now. She learned her way around the department. Patients were the same no matter where you worked. Being in a state of the art department was heaven after her time in Africa.

Friday was slow, although she knew better than to ever say the 'q word'. Nothing could get you dirty looks from new coworkers faster. Everyone knew better than to say it was quiet in the department. While she wasn't superstitious, she agreed with that one.

She dictated her note for a seven-year-old boy who thought he could fly. Thankfully, the bushes surrounding the garage broke his fall. Tommy wanted to be Superman, red cape and all. His older brother, Danny, had dared him to jump off said garage roof. Tommy learned about gravity, earning a fractured ankle for his effort. She wasn't sure which of the boys was in more trouble. She reminded their poor, frightened mother that it could have ended much worse. Charlie waved good-bye to the family and watched Tommy learn to navigate on crutches. That might slow Superman down for a bit.

"Oh, that feels so good," sighed Elizabeth, lowering her bulky frame into the chair next to Charlie. "Not that I'm going to tell Sam, who already wants to wrap me in bubble wrap, but these days are getting longer and harder." She rubbed a hand over her belly and leaned back in the chair.

She bit back a laugh at the sight her friend made. "Hate to be the bearer of bad tidings, but you still have a way to go."

Elizabeth blew an ebony curl from her face. "Don't I know it. My due date is July seventeenth. I'm hoping to stop working by the end of June. But that seems like a million years away right now." She shifted her weight in the chair.

"I'm sure it does, but it's only eight weeks. Pace yourself."

Elizabeth pulled a face. "Believe me, I am." She rubbed her belly. "Peanut here isn't giving me a choice. The other doctors have been wonderful. I'm not doing any more night shifts. And I'm limiting myself to eight-hour ones instead of ten or twelve. That helps."

"I know what you mean about nights. I'm doing three next week." The look on her face told exactly how she felt about that.

Elizabeth laughed. "Sorry about that. I know it means everyone else has to do more."

"It's fine. I don't mind doing nights. It's the sleeping during the day that I hate. I never got good at that. Luckily, Katie was a night shifter too. She has fabulous black out curtains in the bedroom."

Elizabeth nodded, a suspicious smile spreading across her face. "Speaking of the Fitzgeralds, how's it going with Brendan?"

Charlie tried to act cool but failed miserably. She glanced around to ensure they were alone. Gossip mills thrived in hospitals. "Fabulous." She felt a blush spread across her cheekbones.

Elizabeth clapped her hands together. "I knew it! Tell me everything."

"Shush. I don't want to be the next topic of conversation around here. Besides, it's very new. As in this week."

"Really? I would swear there were sparks with you two from the moment you met."

"Oh, there were. But we're both being cautious for obvious reasons."

Elizabeth tilted her head. "Obvious reasons?"

Charlie blew out a long breath and turned her chair to face Elizabeth. "He's very careful about dating because of the girls. And I, well, that's a long story."

Elizabeth rolled her chair closer until her knees bumped Charlie's. "And you? What?" Her mouth turned downwards and her shoulders drooped. "I know there's something going on with you. Something you haven't been able to tell me yet. I'm here for you."

Tears sprang to her eyes. She took Elizabeth's hands in hers. "I know that, Elizabeth. And I'm thankful. The time has never been right." She glanced at her friend's pregnant belly. "But, I'm dealing with it. Really."

Elizabeth grasped her hands and squeezed. "My being pregnant has nothing to do with this, Charlie. I'm here for you, no matter what. As you were there for me in Los Angeles."

Charlie pulled her hands free and swiped at the tears that had leaked from her eyes. She offered up a watery smile. "I know, Elizabeth. And I will tell you. Everything. But in my own time."

"Okay, then. So, back to juicy details about Brendan." She screwed up her face. "On the other hand, he's like a brother to me, so not so juicy."

She laughed and hugged her friend. "I wasn't going to tell you anyway. Let's say that he and I are having fun. I care about him, Elizabeth. More than I wanted to right now. But that's life."

"I know it's tricky with the girls, Charlie. But he's a great guy. He'd never hurt you. And you are the only woman that I know of who's met his girls. That has to mean something."

"It's not like he had a choice. I already met them before we ever got involved. Let's say it's early days. He invited me for a bar-b-q tomorrow."

Elizabeth's clear blue eyes brightened. "That's great! I want to hear all about it on Sunday!"

*****

"When is Charlie getting here, Daddy?"

Brendan looked down at Kerry, pulling on his hand. He thought the same thing. "Anytime now, honey. Where's Abby? Did you guys pick up your room?"

"Yes, Daddy," answered Abby, running into the kitchen waving a piece of paper. "Look what I made for Charlie. Do you think she'll like it?"

Brendan took the offered paper. On it were three shapes. One had long yellow hair and was obviously Charlie. The other two blobs could be dogs. In a certain light. "Are these Fred and Ginger?"

Abby screwed up her face. "Of course, Daddy. Don't they look like Fred and Ginger to you?"

He had guessed only because there were two blobs. "I guessed right! Yay for Daddy. Now, are you sure your room is decent?"

Both girls grinned from ear to ear. "Yes, Daddy," piped Kerry.

"We want Charlie to like us," offered Abby.

Unease gathered in the pit of his stomach. He crouched down to their level. "Girls, Charlotte likes you guys already. You don't have to worry about what your room looks like."

"But we want her to be our Mommy. If our room is perfect, maybe she will."

The disquiet grew to boulders rolling around in his stomach. He grabbed one hand from each girl. "Kerry, Abby, I need you to listen to me. Charlie is our friend. We like her, and she likes us. That doesn't mean she's going to be your Mommy." He glanced to each solemn face. "Please don't ask her to be your Mommy. Do you understand?"

Each girl nodded, their mouths downturned. "Everyone else has a mommy. All the kids in school do."

Kerry nodded. "And that mean boy, Dean, told me it was my fault we don't."

Brendan's heart clenched. This was what he had dreaded for years. "Listen to me. Both of you. It was never your fault. Not everyone should have children. Your mother, uh, is one of those. And I'm the luckiest guy in the world! I get to have you guys all to myself." He reached out and hugged both girls, careful of Abby's cast. "And we do all right, don't we?"

"Yes, Daddy," both girls answered. They hugged him harder.

The doorbell sounded, almost drowned out by the barking of both dogs. "That's Charlie. Why don't you guys go let her in."

The two girls, unhappiness forgotten, ran out of the kitchen. Fred and Ginger followed on their heels. Brendan stood and wished he recovered as quickly. This was the conversation he had dreaded since they were born. His heart ached with the knowledge that they had not come to him earlier with these fears.

"Hello, Brendan."

He turned at the sound of her voice. Charlie stood in the kitchen doorway, a pink box from De Luca's Bakery in her hand. She wore her hair loose and a simple sundress that skimmed her knees and left her shoulders bare. She was a vision. He wanted to pull her into his arms. But Brendan was very aware of two sets of eyes watching him.

"What did you bring us?" Both girls spoke at once. Their faces were wreathed in grins.

"How do you know this is for you? It might be for Fred and Ginger."

"Charlie," Abby cried. "Dogs don't eat people food. Well, not from a bakery."

Brendan laughed out loud. "Luckily, I'm not a dog. What did you bring us, Charlie?"

"Well, I promised to not cook anything, since I'm terrible at it. So, I brought a cherry pie."

"That's our favorite," yelled Kerry. "How did you know?"

"I'm very smart," replied Charlie in a serious tone. Then she laughed. "Actually, I asked Kat."

"Here, let me take that." Brendan reached for the bakery box, brushing her hand as he did. Her skin was warm and soft, and the contact stopped him in his tracks. He had never felt this kind of attraction with anyone. *Best not to think along those lines with the girls here.*

"I hope you brought your appetite. The girls and I have planned a huge menu."

"Never a problem. You know my appetite by now." She laughed at the expression on the girls' faces. "If you're not careful, I might eat your pie."

Both girls shrieked, sending the dogs into another round of barking. "Girls, why don't you take the dogs into the yard?"

"Okay, Daddy," agreed the twins.

When they were outside, he turned to her. His voice was rough when he spoke. "I don't know quite how to say this, so I'm just going to. Before you arrived, the girls asked me if you're going to be their Mommy. In fact, they cleaned their room to impress you."

She gasped. "Oh, Brendan. I'm so sorry. I never meant to make this harder for you. Or them. Should I go?" Concern clouded her eyes.

He reached out, placing his hand on her arm. "No, of course not. I wanted to warn you in case they mentioned it to you. This is why I've never brought anyone home before now. And they've been getting some tough questions from a kid at school about why they don't have a mother." His features hardened. "I had no idea."

She nodded. "I can't imagine how difficult this is for you. I've never dated anyone with children. I don't want to give them the wrong impression. What should I do?"

Her concern for his girls touched him. "There's nothing for you to do. I only mentioned it in case they did. I explained to them that you are their friend. And mine." He dropped his eyes to the ground for a moment. "I don't want the girls to know about us yet. Is that okay with you."

"Of course, Brendan. Whatever you think is best. The last thing I would ever do is anything to hurt them. Or you."

He knew that was true. The irony is that Charlie already cared more about the girls than their mother ever did. He cleared his throat. "Why don't I get things going with the grill?"

She nodded. "Can you point me to the bathroom?"

"Sure. We have a half bath around the corner near the stairs."

"Thanks. I'll be out in a minute."

Brendan stepped forward, closing the distance between them. He kissed her cheek. "Thank you for understanding." He turned and went out the sliding door to the patio.

*****

Charlie held her breath until she found the powder room. After closing and locking the door behind her, she let out a huge, pent up breath. She needed a few minutes alone to digest what Brendan had told her. She turned on the water, splashing some on her face to cool it.

What was wrong with Jillian? Those precious girls deserved so much better than that. She blotted her face with the hand towel and stared into the mirror. Her own would never be named mother of the year, but at least she had been there.

Charlie stared into the mirror, trying to make sense of this. She longed for precious little girls like Kerry and Abby. Her stomach clenched at the unfairness of life. She wrapped her arms around her abdomen. The knowledge that she would never have children of her own tore through her. The violence in Africa had robbed her of much more than sleep and peace. Tears rolled down her face.

Like many people, kids had always been a vague notion for her future. After she found someone she'd want to have them with. No one she had dated ever came close to being that person. Until now. Brendan was such an amazing father. The kind of man any woman in her right mind would want. And here she was, barren.

Bullets had ripped low through her abdomen, destroying everything in its path. The trauma surgeon had been lucky to save her life. Unfortunately, nothing could be done to save her fertility. They had performed a total abdominal hysterectomy. What if Brendan wanted more children?

Charlie straightened up to her full height. She dried her tears and blew her nose. Crying over what was wouldn't help. She had accepted her lot over the past few months. Moved on. But meeting Brendan dragged the reality back to the light. She washed her hands and dried them on the hand towel. Brendan would think she had gotten lost. She opened the door to find four sets of eyes staring at her; two human and two canine.

Putting on a bright yet fake smile, she looked at the kids and dogs. "I wasn't gone that long." Fred bayed his Basset Hound sound as if to disagree.

Abby tapped her foot. "Kerry and me have been waiting here forever, Charlie." Her sister nodded in agreement.

"Kerry and I," she corrected.

Abby blew a chunk of blonde hair out of her eyes. "That's what I said. Anyway, we're dying to show you the tricks we taught the dogs." Each girl grabbed one of Charlie's hands and led her to the backyard.

"I see they found you," Brendan said from his station at the grill. "Girls, I told you to not bother Charlie while she was in the bathroom." His serious tone completely lost on them.

"We waited until she came out. Didn't we Charlie?"

She laughed and nodded to Kerry. "That's right, Brendan. They were waiting for me in the hall. All four of them." She winked at Kerry and Abby. "And they're not bothering me."

"We told you, Daddy." Kerry pulled her hand, leading her to a chair.

The little girl ran into the yard and came back with a bright, pink hula hoop. "Watch, Charlie." She held the hoop several inches off the ground and called Ginger. "Okay, Ginger, like I showed you. Jump." The little dog jumped through the hoop, clearing it easily.

"Good girl, Ginger. I knew you could do it." Ginger ran circles around Kerry, pink tongue hanging out in the heat.

Not to be outdone, Abby stood in front of Charlie. "I've taught him how to sit." She called Fred to her. The Bassett, who had been eyeing the grill at Brendan's side, heaved himself up and lumbered to Abby, sitting at her feet. Abby frowned. "Fred, you're 'posed to wait for me to tell you to sit." The brown and black dog sank to the patio with a sigh, rolling over to expose his belly for some rubs.

Charlie clapped. "Wow, Abby, you've already taught him two things."

Abby's face brightened. "I did, Charlie. I taught him to lay down." She fell to her knees and rubbed Fred's stomach. His sigh of contentment made everyone laugh.

Charlie felt the weight of Brendan's stare and looked up. Sure enough, he looked at her over Abby's head. He mouthed the words *thank you*, and she nodded. She watched the girls play with their dogs. Her heart pounded as she thought of his ex-wife. She didn't know Jillian, and didn't want to. Charlie couldn't imagine how the woman could walk away from such precious children. It wasn't fair, she seethed. She wrapped her arms around her lower abdomen and turned away from the scene.

"Who's ready for hamburgers and hotdogs?" Brendan stepped away from the grill carrying a platter with both. The scent carried on the breeze, making her mouth water. "I am," she responded.

Fred and Ginger barked. The sound of little girl laughter filled the air. "They want some too," responded both girls in unison.

Brendan waved a grilling tool at them. "Girls, we've talked about this. They have their own food. And Fred still needs to lose a few pounds."

"But Daddy, look how sad they are," cried Abby. Charlie thought the dogs looked more hopeful than sad but held her tongue.

"Abby, Fred has already eaten. He's not hungry."

Charlie's lips twitched at his tone. He was in danger of losing this argument. And a hot dog or two. "Abby, your father's right. Fred could stand to lose a few pounds. You and Kerry want him to live a long life, right?"

She had both girls' attention now. "Being overweight makes Fred unhealthy. But with the right diet and exercise, he can live to be an old man. And I know that your daddy went to a lot of trouble to get the best food for him and Ginger."

"Sorry, Daddy," both girls said. They turned their attention to their own plates.

Brendan picked up his sweet tea, grinning into the glass. She guessed he was pleased with her. "You owe me," she whispered to him.

"Oh, I can think of ways to repay you." The air thickened between them as the full meaning of his words washed over her. She smiled and took a large bite of her hamburger.

Charlie put down her food and sat back to watch the girls. She had not spent a lot of time around children, other than her patients. Abby and Kerry were adorable. Their innocent faces flashed. They talked a thousand miles per hour. The girls chatted about everything from the dogs to school friends. Charlie tried to keep up.

"Exhausting, isn't it," Brendan asked. He nodded towards the girls.

"Do you read minds? I was sitting here wondering how I would ever keep up with them.'

"It's not easy. That's for sure. It's almost like they have their own language when they're chatting like this." He smiled at his daughters. "Luckily, they keep each other entertained. Tell me about work. Are you settling in?"

"I love it! Everyone has been so wonderful and welcoming. Of course, being back with Elizabeth is the very best part. It's like we were never separated. She's the reason I made it through our residency relatively sane."

"Are you talking about Aunt Elizabeth, Charlie?"

She didn't realize the girls were listening. She smiled at the ketchup smeared across both, small faces. "Yes, I am. Your Aunt and I go back a long way."

"Use your napkins, girls," Brendan advised. "Charlie went to school with Aunt Elizabeth in California. They've been friends for years but living far apart from each other."

Charlie nodded. "That's right. Elizabeth is my very best friend in the entire world. I'm so happy that we're living in the same place again."

Kerry and Abby threw their arms around each other. "She's my best friend," they both blurted. Abby screwed up her face. "I'm never leaving Kerry."

Charlie smothered a laugh. "There's no reason for you to, Abby. But your Aunt and I wanted to do different things. She stayed in California before moving back here. I went to Chicago for a while before working in Africa. But it's all good. We're back together again."

"And you're never going to leave, Charlie. Right?" Kerry's bottom lip quivered a bit.

Setting down her glass of tea, she faced the girls. "Windsor Falls is my new home. Soon, I'm going to buy a house here."

"Our mother left us," added Abby. "She's in Texas. Wherever that is."

"We've never met her," Kerry said.

The stark simplicity of their words hurt Charlie's heart. Jillian's selfish nature struck her once again. What could be more important than these two? She forced a smile on her face. "Well, she doesn't know what she's missing. I think you two are the most adorable little girls I've ever met. In fact, I think this calls for cherry pie. Who would like to bring it out here for me?"

"I would, I would," cried Abby and Kerry before dashing off to the kitchen.

"Thank you," breathed Brendan, taking her hand in his. "You handled that so well."

Her eyes hardened. "I'm sorry to judge someone I've never met, but their mother makes me sick. She doesn't deserve them. How could she leave them?" Angry tears glistened on her eyelashes.

He rubbed a thumb over the palm of her hand. "I've asked myself that every day since they were born. Still don't have an answer. I had no idea what she was like before we married. I knew she was vain and self-centered, but I had no idea to what depth." He ran his other hand through his hair. "But, I can't say I regret anything. I wouldn't have my daughters otherwise."

She leaned in and placed a soft kiss on his cheek. "You're a wonderful father, Brendan Fitzgerald. Those girls are lucky to have you."

He shook his head. "I'm the lucky one, Charlie. Every day, I am thankful for them." His blue eyes darkened. "But I worry about them not having a mother. I always thought we were fine, but they're getting older. And now they're starting to question things. How can I tell them their mother wasn't interested in them?"

"I don't know the answer to that," she answered in a subdued tone.

The somber mood ended with the girls' return. Kerry carried the pie with both hands, setting it on the table. Abby had a butter knife and paper plates in her good hand. "See, Daddy, I didn't bring a sharp knife." She turned to Charlie. "Daddy always warns us to not touch the sharp knives."

"Daddy is very smart. No more trips to the ER for you, young lady." Charlie sliced the pie and handed out pieces.

"Let's hope not. I'm still recovering from the fright you gave me." Brendan sliced the pie and handed out pieces to everyone. "Have you started house hunting?"

"Haven't even thought about it. Katie is fine with me staying in her house for as long as I need. She's not in a rush to put it on the market."

"Takes some pressure off you."

Kerry and Abby inhaled their small pieces of pie. "Daddy, we're done." Both girls stood, empty plates abandoned on the table. "Can we go in and watch a movie now?"

Brendan glanced at his watch. "It's still early. Okay, girls." He raised a hand when they started to scamper off. "But not before you bring your dishes into the house, please."

Kerry and Abby grabbed their paper plates and other debris and left in a flurry of "see you".

Charlie watched them leave before turning back to Brendan. "Seriously, how are you not exhausted all the time? I already need a nap."

Brendan chuckled. "You have no idea. I could rule the world if I had their energy. Our schedule is crazy. With work and school, the week days fly by. We spend a lot of time doing stuff together on the weekends. Luckily, my whole family lives in Windsor Falls." He pulled a face. "And even though that can get a bit much, I'd be lost without them."

"I can only imagine." She searched his face before continuing. "This is none of my business, so feel free to tell me to butt out. Now that the girls are mentioning their mother, how are you going to deal with it?"

He leaned back in his chair and sighed. "I have no idea," he answered in a rough voice. "They mean everything to me and nothing to her. How is that possible?"

She pulled her chair closer to his and placed a hand on his arm. "I don't know." She thought about the way she had been raised. "Not everyone should be a parent. There should be a test. Like getting a driver's license."

He nodded and covered her hand with his own. The feel of his hand sent waves of pleasure to her girl parts. Not the right time. She cleared her throat. "And you've never heard from her again?"

"Not a word. Never a birthday or Christmas card. No phone calls. I don't get it."

Kerry appeared at the sliding door. "Come on, Daddy. Aren't you going to watch Frozen with us?"

Brendan groaned. "Again?"

Abby appeared next to her sister and laughed. "He loves it just as much, Charlie. Even does the snowman's voice. Don't you Daddy?"

"Well, I'd love to hear that." She stood up and gathered her dinner dishes. Brendan helped. "We'll be in after we clear this up."

The girls turned and ran back in the house, giggling as they went. He shook his head. "You don't have to do this."

Charlie's eyes lit up. "Are you kidding me? I love Olaf! Can't wait to hear your interpretation."

He groaned, sliding open the door. "Great."

Chapter Fourteen

Two hours later, Brendan glanced over at Charlie. She slept next to him on the couch. The twins were also asleep, lying on large pillows in front of the television. Charlie's face was relaxed in sleep. Her lashes fanned her cheeks. Her blonde hair spread behind her on the couch cushions. Now that he knew how soft it was, he was dying to run it through his hands. But the girls were right there.

He should wake everyone, but he didn't. She wore a half smile, and he wondered if she was dreaming. About him. She had been great with his girls, talking to them on their level and including them in everything. Not all adults did that. She had also listened to him when he vented his frustration about their mother.

In fact, Charlie had been great tonight. She didn't balk at sitting through a full-length kids' movie. She roared with laughter at his lame attempts to imitate Olaf. Something warm settled around his heart. He had been careful to shield the girls for so long. Now he wondered if that was the best choice. The girls were crazy about Charlie, and it was obvious that she felt the same about them.

He leaned into her, brushing a lock of hair from her face. She sighed and settled further into the cushions. They had only known each other a short while. And yet Brendan wondered if Charlie might be the right woman for him. For them.

"Did I miss the end?"

Her whisper broke his reverie. His mouth curled in a smile. "Yes, you did. But don't worry. They all lived happily ever after."

"Oh good. I love a happy ending. And they're so rare in real life."

He raised a dark eyebrow at her tone. "Didn't take you for a cynic. My parents have been married for over forty years. Donovan and Nora for more than twenty."

Charlie sat up straight and stretched. He lost all thought as the thin strap to her sundress slid off one, creamy shoulder.

"I'm a realist, not a cynic. My parents have been married for over forty too, but that's not a reason to celebrate."

Brendan took her hand in his. "That bad?"

"They have the American equivalent of an arranged marriage. The two families have known each other for generations. That doesn't mean it was the right choice for either of them." She squeezed her eyes shut for a moment. "I can't remember a time when they weren't fighting. Or not speaking to one another." She let out a humorless laugh. "And my mother wonders why I resisted her matchmaking."

The muscles of his stomach tightened. He didn't know much about her family, other than that she was from Charleston and an only child. Her comments about her parents' marriage echoed Jillian's family. He tamped down the rising unease. Outside of physical appearance, nothing about her resembled Jillian. She certainly didn't scream money to him.

"You're kidding, right?" He held his breath and waited for her to answer.

"I wish I was. I'm thirty-seven, Brendan. And a *spinster*, according to my mother. She's never forgiven me for not marrying Edward Carlisle. Huh! I knew in kindergarten that I would never marry him. He may be a high-powered attorney, but he's also on his third wife. And likes the ponies a bit too much from what I hear. Good thing I ran away to medical school."

Brendan tried not to wince at her tone. He folded her in his arms, tucking her head against his chest. "Good thing for me. Otherwise, Edward Carlisle might be bloodying my nose about now."

Her laughter rumbled against his chest. "I'm sure you could take him. Sorry. My family is a bit messy. And they still think I'm coming home."

Brendan's heart stuttered at her words. Even though he believed she was happy here, the thought of her leaving scared him. Wasn't it too soon for such thoughts? He wrapped her back in his arms and made some soothing noises to her. Or maybe himself.

"The girls and I are happy you're here. And staying." He couldn't help but add that last part. He rained soft kisses on the crown of her head. He wished the girls were spending the night at this mom's. He wanted to wrap his entire body around Charlie and never come up for air.

As if reading his thoughts, she squirmed closer to him, molding her curves to him. She planted a line of kisses along his jawline. She sighed before pulling away from him and standing.

"Where are you going?"

"Home. Before I do something that is definitely not rated G." With a wicked grin and a waggle of her fingers, Charlie walked out of his house.

He stayed where he was and watched the girls sleep. The dogs were wrapped around their respective little girl. They were his life. His whole life. Had been since the moment Jillian announced her pregnancy. Could he risk including Charlie? Still early days. But for the first time, Brendan pictured himself getting married again. Having another child or two. Something settled in his chest. He smiled in the semi-darkness and got up to wake the kids.

*****

Charlie hummed an old country song under her breath while she drove home. The temperature had cooled, and she rolled down her window. She'd always loved the feeling of the wind in her hair. She smiled in the darkness, thinking of the evening with Brendan and his girls. Curling up on the couch with Brendan was a slice of heaven. The bowl of popcorn made it even better. Kerry and Abby had watched the movie from the floor. Each curled up around their dog. Adorable.

Charlie dreamed of more nights like that. Her parents had never spent an evening like that with her. They had 'important' things to do and popcorn was fattening.

More than anything in the world, she wanted that. A family. A place to belong. She had found the place. And Brendan came with a ready-made family. Her heart fluttered. Kerry and Abby were amazing little girls, and she was already half in love with them.

She laughed at her own foolishness. She thought about this because of their earlier conversation. The girls not having a mom had become an issue for the first time. Brendan was concerned with how to handle it. He hadn't proposed, for goodness sake. She was way ahead of herself.

Charlie took a deep, cleansing breath. She pulled into her driveway. He was sweet. And wicked hot. She liked spending time with him. She also liked being with his girls. No reason to put a name on it yet. Paint herself into a corner. Freak either of them out.

She went inside, closing the door behind her. Charlie tossed her keys on the kitchen table and grabbed the kettle. She used to enjoy a glass of wine at night. Chamomile it was. Something to calm her a bit and invite Mr. Sandman.

Her text alert chimed just as the kettle began to boil. She grabbed a mug and poured in hot water. A soothing aroma bathed the air. She mixed in a dab of honey and left the kitchen. Making sure the doors were locked along the way, Charlie headed up the steps. Her phone chimed again, reminding her she hadn't read the text. She'd get to that in a minute.

Stripping off her clothes, she threw them in the laundry basket and pulled on a favorite, old t-shirt. She fluffed some pillows and slid beneath the comforter. Cup of tea on the nightstand, book in her hand. Did life get any better? Charlie was determined to finish the novel from her book club, even though they had already discussed it. She glanced at her phone and her heart raced when she spied Brendan's name.

Had a fun time. Any chance you're free next weekend?

Charlie traced a nail over his name, anticipation swirling in her stomach. She opened her calendar to check her schedule for the next week. She had three night shifts during the week. That left Friday through Monday wide open. Hmmm… She wondered what he had in mind.

I might be. For the right person and plans…

Laughter bubbled up from inside. She hadn't flirted in ages. It felt great. She saw that he was responding and held her breath in anticipation.

Hopefully, I'm the right person. I thought you and I could go to the beach for a few days. Just us.

He wanted to go away with her? Without the girls? A couple of days of alone time with a gorgeous man? Hell, yes. She picked up her cell to respond when it rang in her hand. She startled and dropped it on the bed, laughing at herself. Of course, it was Brendan.

"Hey," she answered. Even to her own ears, she sounded so breathless. "I was about to respond."

"Is it too soon?" His deep, roughened voice curled her toes. She gripped the phone tighter and slid down on the pillows.

"Not at all. I'd love to go to the beach with you. Any particular beach?" Not that it mattered. Charlie had always enjoyed sex but also went a long time between partners. But that was before she met Brendan. Now all she could imagine was being alone with him somewhere. Anywhere.

His deep chuckle came across the line. "Well, yes. A friend of the family, Bailey Saunders, is opening a B&B at Serenity Beach. I thought you and I could go check it out. To be honest, my mom wants one of us to go check it out. See if Bailey needs anything. I offered to go. But, I'd rather take you with me."

The curling toes had become heat in other places. "Sounds like a plan. Sure you don't want to bring the girls?"

After a long pause, Brendan asked, "Do you want me to?"

Charlie tapped her fingers on her thigh, wondering how to answer. Did it make her a bad person if she said no? Did it make her a slut? A nervous laugh escaped her. "Uh."

"Charlie, I'm sorry that I was presumptuous. The girls would love to come."

"No!" More nervous laughter escaped. She took a deep breath. "What I meant to say was I'm happy to go with you." She lowered her voice. "More than happy."

"That's great! How about we plan on leaving early Friday morning?"

"Perfect. I'll be ready. Good-night, Brendan." She disconnected before she could make a bigger fool of herself. Charlie placed the phone down on the bed and picked her book up. After a minute and reading the same sentence five times, she gave up. She picked up her phone again and dialed.

"Hello," mumbled Elizabeth.

"I'm so sorry. I thought you'd be awake. Go back to sleep."

"No, I'm up now. Are you okay?" A muffled yawn sounded in the background.

"Sam will have my head for depriving you of sleep, little mama. It can wait until tomorrow."

Her voice cleared. "Sam is at the store late doing the dreaded inventory, as he puts it. I don't sleep for more than an hour or so anyway thanks to the tiniest bladder in North Carolina. What's up?"

She tried for casual. "Oh, nothing. Brendan asked me to go to the beach with him next weekend. Without the girls. No big deal." She grinned at the shriek that came from her friend.

"What? When? Details. Like right now, Charlie."

She laughed at her friend's excitement. "Geez, and I thought I was excited."

"I'm a married, pregnant woman who hasn't seen her feet in months. Not that Sam isn't creative, mind you. But being swept away for a romantic weekend at the beach? I'm swooning by the way."

"I had dinner with Brendan and the girls tonight. We watched a movie afterward. Then I went home. No mention of the beach. Then he texts me. TEXTS me.

Like it was no big deal. Am I free next weekend?" She noticed her voice reached a pitch only dogs could hear but didn't care. This was Elizabeth.

"Ugh! That's exactly like Brendan. No big deal my ass. This is a very big deal."

"Thank you. I thought so."

"What did you tell him?"

"Have you seen Brendan? He's a sex god. Of course, I said yes."

"Way too much information. Ick. He's like a brother to me, Charlie."

"Fine, but he's not your actual brother. That man is hot. As in smoking."

"Agreed. So, you're going away with him for a couple of days. Without his daughters. You know what that means."

"I certainly hope so," breathed Charlie. "He's yummy."

"Again, too much information." Elizabeth hesitated, clearing her throat before she continued. "But seriously, Charlie, are you ready for this? Is he rushing you?"

Charlie appreciated her friend's concern. "He's not, Elizabeth. I wouldn't let him. You forget how I resisted my parents' wishes for years. I'm excited about going. In fact, I wish we were leaving right now."

Elizabeth laughed. "I bet you do. Hate to cut you short, but my bladder is calling. I'll see you at work tomorrow."

"See you then." Charlie hung up and reached for the light, plunging the room into darkness. She plugged in her phone and set it on the bedside table before curling up on her side. She drifted off to sleep thinking 'life was looking up'.

The week flew by, as Charlie had hoped. She hadn't seen Brendan all week but spoke with him on the phone every day. Her erratic schedule didn't make things easy for them. She needed to pack tonight, but last week she'd made a date for dinner with some of the ladies she met at the book club. At seven sharp, Charlie walked into Between the Covers.

"Hey, Charlie," Jamie yelled in greeting from behind the counter. She turned to Paige and Amy sitting in the reading area. "That'll be twenty bucks from y'all."

Charlie looked from Jamie to the other women, shaking her head. "Why do you owe her money because I walked in?"

Amy didn't bother to cover her smirk. Paige grimaced before explaining. "We, well Amy, thought you might not show tonight."

Swinging her gaze to Amy, Charlie chuckled. "Why wouldn't I make it? We have dinner plans."

"And you're leaving for a hot weekend away with Brendan Fitzgerald in the morning. I thought you'd be home packing. Or at least raiding the local drug store for supplies." The glint in her eye left no doubt of the 'supplies'.

Cursing her fair skin as her face flamed, Charlie declared, "I'm not that kind of woman."

Silence filled the room. Charlie waited until she was sure she had their attention. "I'm not the kind of woman who leaves her girlfriends hanging for a man." She winked at Amy. "I already took care of the other thing."

Laughter exploded from all four women. Paige jumped up and hugged her. "I knew we were going to like you!"

Charlie returned the hug. "I'm so glad. Being new in town sucks." She glanced at the other women. "Should I ask how y'all know about my weekend plans?"

Jamie shrugged. "Small town. Need I say more?"

"No, I guess not. Charleston may have been bigger, but it felt small."

Bells over the door announced someone there. Jamie ducked out from behind the desk to greet a pizza delivery boy. He placed two boxes on the counter, and Jamie paid him. She followed him out, locking the door behind him and flipping the sign to closed.

"Come and get it, ladies," she invited. "I hope this is okay. But after all day on my feet, I'd rather stay here and relax with some carbs and wine. I still have some left over from the last book club."

"I'll grab it and some glasses," offered Paige.

Amy joined Charlie at the counter. They each grabbed a paper plate and a slice of pizza.

Paige came out of the storeroom with a triumphant grin on her face. "Found it." She placed two bottles, one white and one red, plus four glasses on the counter. "Should be enough for us."

Jamie laughed. "Two opened bottles for the four of us? I think not. After all, I only have to make it upstairs and Amy can walk home from here." She pointed at Charlie and Paige. "You two might have to limit yourselves since you're driving."

Uneasiness clawed Charlie's throat at the mention of drinking wine. "Uh, Jamie, you can have my share. Could I get some water?" She waited for the questions, but none came.

"Sure, I have some bottled water in the office fridge." Jamie left the room to get it.

Silence reigned, and the elephant in the room grew larger. Jamie came back, handing Charlie a cold bottle of water. "I don't drink alcohol," she muttered to nobody in particular. "Anymore."

"I gave up sushi," Jamie blurted. "Okay, I never liked sushi, but I thought it was cool to eat it." Her face twisted in a grimace. "Barely choked down one bite. And almost threw it right back up."

Charlie's heart swelled with affection for these women. These new friends of hers. She let out a shaky breath. "I had some trouble in Africa." She pressed her hand to her mouth, smothering a sob. Taking a deep breath, she continued. "I've been at my parents' home for a few months. Recovering. Wine is a staple there. It was becoming a problem for me. So, I don't drink it at all now."

Jamie walked to Charlie's side, squeezing her hand in support. "I love my parents, but I'd drink too much if I had to live with them again."

Paige grinned at her from her seat. "More wine for the rest of us, Charlie."

And like that, it wasn't an issue. Charlie closed her eyes and pressed a hand to her chest. She sniffed back tears. "You guys are the best," she uttered on a half sob. She wiped her eyes and gave them a watery smile. "Warning, I'm a bit of a mess."

"And that makes you like the rest of us," drawled Amy. "Only you have an excuse for being a mess."

"She's right," agreed Jamie. "Here we are, three gorgeous, professional women over the age of twenty-five. And not a committed relationship amongst us. Not that that's how we define ourselves."

"Of course not," replied Paige. "Although spending the day with my small students and nights with my graduate courses is getting old. I wouldn't mind having someone sexy like, say, Brendan Fitzgerald, to curl up with at night."

Charlie laughed, her last tears gone. "I haven't 'curled up at night' with Brendan. In case you were wondering."

"You're splitting hairs. That's what you'll be doing tomorrow about this time." Amy sipped her wine and tapped her blood-red nails against the glass. "I rely on my little mechanical friend for my needs. Never lets me down. Worst that can happen is the battery dies."

Thankfully, Charlie hadn't taken a drink of water. She would have sprayed it everywhere. "Wow. That's honest. Brutal, but honest."

"Sad but true is what it is. I've yet to meet a guy who didn't let me down. No thanks. Don't need the hassle."

There was a story there, Charlie thought. But Amy didn't appear in the mood to tell it. That was fine with her. They all had their stories. She wasn't eager to jump into the gory details of hers.

The four women pulled chairs up to the table and chatted while they ate their pizza. She was glad the conversation lightened. The ladies filled her in on all the latest gossip.

A few hours later, Charlie smothered a yawn. "I'm sorry, ladies. Nightshift the past few nights killed me. I should go."

"That's okay, Charlie. It's a 'school night' after all. Amy and I each have twenty-five little devils to deal with tomorrow."

"And I have a new part timer starting tomorrow," chimed in Jamie. "I should at least look alive." She glared at Paige. "Exactly how many times did you refill my glass?"

"No idea. But you only have to make it upstairs," Paige laughed.

Jamie rose to her feet, swaying a bit. "Have you seen that staircase? It's steep." Her laughter blew the righteous indignation in her tone.

"No worries, Jamie. Paige and I will help you upstairs." Amy turned to Charlie. "I'd tell you to have fun, but I'm sure you're already planning to. Be careful."

"Yes, Mom," replied Charlie, sticking out her tongue at Amy.

Paige laughed and walked her to the door. "I'll lock up after you." She leaned in and hugged her. "I'm so glad you came to the book club. You're amongst friends, Charlie. If you need, well, anything, let us know."

"That means more than you'll ever know," Charlie managed to eke out around the emotion choking her throat. She walked out into the darkness and got into her car. Windsor Falls was the right choice for her. She already had some wonderful new friends. She was working with Elizabeth for the first time in years. Was it too much to ask for a relationship with Brendan and his lovely daughters? She hoped not.

Chapter Fifteen

Brendan jumped back in his truck after dropping off the girls at his Mom's house. They were not happy that he was going to the beach without them. Until they heard that Fred and Ginger were going to Grandma's too. His mother, bless her soul, made it sound like the girls were going to an all expense tropical paradise. Maggie had promised baking cookies, movies, water balloon fights, and more. Abby and Kerry both hugged him goodbye. He smiled at their excitement to start on the fun with Grandma.

He glanced in the back seat of his truck. His lone, overnight bag was on the floor, leaving plenty of room for whatever Charlie brought. Most women packed for a week, in his experience. He drove the few miles to her townhouse. Brendan wondered when Charlie would begin looking for one of her own. He was a little shocked at the disquiet that thought provoked. He liked her in his home. On his couch watching movies with him while the girls sprawled on the floor. Wait. What? Where had that thought come from?

He was still trying to figure that out as he pulled into her driveway. Charlie would run screaming for the mountains if she could read his mind. They barely knew each other. *Get a grip on yourself.*

Charlie locked the door and came down the driveway. She carried a duffel bag over one shoulder. "Where do you want this?"

He pulled his head out of his ass and got out of the truck. He walked towards her, reaching for the bag. "I'm sorry. I would have gotten that. Where's the rest of your stuff?"

She grinned at him. "For two days?" She handed the bag to him. "This is it."

His grin answered hers. "I might be falling in love with you."

Both stood in the driveway, less than five feet apart, staring at each other. Brendan swore he could hear her heart thudding. Or maybe his. What *was* wrong with him? First thoughts of her living in his home. Then this. At least the thoughts had been just that. Thoughts. He stared at his sneakers, unsure what to say, or not, next. "Uh, what I meant was…"

"Should I pick a date?"

"What?" If it was possible for him to swallow his own tongue, he would have. Then he heard her laugh. At him.

"If you could see your face!" Laughter bubbled up from her.

Brendan stood there, annoyed with himself. "When you're through, we can go." Great! Now he sounded like a pouting teen. "I meant to say, we have a long drive. We should go."

She stretched up and kissed him. He felt it to his toes. "I'm sorry, Brendan, but I couldn't resist. Of course, you don't love me yet. You don't even know my favorite flavor of ice cream." Leaving him scratching his head at that one, Charlie walked around his truck and got in.

Brendan did the same. "Mine's mint chocolate chip. In case you were wondering. And what does favorite ice cream flavor have to do with anything?"

She buckled her seat belt, grinning at him. He backed out of the driveway. "That's what I call it when you're getting to know someone. The 'what's your favorite flavor of ice cream list.' You know, like when's your birthday? What's your favorite holiday or season? Dogs or cats? Things like that, superficial but fun facts about someone that you don't know yet."

They came to a red light. He turned to look at her. "September 15th, Thanksgiving, winter, and definitely dogs." He grinned.

"I'm more of a December 1ˢᵗ, Memorial Day, summer kind of gal. You get points for dogs though. Dogs rule, as everyone knows."

"Memorial Day? I had you pegged for more of a Christmas or Valentine's Day kind of girl." The light changed, and he continued on.

She stuck her tongue out at him, making him wish he wasn't driving. "Memorial Day is the unofficial start to summer, my favorite season. It became very important to me when I lived in Chicago. By Memorial Day, I knew I wouldn't be cold again for a while. I hate being cold."

"Noted."

"And Valentine's Day is a Hallmark holiday. I want flowers because it's Tuesday and someone thought of me. Not because it's a national holiday and there's a marketing campaign. Of course, I do love Christmas. Who doesn't? From the day after Thanksgiving until New Year's Day. I love the decorations, especially the over the top, ridiculous ones. The ones my parents looked down on. And gifts are fun of course. But more than anything, I love the way people are a little bit nicer to each other."

Brendan couldn't stop the grin if he tried. Charlie was unique. "It's a shame you're so shy about expressing your opinions," he quipped, tongue planted in cheek.

"If you'd ever met my parents you'd understand. Life is too short. I speak my mind. When it's appropriate. I'm my own person, flaws and all, and I embrace that."

"One of the many things I like about you. Never any doubt where a person stands with you."

"Exactly! Glad we got that cleared up. Now, tell me where we're going."

"Bailey is a friend of the family. She graduated with Aidan and Riley. She and Aidan might have had a moment. Years ago. But then he went off to Charlotte to learn his craft. By the time he got back, Bailey had met Jake. It was a whirlwind thing. Before we knew it, they were married and off to Serenity Beach."

"Wow. That takes guts. She left her home and family. She must love him."

Brendan's face darkened. "Loved. Not long after, Jake was diagnosed with pancreatic cancer. It was a terrible time for both. He died about a year ago. We all thought she would come home. But she's determined to make this work. She and Jake had their plans. The B&B opens next weekend."

"Poor Bailey. That must have been awful for her. She's very brave to stick it out. Finish what they started."

"Brave or foolish. Time will tell. She asked for my professional opinion about a few things with the building. Easier to do that in person, so here we are. You'll like her. She's great, outgoing, funny."

She laid a hand on his arm. He figured she meant to comfort him, but any touch from her electrified him. "Keep that up, and we'll never make it to the beach." He wiggled his eyebrows, making her laugh, and breaking the solemnity in the truck.

"Anything I have to worry about with this Bailey? Not that I'm the jealous type, mind you. I like to be informed." She settled back in her seat. Brendan snuck a look at her profile. She was, hands down, the most beautiful woman he'd ever met. And she was a doctor. Of course, *she* wasn't jealous. Neither was he. Right?

"So, is this the part of the conversation where we discuss our exes?"

Her eyes widened. "Uh, no. I sure hope not."

"Just checking."

She turned in her seat to face him. "Is that what you want to do? I've never seen the sense in that. You have two children, so I know you weren't a virgin."

He barked out a laugh. "Uh, no, I'm not. Are you?"

"You know I'm not. Nor was I when we met. I'm not a nun, but I didn't sleep around either. I'm picky, if you must know. And careful."

"Me too. Good to know, although we probably should have asked before we slept together."

She cocked her head at him. "I don't remember any sleeping."

Brendan felt the corners of his mouth lifting. "True. So, tell me, Charlie the picky woman. Why me?"

"Fishing?"

"No. More curious than anything. You could have anyone you wanted. So, why me?"

She shook her head. "You'd be surprised. I've been told I'm too tall, too opinionated, too bossy. Too educated, if you can believe that. Oh, and I eat too much. Any number of faults have been pointed out."

"You're kidding, right?"

"If only I was. Look, Brendan, I know that I'm pretty. That's genes and luck. Many women are. If someone wants to find fault with you, they will. I'm not shy about my opinion. Some men don't like that. Some men don't like looking up at their date. But that's their problem, not mine."

"I like your height, Charlie. I don't have to bend down to kiss you. Which I would do right now to prove it if I wasn't driving."

"Stupid driving," she agreed on a laugh. "Why wouldn't I want you? Have you looked in a mirror lately? You're gorgeous. That black hair and blue eyes is a killer combination." She tilted her head and stared at him. "In fact, you and Elizabeth would have made beautiful babies."

"Ick. Besides a thirty second period around eighteen, she's always been like another sister to me."

"Well, good. I don't think Sam will share."

"Go on. You were telling me what you like about me. Don't let me stop you."

"I wouldn't want to inflate your ego, but here goes. You make me laugh, Brendan. You remind me to not take my self, or my situation, too seriously. And the way you are with your girls." His heart warmed at her smile. "They obviously love you very much."

"Not even a fraction of how much I love them. They're my life."

"You want the very best for them. Not every parent can claim that."

"I know." Thoughts of Jillian, and her plan for an abortion, turned his vision red. "Not everyone should be a parent."

"Anyway, that's enough of that. Tell me about working for your family business. How's that going for you?"

He launched into a series of funny stories about working with his siblings and father. They moved on to stories from their childhood, and the miles flew by.

Before he realized, they were close to Serenity Beach. "Do you want to stop for lunch or wait until we get there?"

Charlie stretched and yawned. "Sorry. I haven't done night shifts in a while. Lunch later is fine, but I need a drink and a bathroom. And not in that order."

"Me too. And I need gas too. I'll stop at the next place I see." This part of Route 74 had several exits with facilities. Within minutes, they came upon an exit boasting a gas station and convenience store.

"Hope this place is clean," he said.

Charlie shot him a look that women had been shooting men for centuries. The one that said they might not be too bright. "Brendan, I lived in the desert for months. I can handle it."

"And there it is," he joked. "Another of the reasons I like you so much. No fuss."

"I'm pretty low maintenance."

Gross understatement. She reminded him of Elizabeth that way. He slowed at the end of the ramp and turned right. The gas station was another quick right. "I'll get the gas, you go ahead in."

"Not going to argue with you."

He pulled up to the gas pump and watched her walk into the building. The more time he spent with her, the more time he wanted to spend with her.

*****

Charlie finished using the restroom and roamed around the convenience store. She drooled over a candy selection but reached for a pack of almonds instead. She might have excellent metabolism, but there was no point in making it work so hard.

She turned at the bell tinkling over the door. Hidden behind a rack, Charlie watched Brendan walk to the restrooms. If they hadn't been quite so filthy, she might have followed him in. But there was a difference between low maintenance and no standards. She had envied him his ability to pee while standing a few moments ago.

She grabbed a bottled water from the cooler and walked to the counter. The young lady behind it rang up her purchases, and Charlie handed her a twenty. Counting out her change, the woman's eyes widened. Charlie glanced over her shoulder to find Brendan standing a few yards away with his back turned to them.

"Wouldn't mind getting me a piece of that," muttered the clerk.

Charlie glanced again to find Brendan walking towards them. "Nah, he's too pretty. Probably gay."

The clerk glanced at Charlie and longer at Brendan. "That would be a crime."

Charlie took her change. "Thanks," she said and left the store. She leaned against the passenger side of the truck. Although she couldn't make out the words, she watched while he had a short exchange with the clerk. He had an odd expression on his face. She smothered a chuckle.

Brendan clicked his remote, and she opened her door. He was right behind her to give her a hand up. "Something wrong," she inquired. She kept her tone bland.

Brendan glanced over his shoulder at the store before turning back to her. "The clerk in there asked me if I was gay." He helped her up into his truck and shut the door. Walking around to his side, Brendan got in and closed his door. Tension radiated from him. "Not that there's anything wrong with being gay. But, I'm not. Why would she think that?"

"I know," she all but purred. Charlie swallowed a laugh. "It's because you're so pretty."

"That's what she said," he muttered. He started the truck. A heartbeat passed before he whipped his head around to her. "Anything you'd like to share?" His eyes glittered.

That pushed her over the edge. Charlie howled with laughter. Tears rolled down her face until she gasped for breath. She was relieved to see a smile on his face when she finally pulled herself together. "I'm, uh, sorry?"

The side of his mouth twitched. "Doesn't sound like it. Care to explain?" One dark brow arched, almost meeting his hairline.

Charlie pressed a hand into her abdomen and shuddered out a breath. "She scoped you out. I had to say something." Even to her own ears it sounded lame at best. Desperate at worst.

"Some twenty-year-old convenience store clerk I'll never see again 'scoped me out' and you told her I was gay? Why?"

"I don't know." She dragged a hair through her long hair. "Oh, alright. I got flustered and blurted out the first thing that came to mind."

"Flustered?" Confusion flashed across his eyes. "Why?"

She felt the heat spread across her cheeks. "I thought about following you into the restrooms. But they were way to gross to even consider doing that."

Brendan's hands convulsed on the wheel. Heat flared in his eyes before he turned back to the road. "What were you going to do in the men's room?" His voice, rough and low, send all kinds of heat to her belly. And lower.

She leaned across the seat and whispered into his ear. "Something like we did the other night at my house. Only quicker."

"I see," he choked out in a strangled voice. "And you decided to tell me this when I'm driving seventy miles per hour?"

She popped an almond into her mouth and chewed. "You asked."

He glanced at her before watching the road again. "Care to expand on those thoughts? We still have an hour or so."

"Why don't you tell me more about the B&B. Might be safer."

"Chicken."

"No. I don't want to arrive all flustered. I'd prefer to make a good first impression."

"Fair enough. You can tell me tonight. In detail."

Charlie placed a hand on his thigh. The heat radiating through the khaki of his shorts scorched her. She brushed her hand over the bulge in the center. "Oh, there will be lots of details."

His eyes never left the road, but she could see the fierce smile on his face. "Good. I love details."

She fanned herself and reached for the air conditioning. "So, you were going to tell me about the B&B."

Brendan chuckled, a gravelly sound low in his throat that set the flames even higher. "Sunrise House has been in Jake's family for generations. His parents ran it until they died a few years ago. Some sort of accident. Jake never wanted it. But after losing his parents, he decided to give it a go. That's when he met Bailey. And you already know what happened after that."

"So, your friend is staying on to continue her husband's legacy. There's a lot to be said for that. Not everyone would be strong enough to do it."

"It's more than that. Bailey was at loose ends when she met Jake. A little lost. I think this has been good for her. Given her purpose."

"That's understandable. I like the name, Sunrise House. Is it right on the beach?"

"You'll see soon enough."

Chapter Sixteen

Charlie swatted at the fly that buzzed her ear. Her hand connected with solid male. A smile bloomed on her face before she even opened her eyes. She stretched and turned in her seat. "I guess I fell asleep. Sorry." She hid a yawn behind her hand.

"No worries," Brendan whispered into her ear before kissing it. "We're here. You only fell asleep about thirty miles back.

The Atlantic splashed the sand straight ahead. She grabbed her door handle, and a huge, shaggy head appeared almost at eye level with her. She gasped with delight when a large tongue wiped the window. Charlie bolted from the truck and came to a stop in front of the mammoth dog. She offered a closed hand for it to sniff. The great beast snuffled her hand, covering it with his tongue. Charlie patted the course hair on its head.

A shrill whistle pierced the air. "Angus?"

The dog swiveled his head in the direction of the voice, letting out one big woof, but didn't leave Charlie's side. She swore he grinned at her.

"There you are, goofy dog. How many times have I told you that you're not the welcoming committee?"

A petite woman loped around the corner of the building, a smile on her pretty face. She approached Charlie, hand extended. "You must be Brendan's Charlie." Charlie shook hands with her and nodded. "He failed to mention you were gorgeous. I might have to hate you."

Charlie laughed. "Can I still be friends with Angus?"

"He wouldn't have it any other way." Bailey moved past Charlie to launch herself at Brendan. "I like her, Brendan. Well done. Thanks for coming."

"Of course, Bailey. Anything for you." Looking up at the building, Brendan grinned. "Looking good, Bailey. You might not need anything from me."

"Never hurts to get a professional opinion." She turned to Charlie. "I see you've met my roommate, Angus. Don't let him fool you. I feed him. Every day. Won't stop him from trying to talk you out of your bacon though."

Charlie ruffled Angus's head once again. "I've got your number now, Angus." The big dog sat and butted his head against her stomach, almost knocking her off her feet. She leaned in and threw her arms around his neck. "You and I are going to be great friends."

"Come inside," Bailey invited. He grabbed their bags.

Charlie followed Bailey up a few stairs to the wide, wrap-around porch. "This might be my favorite part of the whole house. And I haven't even see the rest of it." She ran her hand along the back of a rocking chair and turned to face the ocean. "The view is fantastic. I can only imagine what the sunrise looks like."

Bailey smiled. "Jake's grandmother named it. She and her husband built Sunrise House in the 1920s. Of course, it was much smaller then. His parents added on to it."

"They did a fantastic job," Brendan said. "Hard to tell where the original ends and the addition begins."

"Yes. Two generations of Jake's family lived here. But he was too stubborn to realize what a wonderful thing he had. Until it was too late." Bailey turned away, facing the see, and gathered herself. Angus walked up to his mistress and leaned into her. Charlie slid her hand into Brendan's. Her heart ached for Bailey.

"That's enough of that," Bailey declared. "I keep telling myself that tears won't bring him back." Her smile didn't quite reach her eyes.

Charlie took a few steps closer to Bailey. "There's no timeline on grief. And the tears are for you, not Jake."

"It's the little things. I miss his smile. It was genuine and could light a room. And sometimes, for a fraction of a second, I forget. Isn't that crazy? I forget he's gone."

"Connor's been gone for over a decade. And I still forget. Something happens, and I can't wait to tell him. And then I remember." He placed a hand on Bailey's shoulder. "It gets easier. I can promise you that. But it never goes away."

Bailey ran a hand through her short hair. "Thank you, Brendan. Nice to know I'm not losing it. Now, how about some lunch?"

"We were going to grab something in town," replied Brendan.

"Nonsense! With the inn opening next weekend, I have enough food to feed an army. How about some sandwiches on the deck?"

Brendan picked up their bags. "Charlie, why don't you go with Bailey? I'll take these up."

Bailey stretched and kissed him on the cheek. "Thanks for coming, Brendan. I appreciate this. You guys have the first room at the top of the stairs. It faces the ocean." She linked arms with Charlie. "You come with me. I'll serve up a side of Brendan stories with that sandwich."

Charlie laughed and let Bailey pull her along, Angus bringing up the rear. "You've got yourself a deal, Bailey. I want all the dirt."

He pulled a face. "Careful, Bailey. I have as much 'dirt' on you."

She shook her head. "No, not even close. Those Fitzgerald boys were always into something, Charlie. Not sure how poor Maggie didn't lose her mind."

The two women entered the kitchen. Angus walked into a small sunroom off the back and stretched out on the largest dog bed Charlie had ever seen. "I wouldn't worry too much about Maggie. From what I've seen, she could run that family with one hand tied behind her back."

"That's true. But it can't have been easy raising all those kids. Joe was so busy building the business, that Maggie handled most of the parenting. Joe called her a steel fist in a velvet glove."

Charlie laughed at the accurate description. "That's perfect. She's amazing."

She smiled at the memory of Maggie hugging her. "My childhood was so different. Life must have been interesting in that household." Her tone held more than a hint of envy.

Bailey burst out laughing. "Interesting doesn't even begin to cover it. You would think six kids of her own was more than enough. But Maggie always took in strays like Sam and Elizabeth. And I was there more than my own home. I'm the same age as the twins, Riley and Aidan. Riley was my best friend growing up."

"And Aidan?"

Bailey's eyes dimmed a bit at the mention of Brendan's brother. "Aiden's a long story."

Footsteps pounding down the stairs heralded Brendan's return. "Hey, where's my lunch?"

He oofed when Bailey's elbow connected with his gut. "We were busy gossiping if you must know. Besides, this is an equal opportunity kitchen." She pulled open the stainless-steel fridge door and pulled out the makings for sandwiches. "I have turkey, roast beef and ham plus all the fixings. Don't be shy. Grab what you want."

"Where are the plates, Bailey?" Charlie looked around, appreciating the painted cabinets. "These are beautiful."

"Thanks! Those are the original oak. I went with white to brighten this room. Painting is great therapy."

The three made their own sandwiches and moved out to the back deck. Brendan held open the door for Charlie who carried a large pitcher of sweet tea outside. She sighed. "How do you ever get any work done? I'd be sitting here enjoying the view all day."

"It is tempting, but there are bills to be paid. I've had it easy until now. Next week comes the test with the first paying customers."

"Don't let her fool you," added Brendan. "Not only has she been getting this place ready, but Bailey is an accountant too."

"Wow! Two whole careers? How do you manage that?"

Bailey laughed. "Says the doctor fresh back from Africa. He's right. I do have my CPA. That's what I was doing when I met Jake. He took me away from all that. I picked up some local clients to make some extra money and to keep my hand in it. Staying busy is my friend."

Charlie nodded. "I hear you. I took some time off after Africa. Stayed with my parents in Charleston. I'm so glad to be back at work."

They finished lunch, chatting like old friends. Charlie liked Bailey and could see why Brendan thought so highly of her. When they finished, Bailey insisted on cleaning up. "You two head out for your tour of Serenity Beach. I insist." Charlie and Brendan protested, but Bailey wouldn't hear it. "Make sure you put on some sunscreen. It's hotter than you think."

Charlie agreed. "I'm very careful with this light skin of mine. I'll be down in a moment, Brendan."

*****

Brendan watched Charlie run up the stairs before turning back to Bailey. He found Bailey grinning at him. "What?" He didn't have to ask. He could see the wheels turning in his friend's head.

"She's terrific. And exactly what you need."

"Oh, and what is that?"

"Someone who's your equal."

He arched an eyebrow. "What does that mean?"

"Women have always fallen all over the Fitzgerald brothers. She's different. She sees more than the pretty face." She patted the face in question. "Please tell me she's not another one you hold at arm's length. Has she met the girls?"

He started to protest, but the look on Bailey's face stopped him. "She met the girls first." Brendan filled her in on the events.

Bailey gasped. "I had no idea. Riley never told me. Is Abby okay?"

"Yes, thanks to Charlie. She jumped in front of a car to save Abby. I can never thank her for that."

"I have a feeling there's more than gratitude at work here. Am I right?"

He tried very hard to not squirm. Bailey was ruthless. Just like his sisters. "She's very special to me. And that's all I'm saying, nosy."

"All ready," announced Charlie. "What did I miss?"

Bailey rushed up to her, throwing her arms around Charlie's neck. "You're a hero. I had no idea." She gulped in a big breath. "When I think about what could have happened…"

Charlie grimaced. When would that stop? "I wish I could have caught her so that her wrist didn't break."

He shuddered. "I still have nightmares. So, I'll take the broken wrist."

"Aren't you going to show me the island, Brendan?"

He smiled, shaking off the bad memories. "Yes, I am. Bailey, if you don't mind, Charlie and I are going to take in the sights."

"Not at all. Although, that may take about thirty minutes. Serenity Beach is pretty small, but I love it."

He grabbed his keys from the kitchen counter. "Let's go." He kissed Bailey's cheek and led Charlie out to his truck, helping her in.

He started the truck but looked at her instead of pulling out. "That makes you uncomfortable, doesn't it? Being called a hero."

She squirmed in her seat. "It does. I'm not a hero, Brendan. I was in the right place at the right time. And I've been thankful for that every day since."

"Me too," he answered. He decided to drop it. Each day he spent with Charlie made him fall a bit more in love with her. He waited for the doubts to come. But nothing happened. No other woman had ever made him reconsider his plans. And that didn't scare him. Something to think about.

"Where'd you go, Brendan?"

He turned his head and grinned at her. "Nowhere worth mentioning."

He turned on to what served as Serenity Beach's main street. "This is Ocean Way. Kind of the heart of the town."

Charlie turned to look out the window. "I love it," she exclaimed and clapped her hands. "Look at those cute little shops. I could do some damage here once I buy a house." She continued to ooh and ah at every place they passed.

Brendan's heart sunk. He didn't want to think of her buying a house, even though he knew that was ridiculous. Best to keep that thought to himself before he scared her away. "Would you like to get out and look around?"

"Of course."

He turned down a side street and then into a municipal parking lot. They got out, and he took her hand in his. "I've always liked Serenity Beach, even though I haven't been in a few years. Other than for Jake's funeral, of course. The girls love the beach."

"I'm sure they do. You couldn't drag me off it when I was their age. I loved to build castles and collect shells. Even though my mother yelled at me to stay out of the sun." She shook her head. "She was always on me about something. I'm glad you're not like that with Kerry and Abby."

He laughed. "You've met my daughters. And my mother. All three would have my head if I tried." He stopped and kissed the hand he held. "I can't imagine being the kind of parent yours were. I want my daughters to be individuals. Know their own strengths and weaknesses. Not to conform to what someone thinks they should be."

"Good for you. I would have a better relationship with my parents if they saw things that way." She stopped in front of an ice cream store. "I don't suppose you'd like to buy me an ice cream cone?"

He grinned at her. "I might. For a fee."

"A fee, huh? And what might that be?"

"A kiss." Brendan moved closer to her until they were only inches apart.

"My mother warned me about boys like you," she drawled. She grabbed the front of his shirt, pulling him into her for a brief but hot kiss. She stepped back grinning. "Luckily, I never listened."

"Thank goodness for that." He placed her hand over his heart. "Feel what you do to me."

"Later, I'll show you what you do to me." Her wink hinted of things to come. "Now, I'd like that ice cream cone."

He laughed and resisted adjusting his shorts. The thought of later had him worked up. He held open the door for her.

"Welcome to Curley's."

Brendan blinked at the large man who had bellowed the welcome from behind the counter. "Are you Curley, by any chance?" Doubt tinged his voice. The man could be a double for Mr. Clean.

A loud laugh shook the man. "I am indeed." He gestured to his shaved head. "Don't let this fool you. I used to have curly hair half way down my back. But that was another time. What can I get you folks?"

Charlie stepped up to the counter and surveyed the choices. "They all look good. What do you recommend?"

"Well, I made them all, so I recommend them all." He looked her up and down until Brendan thought he'd have to step in. "You look like you can handle a little adventure. How about Tropical Paradise? Little bit of coconut. Little bit of Pina Colada. Lots of fun. Care for a sample first?"

Charlie shook her head. "I trust you, Curly."

The big man laughed. "I like you already." He started to scoop he ice cream onto a cone. Where are y'all from?"

"Windsor Falls," she answered.

Curly tilted his head. "Really? I could have sworn I heard some Low Country in there. And maybe something else entirely different."

"I get that a lot. You can take the girl out of the Low Country but not the Low Country out of the girl. The entirely different would be Los Angeles, Chicago, and most recently Africa."

He nodded but didn't blink an eye. "Yep, knew I heard other places in there." He gestured to Brendan with his chin. "What can I get for you, sir?"

"No recommendations?" Brendan winced at the tone of his voice. Curly was in his fifties. But Charlie was beautiful. He couldn't blame Curly. Didn't stop him from wanting to punch him.

Curly raised an eyebrow. "My partner's name is Mike, if that helps." He considered Brendan, as he had Charlie. "Perhaps Carolina Hurricane? It's got a bit of everything thrown in."

Brendan's face burned. "Carolina Hurricane sounds great."

"No worries, man. She's beautiful. I'd hit on her. If I was straight." The big man scooped up Brendan's ice cream and handed it to him.

He paid for both. "Thanks, Curly."

"Come again," replied the owner with more than a little laughter in his tone.

Brendan held the door for Charlie. He noticed she tried very hard to not laugh. He had to give her credit for that. Until she burst out laughing when they got outside.

"You thought he was checking me out?"

"In my defense, you are beautiful."

She squeezed his bicep. "Oh, Brendan, you're adorable when you're jealous."

"I'm not jealous." He wasn't a stupid man. He knew how ridiculous that sounded. "Okay, maybe a bit."

She shook her head and held her finger and thumb about an inch apart. "Maybe a little."

They strolled down the street, Charlie looking in each window they passed. He ate his ice cream cone. Curly had chosen well. Brendan thought about the exchange. He wasn't jealous by nature. At least he never had been before. Not even when Jillian flaunted herself for all the world to see. Interesting.

"Perfect."

Charlie's voice brought him out of his thoughts. "Sorry. What's perfect?" he noticed they were stopped in front of a surf shop.

"I want to get the girls something. This looks like the place." She walked inside, giving him no choice but to follow.

"How about a shirt? Or a stuffed animal. What do you think?"

He thought she was remarkable. "Either is fine, Charlie. They'll love that you brought them something."

"You're not helping," she muttered and looked through a rack of children's' shirts. "Maybe one of each."

"Anything you get will be fine. You don't have to do this."

She gave him a look. The one that said he might not be that bright. "Of course, I'm going to get them something."

After a few moments, she held up two shirts. "Are these the right size?"

The first thing Brendan noticed was the color. One was green. The other pink. His daughter's favorite colors. He glanced at the tags. "They should be fine."

"Good. Now for some stuffed animals." She walked away, browsing as she went. She stopped in front of a display that held tiny soft purses, each with a dog sticking out of them. "Perfect," she squealed. She chose two and headed towards the counter.

Brendan watched Charlie pay for her purchases and wondered how he had gotten so lucky. She was a beautiful woman, inside and out. Something loosened in his chest. Unfurled. He'd been alone since Jillian, unless you counted the brief encounters he had. Being a dad meant everything to him. But it was exhausting. And lonely at times. He took her hand again as they exited the store. She made him feel like he wasn't alone anymore.

*****

Charlie stretched and yawned before sitting up on the side of the bed. After walking around Serenity Beach, Brendan drove them back to the inn. She begged off to take a nap while Brendan looked at the inn with Bailey. Night shifts this week had wrecked her sleep. The two-hour nap refreshed her.

She could hear the others talking on the back deck through the partially opened window in their room, even though she couldn't make out their words. She moved into the bathroom to splash some water on her face. After dragging a brush through her hair and pulling it up into a messy bun, she went downstairs to join them.

Charlie grabbed an apple on her way through the kitchen. Bailey was glancing at Brendan's phone. "My gosh, the girls are huge," she exclaimed.

"Before you know it, they'll be off to college." He sighed. "Sometimes, I wish I could freeze time."

"Any plans on having more children?"

"If you had asked me a few weeks ago, I would have said no. But now, who knows? I never planned on having more, but then I never planned on meeting someone."

"That serious already? Wow!"

Charlie grabbed the door handle, but panic stopped her in her tracks. Her heart clenched. This thing with Brendan was speeding out of control. She had to tell him. That thought made her stomach churn. She never meant to get so involved with him, but here she was. She needed to tell him before it was too late.

She placed the apple back in the bowl and headed upstairs. She heard the backdoor open, so she turned around and came down again, bright smile plastered on her face. "Hey," she called to Brendan. "I'm finally awake. Sorry about that."

He smiled when he saw her and walked over to kiss her cheek. "I'm glad you got some rest. Are you still up for going out tonight?"

"For fresh seafood? Of course." She looked down at her wrinkled clothing. "I'd have to change first though."

Brendan glanced at his phone. "We have plenty of time."

Bailey walked into the kitchen behind him. "Hey, Charlie. Did you have a nice nap? We steered clear of that room. I hope we didn't wake you."

She shook her head. "Not in the least. I worked nights this week, which always messes with my sleep rhythm. Sorry to be a party pooper."

"You didn't miss anything. Bailey gave me the grand tour, including every nook and cranny."

Bailey punched him on the arm. "Can I help it if I love this place?"

"I'm only kidding. The house is gorgeous and will make a fantastic Inn. I couldn't find anything that needed fixing."

Bailey smiled. "I was hoping you wouldn't. I feel better hearing it from an expert though. Besides, you guys are my first unofficial guests. Wait until you see breakfast tomorrow."

Charlie's stomach rumbled. "All this talk of food is killing me. Why don't I go get changed for dinner?" She turned and left the kitchen without waiting for an answer.

Alone in their room, she walked into the adjoining bathroom. She stared at her reflection in the mirror. Keeping secrets from Brendan, especially ones as big as hers, didn't work for her. She blew out a breath and grabbed her toothbrush. She thought about the situation while she cleaned her teeth. Jillian had come from money. It was obvious he had not fit in with them. Charlie worried about his reaction when she told him about her family.

Knowing she should have told Brendan already didn't make this any easier. With his history, Charlie knew he'd have seen her differently. As many others had. Plus, she didn't associate herself with that aspect of her background. Yes, she had more money in the bank than most would see in a life time. But she never touched it for herself. She lived off her salary, which was more than enough.

Doubt crept in, threatening to steal the fun of the weekend. If this relationship continued in the direction she hoped, Brendan would find out. That combined with her inability to have children was beginning to take on a life of its own.

She rinsed her mouth and turned away from the mirror. Rummaging through her overnight bag, Charlie found the one sundress she had packed. The wrinkle resistant material made it a favorite of hers. She paired it with a light sweater in case the night air grew chilly and slid her feet into sandals.

Walking back into the bathroom, Charlie examined her face in the mirror. Her skin glowed from the sun today, so she only added lip gloss and some mascara. For a finishing touch, she spritzed on perfume before heading down.

"Wow," exclaimed Brendan, from the base of the stairs. "You look beautiful. I'm going to run upstairs to change. Be right back." He passed her on the stairs, touching her hand.

"I can save on electricity when you two are here," Bailey joked.

Charlie turned to the other woman. "What?"

Bailey laughed. "Kidding. But you two do have a lot of spark between you." She sighed a bit. "I miss that."

"I'm sorry if we're making you uncomfortable." The last thing she wanted to do was make Bailey sad.

Bailey touched her arm. "Please don't worry about that. I miss Jake. Everyday. But life goes on. It's been over a year, and it has gotten easier." She pulled a face. "I don't curl myself into a ball and cry myself to sleep every night."

"You're still young. Do you ever think about getting married again?"

Bailey shook her head. "I don't know. Not sure I could risk that pain again. But, I liked being married. Loved it, really. The companionship. The not being alone at the end of the day."

"The sex," added Charlie.

Bailey smirked. "Yes, the sex. Can't forget about that." A wistful look crossed her face. "I do miss the sex."

"Me too." She laughed at the look of surprise on Bailey's face. "I mean before Brendan of course. It had been quite a while."

"Did I hear my name? All good I hope." Brendan appeared in the doorway to the kitchen, wearing a pair of khakis and a polo shirt matching his eyes. He walked over to Charlie's side. She inhaled the scent of him, tangy and clean male. Her girlie parts appreciated it.

Both women laughed. And ducked their heads.

He looked from one to the other before shrugging his broad shoulders. "I give up. I'm going with the theory that it was all good. Bailey are you sure you won't join us for dinner?"

She shook her head. "You don't need a third wheel on your date." She held up a hand when he started to protest. "I'm fine. I have a date of my own. With the accounting program on my computer. I need to finish up some stuff for clients. Once Sunrise House opens, I won't have much time for that. For now, I'm only keeping a few clients I can handle with minimal time commitment."

"We're off then. See you later."

The touch of his hand at the small of her back made Charlie wish they were headed upstairs. He helped her into his truck. She twisted her hands in her lap, thinking about the things she needed to tell him. She made an instant decision. It could all wait until next week. She would enjoy this time with him. Once he found out what she had to say, things might never be the same.

Chapter Seventeen

Brendan raised his frosty glass of local IPA to his lips, watching Charlie over the rim. Something bothered her tonight. Had been since she got up from her nap. She played with the edge of her napkin and seemed a thousand miles away.

"Do you not like the crab dip?"

She started. "What?" She looked down at the appetizer in question. "Sorry. I guess I'm still tired." She scooped up some crab on a piece of the crusty French bread provided. "Mmmm."

Brendan almost moaned aloud when she licked a spot of dip from the corner of her mouth. He loved to watch her eat. Since the crab was not an issue, he wondered what might be. He hesitated to ask. The weekend had been going so well, and he wanted it to continue. Still… "Are you sure nothing's bothering you? You seem preoccupied."

Her mouth curved in a dazzling smile. She would have fooled him too. If it had reached her eyes. "I'm fine." She looked around the restaurant. "This place is great. Have you been here before?"

He didn't believe her, but this wasn't an interrogation. "Can't take the credit. Bailey told me about it. It's new. A friend of hers owns it."

"Serenity Beach reminds me of Windsor Falls. Except for being at the beach instead of in the mountains. It's the community feel to it. People know each other. Care about each other. It's nice."

"You're right. I guess I never thought of it that way. We all thought Bailey would come back home after Jake died. But this is her home now. She told me how people in the community supported her."

"That makes all the difference."

A waiter approached the table, delivering their meals. Charlie picked up a fish taco. "Haven't had good ones since Los Angeles." She took a bite and smiled around her mouthful of food. "That was worth the wait."

Now that was the Charlie he had come to know and. And what? Love? Wasn't it too soon? He watched her eat. His own food grew cold. All his plans turned to dust. And the funny part was, he didn't mind. He picked up his fork and took a bite of the Mahi Mahi on his plate.

"That's delicious. I'd ask you how yours is, but you haven't come up for air yet," he joked.

She picked up her napkin from her lap and wiped her mouth. "This is amazing."

"I'm so happy to hear that." He looked up to find a man in his early forties standing next to their table. The next thing he noticed was the man's attention focused on Charlie.

"I'm Jeff Henderson, owner of the Crazy Turtle. Welcome."

Charlie smiled at Jeff. "The fish tacos are so good. I was telling my boyfriend that I haven't had them this good since I lived on the West Coast."

Brendan's insides flopped at the word 'boyfriend'. "The Mahi Mahi is great also," he added to the conversation. He could be generous now that Charlie had staked her claim.

"I'm glad," chimed in their host.

Brendan squelched a laugh. The man's super bright smile had dimmed a bit. Too bad.

"I understand you're a friend of Bailey Saunders. She and Brendan go way back. We are staying at The Sunrise House this weekend. She recommended we come here for dinner."

"Yes, Bailey and I met through the local business owner's group. I'm happy for her opening next week and wish her all the success in the world. Please let me know if I can do anything for you."

Charlie watched him walk away before smirking. "No lack of confidence there. Did you see the way his face dropped when I mentioned you were my boyfriend?"

He reached for her hand, turned it over, and kissed her palm. "I noticed." He looked down at their plates. "Hope you weren't thinking about ordering dessert. I have other plans."

Her eyes blazed. "I can think of another form of dessert I'd rather." She never broke their gaze.

Brendan flagged their waiter. "Check please."

She laughed low in her throat. "In a hurry, Brendan?" She traced one fingernail across his palm, sending sensation up his arm. And to other parts of his body.

"What do you think?" His voice was a low growl. "Screw the check." He stood up, throwing some bills on the table. Helping her from her seat, he wrapped an arm around her waist. "Less than ten minutes to get back to the inn," he whispered in her ear.

"Might be too long," she answered.

Out in the parking lot, Brendan led her to his truck. Before opening her door, he trapped her up against it, arms on either side of her. He plundered her mouth with his own. Her lips opened on a sigh. He didn't hesitate. His tongue slid inside, drawing out sounds from deep within her. One hand dropped from the truck and made a path up the silky material of her skirt. The feel of it, along with the firm flesh underneath, was almost his undoing. He tore his mouth from hers and laid his forehead against her. He could feel the rapid beat of her heart against his own chest.

"Not that I wouldn't want to follow through with this right here," he ground out. "But we have a nice big bed waiting for us." Brendan placed a kiss on her forehead and helped her into the truck.

When he got into the driver's seat, she slid towards him, placing a hand on his thigh. "Hurry," she urged.

As if he needed any prompting. "We'll be there before you know it. This is a small island. Thank God."

Charlie laughed at his tone. "I second that."

The ride back to the inn took no more than six minutes, but the bulge in his pants made it seem more like thirty. He said a quick, silent prayer that Bailey was an early to sleep kind of girl. He pulled into the parking lot on the side of the inn and threw the truck in park. She jumped out her side before he could even turn off the ignition.

He met her at the front of the truck and pulled her into his arms. Freeing her hair from the bun she had arranged it in earlier, Brendan tangled his hands in her long tresses. The silken strands were binds holding her to him. Brendan took advantage and pressed his mouth to hers.

Charlie met his passion with her own, pressing her body along the length of his. Brendan was sure they might combust right there in the parking lot. He deepened the kiss, flattening her against the hood of his truck. A moment of sanity whizzed through his brain, and Brendan straightened. He peered into her glazed eyes. "This parking lot isn't any better than the last."

She half sobbed, half laughed. "You're right of course. Good thing one of us is thinking."

"I want you naked, under me, on the bed. That's my only thought." Her hand trembled in his. He led her into the inn and up the stairs. He almost ran by the time they reached their room. He closed the door softly, loathe to wake up Bailey.

She kissed him and then placed one finger on his lips. "Give me a second. I'll be right back. Be ready."

He nearly choked at her command. Ready? If he was any readier, it'd all be over with. Hearing the water turn on in the bathroom sink, Brendan figured he only had a few moments. Hoped, anyway. He stripped down to his underwear and turned to the bed and grinned. Bailey had turned down the covers, leaving chocolates and condoms on the pillow. He moved them to the night stand and slid under the covers, propping himself up against the headboard.

*****

Charlie removed her sundress and turned to the mirror. She splayed a hand against her lower abdomen. The scars were fading but still there. They were a part of her, a part of her history. She didn't mind them but still hadn't told Brendan about what happened to her. A cold whisper of unease slithered through her. Just one of the things she needed to tell him.

Shaking off the bad vibe, she brushed her teeth. Then she donned the lingerie Elizabeth had insisted she buy. Glancing down at what little she was wearing, Charlie was glad she listened to her friend. The pale peach silk covered the bare minimum while leaving some room for imagination.

Turning off the light, she opened the door and hesitated while her eyes adjusted. Moonlight filtered in from the windows. Brendan sat upright in the bed, the sheets drawn to his hips. A smile on his handsome face. She crossed the room, eager to get to him.

His eyes travelled down and back up the length of her body, appreciation dancing in them. He held out one, tanned arm. "Dessert as promised," he murmured.

She spied the two heart shaped chocolates in his outstretched hand. "You think of everything."

"I wish I could take the credit. These are from Bailey. Along with those." He flicked his chin to the bedside table.

"Oh my," she mumbled, feeling color sweep her cheeks. "*She* thinks of everything."

He reached into the single drawer and pulled out a string of condoms. "So do I. In case you were wondering."

"And more than a bit confident. That's a lot of condoms."

Brendan glanced at the half dozen in his hand. "Better more than not enough," he quipped. He dropped the condoms, reaching up to pull her to the bed. "Why are we still talking?" He smothered any answer she may have had with his mouth. She stripped back the covers and climbed onto the bed, straddling him. She felt him harden against her. She deepened the kiss, running one hand along his length. "No words needed," she whispered into his mouth.

Charlie squealed as he flipped her onto her back. His hot mouth burned a trail down her jaw and across her collarbone, nipping his way south. He slid the silky material aside, bearing her breasts for his view. "Beautiful," he whispered before lowering his head to one taut nipple. Brendan sucked it into his mouth. His large, work-roughened hand teased the other one.

She moved on the bed, grabbing a fist full of the sheet. Her hips arched into him, telling him what she wanted, needed, without words. She tossed her head on the pillow, blonde hair spilling across it.

He switched to her other nipple, sucking and then pulling back to blow across the already puckered flesh. "Tell me what you want, Charlie."

She raised her head from the pillow to look him in the eye. "I want you, Brendan. All of you."

He grinned before lowering his head to her overheated skin. He kissed and sucked his way down across her body until he reached the series of scars. He kissed the raised flesh. "Why didn't you tell me?"

"I haven't told anyone. Not even Elizabeth."

He nodded before lowering his head. He kissed his way along the ridges of her flesh before heading further down. She dug her heels into the mattress when he found the spot. It was all she could do to not fly off the bed. He circled her tiny bud with his tongue, over and over again, before sliding one finger inside. The tension built as Charlie raised her hips to him. "Please," she begged in a broken voice.

"Your wish is my command." Brendan slid another finger inside of her, increasing the pressure. Her muscles tensed. "That's right, baby. Let go."

Charlie didn't have a choice. She flew apart before floating back down to earth. "Wow. Just wow."

He grinned. "And we're nowhere near done."

"You're right about that. With a wicked grin, she stretched her hand over to the nightstand. Grabbing a condom, she wiggled out from under him, making sure he felt every inch of it.

"You're killing me," he grated from deep in his throat.

"That's the idea." Charlie ripped open the condom package and rolled it down the length of him. He lay very still, breathing hard and eyes squeezed shut. "Just another moment," she crooned near his ear. She pressed him down into the mattress and climbed on top of him.

Brendan opened his eyes and watched Charlie lower herself upon him. "Don't ever stop."

She laughed. "I take it you like that."

He pressed his hips up to meet hers. "What do you think?"

"I think there's no more need for talking." She lowered herself, taking all of him within her. Their eyes met and held. Emotion she wasn't ready to deal with welled up inside her chest. Charlie hadn't planned on this. And God knew her life was a bit of a mess right now, but she loved him.

Rather than think about that, she lost herself in the feeling. In one smooth move, Brendan flipped her under him and drove home. She gasped aloud at the sensation. Her breath reduced to panting. The tension that had barely ceased from her last orgasm mounted again. "Brendan," she whispered, able to do no more than that.

"I'm right there with you." He ground his hips into her, proving the point.

Charlie locked her ankles around his lower back and tilted her hips, straining to hold every inch of him. His next thrust sent her spiraling over the edge. She dug her nails into his back to ground herself.

"Open your eyes for me, baby."

She did as he asked, meeting his gaze. And she was lost.

"That's the way. I need you with me, Charlie." He fell silent as he followed her into the void.

He collapsed on the bed next to her with his arm across her belly. "I may have died."

Better to keep it light, she figured. "If that was death, then I'm okay with it."

Brendan heaved himself off the bed. Leaning down, he kissed her shoulder. "I'll be right back." He walked towards the bathroom.

Grateful for a moment to pull herself together, Charlie reached for the sheet to cover herself. She tucked it above her breasts and rolled away onto her side. Love? Where had *that* come from? Sure, she liked Brendan a lot. And his daughters were amazing. But love? Was she ready for that? A bitter sound ripped from her throat. Love wasn't about convenience.

"That's a serious look considering what we did." Brendan slid in behind her, pulling her body back against his chest.

Without warning, tears leaked from the corners of her eyes. She wiped them away with the heels of her hand.

"Charlie?" Brendan rolled her away from the edge of the bed until they faced each other. She could feel the wetness on her cheeks.

"I'm sorry. I'm such a mess." She shocked herself by sobbing against his hard chest.

Brendan gathered her in his arms, making soothing noises. "It's okay, honey."

After a few moments, she hiccupped and gathered herself. Brushing the hair out of her face, she sat up clutching the sheet to her. "I've been hanging around Elizabeth too much. All those pregnancy hormones. She cries at the drop of a hat." She gave him a watery smile.

He hauled himself up until they were both sitting, facing each other. He tucked a wayward strand of hair behind her ear. "Talk to me, Charlie."

Because his voice held a tenderness she didn't expect, she did. "I've fallen in love with you," she blurted. She gasped at her own words but rushed on. "I know that's crazy. We barely know each other. And you have the girls to consider. And

I moved here a few weeks ago. I'm still settling in at the hospital and don't have a permanent home. Then there's the PTSD and therapy. Ugh! What could I possibly have been thinking?"

He smiled at her. "Charlie, it's okay. Take a breath."

She did so. A big one. Then she poked him in the chest. Hard. "It's your fault you know. You with the beautiful face and to die for body. Not to mention the adorable daughters. And Fred and Ginger. How could I not fall in love with you?" She poked him once more for good measure before burying her heated face in her hands. She willed herself to not cry again.

He rubbed his chest. "Is it safe to speak? Or are you going to poke me again?"

She uttered a sound from behind her hands; half sob, half laugh. "I suppose."

"You're right. We don't know each other long. And you just got here. And I have the girls to think about. And yet."

She dropped her hands from in front of her face. Hope, the barest trickle of it, bloomed in her chest. "And yet?"

"And yet, you're all I think about, Charlie. I've had that very same conversation, over and over, in my head. And I love you more than you could imagine."

She held her breath, afraid something would ruin this perfect moment. "You love me too?"

"Why do you sound so surprised? How could I not love you?" He held her hands in his. "From the very first time I saw you, Charlie, I felt like someone hit me in the chest with a bat. You took my breath away. But it's so much more than that. I watch you with the girls. See how much you care for them, and it warms my heart. I wasn't looking for love. I wasn't looking for you. But here we are. And I wouldn't have it any other way."

She should tell him what she needed to. About her family. And what had happened to her in Africa. About her inability to have children. But the moment was too perfect. She couldn't risk ruining it. A finger of doubt wormed itself into her brain, but she ignored it. There would be plenty of time later.

She stood and placed her hand in his. "Let's give that lovely oversized tub a try." He smiled as she pulled him into the bathroom. There was no more talking for a long time.

Chapter Eighteen

Sunshine pouring in through the open blinds awakened Charlie early Sunday morning. She rolled over and groaned. Long unused muscles protested. They had spent more time in bed than out this weekend. She blushed when she thought of their hostess. Bailey must be wondering if they were still alive.

She started to edge out of bed when a large hand wrapped around her wrist. "Where do you think you're going?" She could hardly make out the mumbled words from under a pillow.

"Shower. We have to go home today." Her tone told exactly how she felt about that.

He rolled over on his back, causing the sheet to slip lower on his torso. She stared. Couldn't help it. The man was all ripped abs and broad chest. "You could shower with me. Save water and all that."

A wicked grin spread across his face before his eyes even opened. "Can't imagine we'd save any water. But I'm game if you are." He slid his hand down her back, cupping her bottom.

She jumped up from the bed and ran to the bathroom. "Better hurry while there's still hot water."

She hadn't made it to the door when he caught her. Brendan picked her up, carrying her to the shower. He kicked the bathroom door closed with his foot. It was a long time before they made it downstairs to breakfast.

Bailey looked up from the sheets of paper spread in front of her, grinning from ear to ear at Charlie. "Came down for sustenance?"

"Coffee. I need coffee." She spied a basket of muffins. Her stomach growled in appreciation. "And I'll love you forever if I could have one of those muffins."

Bailey got up to grab a plate. "Where's Brendan? Did you finally wear him out?" She grabbed the basket and placed it along with a plate and knife in front of Charlie. "I recommend the plum jelly, but I have several flavors. They're all home made on the island."

Charlie poured herself a cup of coffee. "Um, I needed that." She broke off a corner of the muffin and popped it in her mouth. "Oh. There aren't any words."

"Thanks. I guess you like it."

"Like doesn't even cover it." She reached for the plum jelly and slathered some on a piece of muffin. "Not sure how it could taste any better." She took a bite and smiled. "Okay, I was wrong. That's amazing."

"I'm using local products whenever I can. Fresh produce, meats, seafood, etc. We all try to."

"That's smart business."

"Yes, and friendship as well. There are many small businesses on the island. Everyone tries to help each other out. The people here are wonderful."

"We loved the restaurant the other night. The owner was, uh, colorful."

Bailey laughed. "Meet Jeff, did you? He's harmless, for the most part."

"Bit flirtatious. So, I introduced Brendan as my boyfriend. That put him off a bit."

"Yes, he is that. Jeff likes to 'play the field', or so he says. I think he's lonely. But, he'd do anything for me."

"Wasn't fond of him checking out Charlie," offered Brendan as he walked into the kitchen.

Charlie took in his shorts and t-shirt, molding to his chest. His hair was still damp from their shower. If Bailey wasn't standing there, she might have jumped him. She passed him the basket of muffins instead.

"Seems like your *girlfriend* put Jeff in his place."

He glanced at Charlie, a huge smile on his face. "Yes, she did. Saved me from going all caveman on him."

His girlfriend almost blew a mouthful of coffee across the breakfast bar. "Wow. Who knew you had an inner caveman?"

"Not me," piped up Bailey.

"Kind of took me by surprise." Brendan looked at Charlie, his gaze simmering with a heat she felt to her toes. "I That's what happens when you love someone."

Bailey fanned herself before leaping up and hugging Brendan and Charlie. "I'm so happy for both of you!"

Charlie fidgeted with her knife. She would feel so much better if she had told him what he needed to know about her. They had a long car ride home soon. That would be the perfect time.

She realized Bailey was talking to her. "I'm sorry, what?"

Bailey smirked. "Guess you're lost in the fog of new love. I asked when you guys were taking off today."

"Oh, soon. Not that I want to leave. Ever. But, I have a shift in the morning and am lacking groceries in my kitchen. Whenever Brendan is ready I guess."

He took a sip of his coffee. "She's right. The girls have school tomorrow, and I have to get them from my mom. They always act like they'll never see each other again. Even though they live less than five miles from us."

"How is your Mom? I miss her. Send them my love. Please tell them to come down for a few days."

"I will. They'd love this place. I know they love Serenity Beach."

He got up and rinsed his coffee cup and Charlie's plate and mug. "We should go."

Charlie stood and hugged Bailey. "I'm so pleased to have met you, Bailey. Sunrise House is gorgeous. I'll be back. I can't wait to hear about all the success you have." The two women exchanged phone numbers, promising to keep in touch. Charlie felt like she'd made another good friend.

She and Brendan went back to their room. Funny how she thought of it that way after the weekend. "We get this room again when we come back."

He closed the door and walked her backwards to against the wall. "Yes, we do," he murmured as he lowered his lips to hers.

The heat that always remained under the surface exploded the moment he touched her. Charlie put everything she had into the kiss, wrapping her arms around his waist and pulling him to her. When they finally came up for air, Brendan's eyes were glazed. "If we don't leave now…."

"I know," he groaned. "You'll have to keep your hands off me then."

"Ha," she replied. "Who started that one?" She walked into the bathroom and brushed her teeth. When she looked up, her eyes met Brendan's in the mirror.

"I do love you," he told her.

Charlie turned and walked into his arms. "I know you do. And I love you. Who cares if it's fast and crazy?"

"Exactly." He kissed her forehead and took his turn at the sink.

The doubt that had been niggling at her all since last night bloomed inside her chest. Her heart pounded. They needed to talk. She finished packing, the unease growing.

Brendan walked out of the bathroom. "I've got the bags. Can you grab my car keys, please?"

She nodded and plucked his keys from the dresser. Taking a quick look around, Charlie ensured they had everything. They went back downstairs and out onto the deck. Bailey sat in a rocking chair, watching the waves roll in and out.

"It's time, then." She stood and hugged both. "Make sure it's not so long this time, Brendan. And bring my favorite girls with you."

"We will, Bailey. We'll come back this summer with the girls. Make sure you have room for us. I'm sure this is going to be a wild success."

"Your lips to God's ears."

Angus came down the porch stairs and sat at Charlie's feet. His big soulful eyes pulled at her heart. She wrapped her arms around his shaggy neck. "I'll miss you too, Angus," she assured him. He gave her one deep bark. She leaned down to kiss his head

Bailey stoked the length of the dog's back. "Don't worry, Angus, I'm staying with you." Angus licked her hand.

"Okay. We're going now before we head back in for more muffins." He gave Bailey a final hug and opened Charlie's door for her. She waved and got in.

They drove off the island towards Highway 74. She turned to Brendan. "Thank you so much for bringing me this weekend. I can't believe I've never been here before. I spent my whole childhood at the beach, but always in South Carolina."

"Where did you go?"

"Mostly Sullivan's Island." She didn't mention the gorgeous home her family had there. The 'beach cottage', as her family called it, was the best part of her childhood. She spent her summers there, usually with some of the family's staff. Her mother travelled back and forth to their home in the city for this event or that function. Her father did nothing but work, only venturing out to the island on the occasional weekend. That suited Charlie just fine. Miss Suzi had been her favorite. So much more than a nanny, Miss Suzi had been her constant companion. A safe harbor in the storm that was her parents' miserable relationship.

"Hmm," was his only reply.

She wasn't sure what that meant and changed the subject. "I hope the girls like their souvenirs."

Brendan glanced at her. "They will. No doubt. That was very thoughtful of you."

"It was nothing. They're so adorable. I can't wait to get to know them better."

"They'll like that too. They talk about you all the time, Charlie. And I told you their comments about you being their mother."

His tone was light but she felt a hint of reservation. "I know it's still early days, but I'm looking forward to spending more time with them."

"I want that too, Charlie. But this is unfamiliar territory for me. They've never met anyone I had a relationship with, as you know. I want to take this slowly, make sure we're doing it the right way."

She rubbed the back of her neck. "I wasn't suggesting a sleep over. I want them to get to know me. That's all." She turned to watch the passing scenery.

He rubbed her shoulder. "I'm sorry. I'm not trying to be difficult. Or keep them away from you. I want them to get to know you, love you like I do, before we take things further."

"That's smart. Take it slow."

"Exactly." He snuck a glance at her before looking back at the traffic. "Speaking of family, when am I going to meet yours?"

"Not until you have to." The thought of that meeting sent a chill through her bones. The Fitzgeralds were such down to earth, real people. And her parents weren't. It wouldn't go well. She glanced at Brendan long enough to see one dark eyebrow raised in question.

"Never? Won't they be coming to visit? Windsor Falls is only a four-hour drive."

"It may as well be on the moon," she muttered. She pulled herself away from the window and faced Brendan. She traced a pattern on his thigh with one finger. "Ask Elizabeth some time. She's met them."

"I'm asking *you*, Charlie." He removed his baseball hat and ran a hand through his hair, mussing it. "Are they that bad? Or is it me?"

"Of course not, Brendan. You're wonderful. I've told you what they're like." Charlie gritted her teeth, trying to figure out how to explain them to him. "They're not bad people. But they're shallow and self-centered. My parents have the worst marriage ever. But Averys do not divorce. They stay together, making themselves and everyone around them, miserable. They won't like Windsor Falls. It's too small. Exactly what I love about it. They won't like you, because you're not the one they picked for me. Hell, Brendan, they don't even like me." The acid in her stomach turned to a forest fire. The mere thought of them meeting, and snubbing him, made her sick.

He picked up her hand and placed the softest of kisses in her palm. "How did you turn out so well?"

"You always know the perfect thing to say." She leaned in and kissed the side of his face, the stubble tickling her lips.

"Thank you, but I'm serious. Charlie, you're the most grounded person I know. Nothing like how you're describing your parents."

"Ha! That's just the façade I keep. Under it, I'm a mess. And I escaped at eighteen." She was about to tell him about Miss Suzi. But that would lead to more questions. She had to tell him. But not yet. She feared bursting their bubble of happiness. She gnawed her bottom lip.

Brendan shook his head. "Eighteen years is a long time to be influenced. It's because you're your own person."

She laughed out loud, not altogether with humor. "I'm definitely that. Warts and all."

"Well, I like you. Warts and all. I'm not worried about meeting your family. And you can borrow mine anytime you want."

Charlie released a breath she didn't realize she was holding. One bullet dodged. At least for now. "Anyway, it's too nice of a day to spend talking about my parents." She leaned forward and turned on the satellite radio to a country station. She sat back and listened to Toby Keith sing about liking him now. Seemed appropriate.

The rest of the drive flew. They stopped for lunch at a roadside diner. Charlie napped again, waking as he pulled into her driveway. He got out and grabbed her bag, walking her to the door. Bending down, he brushed his lips across hers. "I wish I could come in. But I have to run home and then grab the girls after dinner."

She wound her arms around his neck, pulling him for a last kiss. "That's okay. I've put off grocery shopping for too long. And then there's all the laundry to catch up on."

"Ah, the glamourous life of an ER doctor, "joked Brendan.

"You have no idea." She unlocked the front door and gave him one last kiss. She pulled a bag out of her duffle. "Do you want to give the girls their gifts?"

"No, you can do it when you come over for dinner tomorrow. You're working days, right?"

"I am. Should be done by four or so. Text me when you get home."

"That's a date." Brendan gave her one more scorching kiss before heading to his truck.

*****

Getting in, he noticed the missed calls from his mother. Four of them. His heart jumped. He hit the preset for his mother as he backed out of Charlie's driveway. He didn't notice Charlie waving from her front porch. His mother answered on the first ring.

"Brendan, thank goodness. Where are you?"

"I just dropped off Charlie. I was going to head home before I picked up the girls. What's wrong, Mom. Are Kerry and Abby okay?" Icy hands clutched his heart.

"The girls are fine. I'm sorry to have scared you like that. They're out with Katie and Riley at the store. There's a woman here looking for you." His mother's voice dropped to a whisper, increasing his concern. "She says she's your ex-wife."

Disbelief flooded him, making him speed through a yellow light. "What?" Jillian? In Windsor Falls? Why?

"She says she came to see the girls. Why now, after all this time?"

Brendan spoke through gritted teeth. "She must want something, Mom. Don't say one word to her. Call Katie and make sure she doesn't come home with the girls. I'll be there in under ten minutes." Brendan ended the call and concentrated on getting to his mother's in one piece. He had always feared this day.

Chapter Nineteen

Brendan yanked open his mother's front door. He froze at the sight of his ex-wife seated in the living room. For a second, she looked so much like Charlie that he blinked. But the superficial similarities of height and long blonde hair faded. Jillian was an empty shell next to Charlie.

"What are you doing here, Jillian?" His voice dripped with ice and disdain.

She turned, fixing her gaze upon him. And that's where the similarity ended. Hers were hard, calculating. Charlie's were warm and inquisitive. "Why, Brendan, I thought you'd be pleased to see me." She closed the distance between them, placing one hand on his bicep. "After all, it's been a long time," she drawled.

He shrugged his arm, dislodging her hand. "I know exactly how long it's been. Six years without so much as a birthday or Christmas card."

"I sent you a letter a few weeks ago, Brendan. Didn't you get it?"

A vague memory of ripping it into pieces came to mind. He smiled grimly. "Didn't read it."

"Well, if you'd bothered to read it, you would have known I was thinking about the girls. How are they?"

"Kerry and Abby are fine. They're happy and healthy, no thanks to you. Now I'll ask you again. What do you want?"

Jillian arranged her beautiful face into a pout that would have gotten to him years ago. But that was before she threatened to abort the girls. "Maybe I've come to realize the error of my ways. Maybe I came to see my girls."

Brendan's jaw tightened until he feared his teeth would crack. "Your girls? Forgive me if I'm a bit cynical. After all, you signed away all rights to them and never looked back. Six years have passed. Why now?"

"Brendan, give her a chance to explain."

He whirled on his mother, who had been standing in the kitchen doorway. How could she be taking that woman's side? "She's had six years to explain, Mom." He turned to Jillian, taking her by the arm. "This is something we need to discuss in private." Brendan led her to the front porch, pulling the door shut behind him.

Ever the cool one, Jillian pulled her arm free and put some distance between them. "I can understand why you're surprised. But I have a right to see the girls."

Red blurred his vision. "No, Jillian, you don't. You signed away the rights to *my daughters* the day they were born."

Jillian crossed her arms in front of her, the sun flashing off the large diamond on her left hand. "You're getting married again," Brendan said.

She glanced at the rock on her finger. "Yes, I am. In the fall."

"And how does that have anything to do with my daughters?"

For the first time, Jillian looked less than confident. "Phillip, my fiancée, can't have children. His first wife left him because of it. My parents told him about the girls."

Fury and dread warred within Brendan. "I still don't understand what that has to do with Kerry and Abby."

"He wants heirs."

Brendan's heart lurched within his chest. "Kerry and Abby are my daughters. Mine alone. I'm not sure what your plan was for coming here, but you can take yourself right back to Texas."

She reached into her purse and pulled out a card, handing it to Brendan. "I had a feeling you'd be unreasonable. We can do this the easy way or the hard way,

Brendan. My parents will back me all the way. Do you really want to put the girls through that? I'm staying in town for a few days. Here's my number. Call me when you've come to your senses."

She turned and walked away. Brendan watched here get into a rental and drive off, before he glanced down at the card in his hand. The full reality of her words hit him. He heard his mother speaking to him, but she sounded as though she was speaking from the bottom of a deep well. He staggered to the porch and sat, sinking his head into his hands. How could he stop Jillian?

*****

Charlie pulled her phone from her scrub top pocket for the thousandth time that afternoon. Still no reply from Brendan. She had been busy all day, without much time to think about it. But now her shift had almost ended, and they were supposed to have dinner. She had left him a quick voice mail message around noon. She shook off the bad feeling and went to see another patient.

An hour later, and still no reply, she sat behind her computer screen, staring at her phone and willing it to ring.

Elizabeth lowered herself into the chair next to her. "Are you expecting it to do something?"

Charlie rolled her eyes. "I feel like I'm back in high school. 'Why hasn't he called?' Ugh." She turned back to her computer, trying to concentrate on updating a patient's chart.

Elizabeth rolled her chair closer to Charlie's and placed a hand on her friend's shoulder. "You haven't heard, then. Jillian showed up last night. It didn't go well."

A heavy stone landed in her chest, making it hard to breathe. "What? Why? I thought she's had nothing to do with the girls since they were born."

Elizabeth nodded. "That's just it. She hasn't. I don't know all the details, but it can't be good. I thought he would have told you."

Why *was* she hearing this from Elizabeth and not Brendan? Her heart squeezed in her chest. "It must have happened after he dropped me off yesterday afternoon."

"Call him, Charlie."

"That's the problem. We were supposed to have dinner tonight, and texted him to find out what we're doing. He hasn't responded." She rubbed her forehead. "I didn't even know about Jillian being here. "I'm sorry. I have no idea what's going on or why he's handling things this way. Give him some time to deal with whatever it is. He's not going anywhere."

She blew her a piece of hair out of her eyes. "That's all I can do." She wasn't happy with the situation, but she respected Brendan. She didn't know much about his ex, but what she did disturbed her. She focused on documenting her patient's care. She'd already given report to the oncoming physician. Once she finished, she could leave for the night.

"Why don't you come home with me for dinner?"

"Thanks, but I'd rather go home. I have laundry to do and a stack of books I haven't even started yet." Anything to keep her mind off Brendan, she thought.

"Are you sure? Sam's making his famous ribs on the grill." Charlie tried to not laugh at Elizabeth hefting herself out of the chair. "Not that I need to be eating a huge dinner," she said.

Charlie stood up too, giving Elizabeth a hug. "You're eating for two, remember. Besides, you don't need a third wheel. Your days of romantic dinners alone with Sam are dwindling. You'll be the three of you before you know it."

Elizabeth's face lit with her smile. "True. And I can't wait. But I enjoy the just us time. See you, Charlie."

She sat back down to finish her charting. Thoughts of Brendan, and the girls, crowded her mind. What could Jillian want after all this time? Had she finally met Kerry and Abby? Her heart clenched. Those poor girls. She finished up her work and left for the evening. She was back for day shift in the morning.

Climbing into bed later that night, she grabbed a random book from the pile on her night stand. She opened it and settled back against the mountain of pillows behind her. Ten minutes later, after reading the first page several times, Charlie gave up. She tossed the book on the bed and sank back against the pillows. Why hadn't Brendan called her back? Why hadn't he told her about Jillian showing up in town?

Knowing she wouldn't be cracking the new novel, she reached over to turn out the light. The moonlight filtered in, creating enough light for her to watch the ceiling fan rotate. Usually its soft background noise lulled her to sleep. Not tonight. She hadn't been able to turn her mind off. After throwing together a quick meal, she had cleaned the house. Or tried to. But Katie had left it immaculate for her, and Charlie hadn't been here long enough to make any mess.

So here she was, lying in bed and not tired. She picked up her phone, cursing herself for checking yet again. Nothing from Brendan. She glanced through her email, skipping one from her mother. No thanks. She could watch something on Netflix, but she had an early shift in the morning. She needed sleep more than anything. She hit her sleep playlist on her music app and hoped for the best.

*****

Across town, Brendan checked on the girls. One day, they would want their own rooms, but for now Kerry and Abby preferred to sleep together. He had painted one half green, the other pink. A nightlight glowed softly from the wall. Not that they were afraid of the dark or anything in it. Fred and Ginger both raised their heads, acknowledged him with a brief wag of their tails and went back to sleep.

He walked into his bedroom. He brushed his teeth and dropped his dirty clothes in the hamper. It had been a long and horrible day, filled with the usual Monday craziness at work. The knowledge that Jillian was here made it that much worse. His blood boiled at the thought of her trying to take Kerry and Abby from him. This had to end. He left a brief message asking her to meet him. He should have known she wouldn't make this easy for him. Jillian was the queen of games. She had not responded to his call.

Brendan turned out the lights and flopped onto his back in the middle of the bed. Soothing night sounds filtered in from the cracked bedroom window. But nothing helped tonight. For the hundredth time, he thought about Charlie. Guilt clenched his gut. He'd blown off dinner tonight. He hadn't responded to her voicemail or text either. Both bed choices. What could he say? His ex was back threatening to take the girls? He didn't want to drag her into any mess Jillian might be planning. She had enough on her plate. He'd tell her when he figured a way out of this nightmare. Unease trickled through him, but he remained convinced this was the right choice.

He punched the pillow, turning it over to find the cool side. He needed to get some sleep. It had been scarce last night, and he couldn't afford two nights like that in a row. Of course, wishing for something and getting it were two very different things. At least Kerry and Abby had been kept out of this mess. So far.

*****

The medic radio blared. Charlie listened as a nurse took down the details of an incoming patient. Twenty something male, unrestrained driver in a two-car motor vehicle accident. When would people learn, she wondered. Seat belts saved lives. It was a proven fact. But only when used.

Eve, the nurse who spoke with the medics, turned to her. "Did you get all that?"

She sighed. Not what she needed after an almost sleepless night. "Got it, thanks. Suspected femur fracture and altered level of consciousness. Is the trauma bay ready?"

"I'll make sure," Eve said, dashing in that direction.

Charlie knew it would be ready to go by the time their patient arrived. The ER staff at Windsor Falls Memorial worked well together. Each person knew their role and were good at it. They made her job so much smoother.

She grabbed her coffee cup and headed for some much-needed caffeine. With only a few minutes before the patient arrived, she'd have to hurry. Now was not the time to think about Brendan and why he hadn't called her. She had slept poorly last night because of him, but she was a professional. Focus on what needed to be done here. She gulped down some coffee and headed for the trauma bay.

Other staff were waiting. Charlie heard the wail of an ambulance growing closer and then ceasing as it pulled into the ER entrance. She put on her glasses and face shield and gloved up. The medics wheeled her patient into the trauma bay.

"Hey Charlie," Mac said by way of greeting. "Don't have an ID on this one. Male approximately mid-twenties. He was the unrestrained driver. Considerable damage to the front of his SUV. Conscious on scene but altered and confused. Only responsive to painful stimuli now. Glasgow Coma Scale is seven, down from ten upon our arrival. There's a large contusion on his left forehead with some blood loss. He's got obvious bruising on his chest and abdomen and an open fracture of his right femur."

"Thanks, Mac. Let's move him over to the table on my count of three. One, two, three." They moved the patient onto the ER stretcher, and Mac backed theirs away. "Okay, everyone, I'd like another IV started. Let's run some normal saline in. Get him on the monitor please."

Charlie stepped in to do her primary assessment. The patient was too still for her liking. He was breathing on his own with oxygen saturation at ninety seven percent. But that could change in a heartbeat. She palpated his head, looking for signs of a skull fracture and was relieved to find none. Of course, that didn't mean he didn't have a brain injury. His trachea sat midline. However, the large bruises on his chest and abdomen were concerning.

"Let's get x-ray in here and get a trauma series of his head, chest, abdomen, and pelvis. He's going to need a Foley and labs please." She continued her survey down his chest and abdomen, finding more bruising. The patient groaned when she pushed on his lower left abdomen. She noted his spleen may be involved and moved on.

Mac had splinted the man's leg. She pulled off the loose gauze dressing on top, revealing an open fracture of the upper leg. "Well, that's a ticket to the operating room."

"And that's my cue," called Dan Martin. He strode into the room as though he owned it.

Charlie glanced up at the trauma surgeon, relieved to see him. "Welcome, Dan. Glad you're here."

"Glad enough to have dinner with me?"

A few people snickered. Charlie ignored them and Dan. Elizabeth had been right about him. "Finished up my assessment. He has an open right femur fracture. Pulses and color are good distal to it. I'm more worried about his spleen. No seatbelt and there's bruising and rigidity in his right lower quadrant." She stepped aside. Dan approached the patient.

The surgeon ran through his own assessment and nodded. "They never learn." He glanced at the monitors. "Since he's stable, let's get the imaging done before I take him to the OR."

He rattled off more orders to the nurses involved and then approached Charlie. "You never called me for that coffee."

"No, I didn't." This wasn't the first time a fellow doctor had hit on her. Being direct worked best. "I don't get involved with co-workers, Dan." A smile softened her words.

He laughed. "Okay. Fair enough. Thanks for being honest. You can't blame me for trying." He turned back to his patient. "I've got this from here."

That was fine with her. She had more than enough patients to handle. Still nothing from Brendan, but she had dinner plans with the women from the book club tonight. Something to look forward to. They were wonderful, and hanging around with them would take her mind off things.

The rest of the shift passed without incident. She showered and changed in the locker room before heading out for dinner. This would be her second time to

The Sunshine Café. She couldn't help but remember going with Brendan when she first arrived in Windsor Falls.

Charlie pulled into the parking lot in the back of the restaurant. Paige, Amy, and Jamie were standing under a tree, engaged in an animated conversation. It ceased when she joined them.

"Hey! Don't stop on my account." She was joking, but the guilty looks on their faces hit home. "Okay. What is it?"

The three women looked at each other and then anywhere but at her. Finally, Amy spoke up. "Oh, for Pete's sake. We were talking about Brendan and his no-good ex showing up in town. Sorry."

Charlie held up her hand. "I imagine it's big news here. Do you know anything else?" Her face flushed. "Pathetic, I know. But I haven't heard from him," she muttered.

Paige slid her arm through Charlie's, herding her towards the restaurant. "Come on, let's eat. Besides, we want to hear *all* about your trip to the beach."

She let herself be pulled into the conversation, desperate to talk about something other than Brendan's ex. She summoned a smile. "Well, I can't tell you *all* about it." The other women laughed.

"Not fair," called Jamie. "You're the only one with a sex life. Throw us a bone. We're dying."

She waited until they were all watching her. "Well, there is this one thing he does with his tongue." She shook her head. "No, a lady never tells."

There were cries of "no fair" and boo", but Charlie kept walking. The four went in the front door.

"Hello, again, my new friend." Claire Bonet, the owner, rushed up to Charlie, kissing her cheek. "I see you brought some friends."

"Guys, this is Claire, the owner and chef extraordinaire of the Sunshine Café. Claire, this is Amy, Paige, and Jamie. Amy and Paige teach kindergarten, and Jamie owns Between the Covers."

"Welcome, my friends. Amy and Paige, you are very brave women." She turned to Jamie. "I'm sorry to say that I have not been to your store yet, though I do like to read. I'm thinking of writing a cookbook. Putting together some of my family's creole recipes. I'd love to talk with you sometime about that project."

Jamie smiled at her and dug through her purse. She pulled out a slim case. "Here's my card. Call me anytime. I'd love to hear what you're planning. I love to showcase local authors."

Claire clapped her hands. "Wonderful! Now let me find an excellent table for you lovely women." She led them to a large table in an alcove of windows. "From here, you can watch life go by and have an excellent view of the setting sun. Someone will be right here with menus. Can I start you with something to drink?"

"I thought you'd never ask," joked Amy. The women all gave their drink orders and Claire left the table.

"Okay, spill," ordered Jamie.

Charlie laughed as all three women focused on her. "We had a fun time. Brendan's friend, Bailey Saunders, owns a lovely old house she's opening as an inn this weekend. We stayed there."

"She's from Windsor Falls, right? I know the name."

Charlie nodded to Paige. "Yes, she is. Moved to Serenity Beach a few years back."

"And? Those weren't exactly the details we were waiting for, Charlie."

"Really, Amy? I never would have guessed. I will say that the bed was very large and comfortable. Lots of room." She raised her eyebrows up and down. "Same goes for the shower."

There was a moment's pause before the three women burst out laughing. Charlie sat back and watched her friend's reactions. She was so glad to have met these women.

*****

Across town, Brendan tried to check his temper. "You can't be for real, Jillian. These are the same children you wanted to abort. You waltz back years later and expect me to hand them over to you? You've lost your mind."

Brendan paced the length of his porch while Jillian sat on the swing, looking bored. Kerry and Abby were safely tucked away with their Uncle Donovan and Aunt Nora. Brendan didn't want them to even see Jillian. He rubbed his temples, sure his head would explode.

"Brendan, I've already explained. Unfortunately, Phillip cannot have any children of his own. When he found out about the girls, he was eager to adopt them."

"And I'm supposed to what? Hand them over to you because your fiancé needs an heir?" He stopped right in front of her, hauling her by the arm to a standing position. "Let me be very clear. No. You will not ever get the Kerry and Abby. Now go back to Texas and stay away from my family."

Jillian ran one blood red nail down his chest. "I love it when you're angry," she purred. Then her face hardened. "Now let me be clear. I will get what I want. I always do. My family has more money than God. I'll take you to court, Brendan, and I will win."

Brendan grabbed her by the upper arm and walked her off the porch. He stopped at her rented Mercedes. "Get in your car and go home. No judge in his right mind would side with you after abandoning them at birth." Brendan wished he felt as confident.

"Are you sure about that?" Jillian hit the key fob to open her door. "My flight is tomorrow night. Do the right thing, Brendan."

His chest tightened until breathing became difficult. Brendan gripped the porch railing, the wood biting into his palms. He couldn't lose them. Not now. Not ever. He watched her car disappear around a corner. She might have the resources behind her, but Brendan had over six years of parenthood. He was the only parent Abby and Kerry ever knew. That had to count for something.

Brendan went inside, wishing he knew a lawyer. Someone who could give him an opinion on this. He did the next best thing. Picking up his cell, he hit the first contact. "Mom, I need help." Brendan explained the problem. His mother talked a mile a minute about rallying the troops. Her reassurances might not count for anything against Jillian's money, but Brendan felt better knowing he wasn't alone.

Chapter Twenty

Insistent ringing of the doorbell woke Charlie the next morning. She glanced at her phone. Only six in the morning. She groaned as the sound came again. Someone really wanted her to wake up. Years of her medical training kicked in. Charlie threw a robe on over her nightshirt and ran downstairs. She opened the door to a red-faced Elizabeth.

"What's wrong? Come in." Charlie threw open the storm door and escorted Elizabeth inside.

Breathing heavily, Elizabeth came inside and collapsed on the couch. "I'm so sorry for the hour, but I'm on my way into work. I need to talk with you."

That got Charlie's attention. She sank into the couch cushion next to her friend. "Are you all right?"

Elizabeth nodded. "I'm fine. It's about Brendan." In a hurried rush, the tale of his ex and her demands flowed out of Elizabeth. Tears rolled down her cheeks when she finished. Charlie wasn't sure if they were sorrow or anger.

Charlie jumped up and paced the room. "What? The woman who would have aborted them if he hadn't stopped her? She can't stand a chance at getting custody!" Bright spots appeared in front of her eyes. She had never wanted to smash something like she did right now. Jillian's face would do.

"I know it sounds ridiculous, but he's is worried. The whole family is. Jillian's family is very rich and very powerful."

"Those poor girls." Anguish roughened her voice. The thought of anything happening to those little girls gutted her.

"That's just it. No one thinks Jillian could win. Jillian doesn't care about them. She's never even seen them. But she's not above hurting them to get what she wants."

Charlie clenched and opened her fists. Her blood ran cold and then hot at Jillian's lack of feeling for the girls. Who did that? "What is Brendan doing about this?" The beginnings of a plan formed in her mind.

Elizabeth got up from the sofa. "He's meeting with an attorney this morning. Trying to get a plan into place. I have to get to work." Elizabeth hugged Charlie. "I'm sorry to be the one to tell you this, but I thought you should know."

Charlie hugged her friend back. "Thank you. I wish he had told me, but he has a lot on his plate right now. We can talk about it when he feels a bit more in control."

"Please don't give up on him. I know that Brendan cares about you. A lot. This thing with Jillian, the thought of losing the girls, is killing him. He can't think straight. If he was, he would have called you."

Charlie walked Elizabeth to the door. "You're right. I should be patient. Have a good shift."

"Thanks."

She stood there, watching Elizabeth drive off. Her heart raced. Jillian couldn't get away with this. Mind made up, she ran back upstairs to take a shower. Jillian might be from wealth and privilege, but so was she.

Thirty minutes later, Charlie dressed for battle. She drove to The Blue Iris. She didn't know for sure if Jillian was staying here, but it was the nicest place in town. She parked her car and went inside.

Lorna manned the desk. Charlie smiled at the younger woman. "Good morning, Lorna."

"Oh, Dr. Avery. How nice to see you again. How may I help you?"

"Nice to see you as well, Lorna. I'm looking for a guest of yours, Jillian Harrison." She had no idea if Jillian was staying here, but sounding confident couldn't hurt.

"Miss Harrison is having breakfast on the back patio. I'll announce you, Dr. Avery."

Charlie headed for the patio. "No need," she muttered over her shoulder. She walked outside and followed the wrap around porch to the back of the property. There were several wrought iron tables, all empty except one. Charlie stopped when she spied Brendan's ex. A tall willowy blonde, Jillian could have easily been her sister. She shook off her shock and continued to the table, sitting down across from Jillian.

"Good morning. You don't know me. I'm Charlotte Avery, a good friend of Brendan Fitzgerald. You and I are going to have a little chat, Jillian."

The steel in her voice caught the other woman's attention. Jillian perused Charlie over her coffee cup. "Are we? And what do we have to talk about?"

She fisted her hands in her lap at the other woman's bored intonation. "You might think that you'll get your way because you're rich and powerful. Or at least your family is. But that's back in Texas. No one knows you here, Jillian. But they know Brendan. And his family. You won't get those girls away from him."

Jillian raised one perfectly shaped eyebrow. "Whatever gets you through the day, honey." She looked Charlie up and down before laughing. "I guess you're the cheap replacement."

"I'm not a replacement for anyone. I love Brendan. I love Kerry and Abby as if they were my own. You don't care about them. Never have. You may think you can come here and throw your family money around, but it won't work. I'm prepared to back this fight. And I have very deep pockets. So, any advantage you think you have is gone. I suggest you take whatever pride you have left and go back to Texas."

Charlie turned on her heel and strode away. She got in her car and drove a few blocks. Only then did the tears come. And the shaking. Rolling down the windows, she fought for breath. She closed her eyes and concentrated on her breathing. That horrible woman wasn't worth a full-blown panic attack. After a few minutes, her pulse slowed and her breathing eased. She unfurled her hands, staring at the crescents she had dug with her fingernails. Only then did she drive home.

*****

Brendan sat in the office of Alexander Windsor, Esq. and told the whole sorry story. He drummed his fingers on the desk until he drove himself crazy, then fisted his hand in his lap. The attorney scribbled notes while Brendan spoke. When he finished speaking, Brendan sat back in the chair, wasted.

"Is that everything?"

"Yes, that's the whole sordid tale. So, you see why I'm concerned?"

Alex leaned back in his chair. "Frankly, no. Yes, Jillian comes from money. A lot of it. But that doesn't counter what she's done. She planned to abort your children. Then signed away all rights to them on the day of their birth. Not to mention no contact since they were born. She can threaten all she wants, but she doesn't have a legal leg to stand on."

"I understand that. But she has the money to drag this thing on. I don't want my daughters being subjected to that."

"And I understand that. The best defense is an offence. I will send a very strongly worded warning to her attorney this morning. They will know, before she's even had the chance to start something, that we aren't going to take this lying down. Give me the contact information, and it will be out the door in fifteen minutes."

For the first time since he came home to find his ex at his parents' home, Brendan could breathe. Standing up, he reached into his pocket and handed over the card Jillian had given him. Then he shook the attorney's hand. "You have no idea what this means to me, Mr. Windsor."

"Please, call me Alex. I don't have kids yet, so you're right. I can't imagine. But no one comes blowing in here thinking they can mess with someone from this town. I don't care how much money or power her family has back in Texas."

"I came to you, Alex, because of your last name and deep connection to Windsor Falls." Brendan had done a little research in finding a lawyer to fight Jillian. When he learned that a member of the Windsor family practiced here, it was a no brainer.

Alex smiled. "In this case, Brendan, that's the way to play the game. Jillian needs to understand that her family's name, and money, don't mean anything here. If her attorney is any good, he or she will convince Jillian there's no way to win this before they ever get started. Now, let me do my thing. You'll be hearing from me shortly, I imagine."

Brendan thanked Alex again and left the office. He walked out into the early morning sunshine. He needed to talk with Charlie. Wanted to. Brendan had started to call her so many times in the past few days. But this thing consumed him. And it didn't seem fair to drag her into something that wasn't her fight. If Alex was right, this might all be over soon. Then he could explain to Charlie what had happened.

He kept busy all day, driving to different construction sites to check in with his foremen. Brendan was always a hands-on kind of manager, so nobody seemed surprised to see him. Although a ton of paperwork sat on his desk begging for his attention, he couldn't focus. Better to drive around and talk with his employees than to stare at the wall of his office. Every time his phone rang, he hoped to see Alex's name. Or Charlie's. He needed to hear from both.

When Brendan didn't think he could take it anymore, his phone buzzed. Seeing Alex's name on the screen, he excused himself from a conversation with a site foreman. He almost dropped the phone in his hurry to answer it.

"Brendan Fitzgerald."

"Alex Windsor. Great news. It went exactly as I said. Jillian's attorney advised her client that there's no chance in Hell of winning. Once her daddy heard that, he pulled the plug. Of course, the part about the negative publicity helped him to see the light. After all, what kind of person tries to take two little girls away from the only parent they've ever known? Congratulations."

Brendan walked to his truck and sat down. Hard. "I don't know how to ever thank you, Alex." His voice quavered with emotion. "Family means everything to me. I owe you."

Alex laughed. "Pay the invoice when it comes. That's all you owe me. Besides, I enjoyed sticking it to them. Thinking they could come here and try to mess with one of ours. Guess we showed them."

Brendan laughed while tears coursed down his face. He didn't even try to stop them. "Thanks again, man. I owe you."

The two exchanged pleasantries for a moment before hanging up. Relief flooded Brendan's body. The nightmare was over. He called his mother, explaining what had happened, and asked her to pass it along. She was information central for the Fitzgerald family. Next, he needed to call Charlie. But he stopped before hitting send. He needed to do this in person.

Brendan walked back over to the foreman and explained he would be out the rest of the day. They could reach him by phone if necessary. Better yet, call his Dad or one of his siblings. Brendan had plans for the next few hours. And they involved some groveling and a whole lot of love making. His heart soared when he thought of her. He had not handled this situation well, but he would explain. Make amends for it.

His phone rang once more as he got into his truck. He answered without glancing at the screen. "This is Brendan."

"I hope you're satisfied." Sarcasm dripped from Jillian's words.

Brendan slid his phone into the dash holder and started his truck. He pulled out onto the road before responding. "Of course, I am. Kerry and Abby belong with me, the only parent they've ever known. You had no right to threaten me with taking them."

"You didn't mind threatening me with your girlfriend's money, did you?"

Cold seeped through Brendan's bones, despite the warmth of the day. "What are you talking about?"

"Oh, come on, Brendan. Nice touch sending your girlfriend with the 'deep pockets' around to warn me. Very convincing to my father. I'll give you that much. It made him rethink going after the girls."

Bits of past conversations with Charlie whizzed through his mind. The references to an arranged type marriage and summers at Sullivan's Island. He'd never put two and two together, but now blood roared in his ears.

"You lost because you didn't have a legal leg to stand on, Jillian. You gave up any rights to Kerry and Abby when you signed them away. Do not call or ever try to contact the girls again."

Brendan ended the call and drove to Charlie's house. When he arrived, he had no memory of getting there. He slammed the truck into park and ran to her door. She answered after a few moments, a broad smile on her face. But that didn't matter to Brendan.

"Tell me it's not true, Charlie. Tell me you're not like her." He spat the words at her.

Realization dawned in her eyes. Charlie steeped back and motioned him inside. Not wanting to have this conversation on the porch, he stepped in and closed the door behind him. He expected explanations or recriminations from her. He didn't expect fury.

"How dare you compare me to Jillian.? Who do you think you are? I am nothing like her."

Somewhere in the back of his brain, Brendan heard the truth in that statement, but he was too far gone. "Really? You're not filthy rich and think that your money can buy you anything?"

She stepped back as though he had slapped her. "I come from money, like Jillian. I'll give you that. But, that's where the similarities end. There's a reason my family and I don't have much of a relationship. I don't care about the money and the family name. I make my own decisions and live my own life."

His face twisted in an ugly sneer. "And one of those choices was to threaten my ex with your family money and position. Isn't that right, Charlie."

The color drained from her face. "And I would do it again, Brendan. Kerry and Abby are everything to you and becoming so to me. There was no way I could stand by and let that woman take them. I love them. And I love you. And that's what I told Jillian."

He dragged a hand through his thick hair. "You don't get it, Charlie. I told you, from the beginning, about my marriage. You knew how I felt about Jillian's family and money. And yet you never told me about yours. You kept that from me."

"Not because I wanted to. You have to understand," she pleaded. "Yes, you told me what a terrible experience you'd had with all that. How could I tell you about my family? 'Oh, by the way, I come from money too'? Like you would have listened. I come *from* money, Brendan. I don't live that way now. I told you about my parents and how they never approved of me. I didn't fit in with them or their lifestyle." Tears filled her eyes. "I was afraid of losing you. I know I should have told you, but I didn't know how."

"And lying to me was better? I can't be in a relationship with someone who won't or can't be honest. I won't do that again."

Tears flowed down her face. "I'm not Jillian," she sobbed. "You must know that. I went against my family, left them even, to be my own person. To not be like them. Why can't you see that?"

"All I can see is that you lied to me. And then tried to use your money to get what you wanted."

Sobs wracked her slender frame. "What choice did I have? You wouldn't talk to me. I had to hear about this from Elizabeth. I love you and the girls. I wanted to help. But you shut me out."

"It doesn't matter anymore. I can't do this. I can't be in a relationship with a stranger. And that's what you are to me." He turned and left, disgust filling him.

*****

Charlie collapsed on the sofa, curling herself into the smallest ball possible. Hot tears slid from her eyes. How had this happened? She only wanted to help Brendan keep the girls. She wasn't anything like Jillian. She pressed a hand to her heart. He would never forgive her.

She longed to run. To lose herself in the miles, pounding the road until she couldn't anymore. But she wasn't far enough along in her recovery. She could end up doing more damage. So, she paced the downstairs of Katie's home. Darkness filled her thoughts. He would never understand. Never forgive her. Her heart raced. Her breathing became more difficult. The edges of her vision grayed out.

She stood in the kitchen, death grip on the counter and struggled to not fall apart. She could call Elizabeth, but the thought of rehashing this was too much. She needed to not feel anything. Needed oblivion. And there was only one way to achieve that. She had spotted a few bottles of alcohol that Katie left behind. It was a terrible idea, but she no longer cared.

She grabbed a bottle of vodka and a glass and sat at the table. Charlie stared at the label for a full five minutes, battling with herself. Then she filled the glass. The first gulp burned all the way down, but it got easier after that. By the time she finished the bottle, it might as well have been water. Her mind numbed with each sip, and that's all she cared about. Her breathing and pulse slowed. Her vision blurred. She spread her arms on the table top, knocking over the now empty bottle. She lay her head on top of her arms and welcomed oblivion.

*****

Elizabeth knocked on Charlie's door again, dread building. It wasn't like Charlie to not respond. She had called and texted her several times, trying to tell her the good news. Everyone was excited about Jillian dropping her insane attempt to gain custody of Kerry and Abby.

She turned to leave, when she heard a noise from inside. She tried the handle, finding it unlocked. A bitter smell assailed her nose when she pushed open the door. She stepped into the gloom. Elizabeth glanced around the living room before heading into the kitchen. That's where she found Charlie, face down in a puddle of vomit.

Elizabeth's own heart raced as she felt for a pulse in Charlie's neck. It was there but weak. She whipped out her phone and called Katie, thankful the other woman was off today. She told her what had happened and asked her to come. And to bring her fiancé.

After placing her phone and purse on the counter, Elizabeth tipped Charlie back until she sat upright in the chair. At least she could protect her airway. She shook her friend's shoulders. "Charlie, wake up. Charlie! Can you hear me?" She got a moan for her efforts. But at least Elizabeth knew that Charlie wasn't unresponsive. She continued to monitor her pulse and breathing, waiting for Katie and Flynn to arrive.

After what seemed like an eternity, the two rushed through the front door. Katie reached her side first. "What happened to her?"

Icy fear flowed through Elizabeth. "She didn't answer her phone, and I found her this way." Elizabeth kicked the empty vodka bottle aside. "May have something to do with that. I've never known her to drink like this."

"Good thing you called us," added Flynn. He pointed to her soiled clothing. "We need to get her changed. And you're in no condition to help, Elizabeth." Flynn picked Charlie up s though she weighed no more than a feather and carried her up the stairs to the master bath.

Katie was on his heels. "Get her in the shower. We have to clean her up." Elizabeth took Flynn's place. Katie gathered some towels and underwear and pajamas for Charlie. The two stripped her and showered her as best they could. Elizabeth helped Katie towel Charlie dry and put her in PJs. Flynn came back in and lifted Charlie again, carrying her to the bedroom. They decided the recliner would be a better option, so Flynn placed her in it.

Katie grabbed a blanket, covering Charlie with it. She placed a trash can next to the recliner. "She'd be better off if we took her into the ER. We could give her fluids."

Elizabeth shook her head. "I know, but she wouldn't want that, Katie. She just started there. How would it look to be a drunken patient? If I can protect her airway, I'd rather take care of her here."

"I understand. Flynn and I will stay too. Just in case." Katie grabbed her Flynn's hand and led him out of the room. "We'll go down and make a snack. Can I bring you something?"

Elizabeth waved a hand. "I'm fine." She glanced up with tear filled eyes. "Thanks so much for coming. Both of you."

"No worries," answered Flynn.

When she was alone again, Elizbeth turned to her friend. She pushed a hunk of wet hair from her face. "Oh, Charlie, what have you done to yourself?"

"Brendan," sobbed Charlie in response before settling back into sleep.

Elizabeth didn't know what that meant, but he had some explaining to do.

Chapter Twenty-One

Nausea awoke Charlie, and she struggled to get up. Spying a can next to her on the floor, she grabbed it in time to lose the contents of her stomach. Everything ached. Why was she in the bedroom recliner? That's when she saw Elizabeth sleeping on her bed.

She got up and carried the offending basket into the bathroom. She emptied the putrid contents in the toilet, holding back the urge to vomit again, and flushed. She rinsed out her mouth and washed her hands at the sink, unsteady as she went. That's when she remembered the bottle of vodka.

She met Elizabeth's worried eyes in the mirror. She apologized without turning around. "I'm so sorry. It was a stupid thing to do." She sat on the toilet lid and buried her face in her hands.

"Hush now. It's okay, Charlie. The good news is that you're fine. Luckily, we didn't have to take you to the ER."

"We?" croaked Charlie. "Who's we?"

"I had to have help. I couldn't lift you. Flynn and Katie are asleep in the guest room."

"Oh my God," she wailed. "I'm such an idiot. There's a reason I haven't had any alcohol for months."

Elizabeth sat on the edge of the garden tub and picked up her friend's hand. "Please tell me what's going on. I can't help if I don't understand."

Charlie raised her tear soaked eyes to her friend. "Things did not go well in Africa. They tried to warn us what we'd be up against, but we were unprepared. So many children dying from malnutrition, Elizabeth." She closed her eyes and shuddered. "And the parents, hoping you can help them but knowing you'll fail."

Elizabeth stroked Charlie's hair. "It's not failure when the odds are stacked against you. You did the best that you can."

"We all did, but the children still died. By the hundreds. That is failure. And then there was the constant threat of violence. We'd hear gunshots, sometimes all day or night. But always in the distance. They'd bring bloodied, broken people to us, and all we could was make them a little more comfortable until they died." She closed her eyes, but the faces of those desperate people haunted her. "I couldn't save them," she whispered.

"Oh honey, I had no idea." Elizabeth stroked Charlie's hair.

She took a deep breath. "It ended badly, Elizabeth. We always knew about the danger around us, but somehow we felt protected." She laughed bitterly. "Or maybe we didn't think about it. We were too busy trying to keep it together. Too many bodies. Too little supplies. Then one day, that all changed."

Elizbeth hitched in a sharp breath but didn't say anything. She squeezed Charlie's hand.

Her tone flattened as she told the tale of her last day in Africa. "The rebel leaders didn't appreciate what we were trying to do. It didn't matter that we patched up anyone who came along. After sunset, they surrounded our camp. And burned it to the ground. I can still hear the screams." She clutched Elizabeth's hand harder and swallowed. "They shot anyone who survived the flames. Including me. Only three of my team made it out alive." She clutched at her lower abdomen. "But not whole."

Charlie sobbed. "The soldier who shot me was a child, Elizabeth. He couldn't have been more than twelve. A bandana covered his face. But not his eyes. His eyes were wide with fear. He was only following orders. Trying to survive. I remember the burning pain and then nothing until I woke up in hospital. I was flown to one in Nigeria and then a military facility in Germany. It was several weeks before I made it home to Charleston. You can imagine how that went. I still haven't told my parents what happened. They'd only tell me I told you so."

Elizabeth got up and got some water for Charlie, who drank it all down. "What haven't you told me?"

She turned her reddened eyes to Elizabeth. "I can't have children. There was too much damage, and they had to make a choice to save my life."

Elizabeth clutched her swollen belly. "Oh, Charlie, I'm so sorry. I didn't know."

"Of course, you didn't. How could you? And I am so very happy for you and Sam." She closed her eyes. "But it's difficult watching you, knowing that will never be me. And when that horrible woman came along and threatened to take Kerry and Abby away, I lost it."

Confusion clouded Elizabeth's blue eyes. "What do you mean?"

"I love Brendan. And his daughters. I thought we were going to be a family. And then Jillian showed up, threatening to take the girls. I knew she wouldn't win, but I couldn't take the chance. So, I went over to the B&B and told her exactly what I'd do if she tried." She sobbed. "And he found out, before I had a chance to tell him. And now he hates me." She collapsed in Elizabeth's arms, sobbing as though her very heart were breaking.

Elizabeth held Charlie. "He didn't know about your family."

She shook her head. "I wanted to tell him, but he always talked about Jillian and her family with such disgust. I couldn't risk it. Then it felt too late. I didn't know what to do." Charlie hiccupped. "He won't give me a chance to explain. He feels betrayed, Elizabeth. He's never going to forgive me."

"Give him time to cool down. I've never known him to be so unreasonable."

Charlie stood, still a bit wobbly on her feet. She gave Elizabeth a smile that didn't reach her eyes. "I'm tired, Elizabeth. She padded back into the bedroom and stretched out in the recliner. "I'm fine now. Please feel free to go home. Or go back to sleep in the bed. This won't happen again. I haven't had any alcohol in several months. Not since I realized it helped a bit too much to ease the memories. I'm seeing a psychiatrist in town. Despite what you've witnessed, he is helping me." Her words slid off as she fell asleep again.

Late afternoon sun slanted into the bedroom, waking Charlie for the second time that day. She stretched and groaned, rubbing the sore muscles of her abdomen. The bed was empty and the house quiet. She glanced at her phone. After five and several texts from Elizabeth. Nothing from Brendan. She responded to Elizabeth, thanking her again. And assuring her friend that she was alive and well. Her head pounded. Proof she was alive.

She went down to the kitchen and nibbled on a plain bagel before taking some pain reliever. She thought about Brendan, wondering what he and the girls were doing. She couldn't blame that pain in her gut on alcohol. She should have told him when he first mentioned his ex. Showed him that she was different. But she was afraid he wouldn't stick around long enough to listen. The longer their relationship went on, the harder it became for her to bring up. The fact is she feared losing both Brendan and the girls. Ironically, that's exactly what she did.

Looking around the room, she noticed all traces of last night's debacle were gone. Charlie stood and opened some cabinets. Someone had removed all temptation. Not that she would ever be drinking again. Her patients said that all the time, especially after a bad bender. But she meant it. She had never been much of a drinker to start with. Knowing how she leaned on it now made the decision to not drink again an easy one.

Charlie grabbed a bottle of water and sat on the sofa. And allowed herself to feel the pain she feared last night. Brendan had every right to be angry with her, even if she had the best of intentions. But he'd been wrong to shut her out. They had grown very close in a brief period, and he chose to not tell her what Jillian threatened. He knew how much she cared for his daughters. How could he do that?

She decided to cut him some slack. She wasn't a parent. She didn't know, couldn't understand, what he had been feeling. Thinking. He might have been acting in survival mode, trying to figure out a way out of that mess. But understanding that didn't make her feel any better.

Huge tears slid down her face. She didn't bother to wipe them away. Let them come. Today she would start to deal with the pain of what she had lost. She should have told Brendan about her family from the very beginning, when it might not have been such a big deal. It was too late now. He made that very clear.

*****

Elizabeth drove away from Charlie's, sorrow mixing with anger. Her heart ached for Charlie. She couldn't imagine surviving the trauma that her friend had. She placed a hand on her pregnant belly and said a silent word of thanks to the universe. Losing the baby she was expecting with Connor all those years ago almost wrecked her. But knowing she would never be able to have one? That was a pain beyond imagining. She didn't know how to help her friend.

The strife with Brendan made everything worse. She lifted her chin and ground her teeth. That situation she could something about. Before she could change her mind, she headed towards his house. Elizabeth knew this wasn't any of her business, but the pain etched into Charlie's face spurred her on.

A few minutes later, Elizabeth turned onto his street. His truck sat in the driveway. Relief mingled with the acid churning in her gut. What could she possibly say to fix this? Maybe nothing, but she had to try.

She pulled in behind his truck and cut the motor. Elizabeth stayed in her car, giving herself a moment or two to gather her thoughts. No such luck. Her head jerked up at the sound of approaching shrieks of joy.

"Auntie Elizabeth," cried Kerry at full volume.

Abby, not to be outdone, waved her cast. "Look, Aunt Elizabeth, it's all covered with names."

Elizabeth got out of her SUV and hugged both girls. "Hello, ladies. Where is your Daddy?"

Each girl took one of her hands and led her into the house. They both screamed for Brendan at the top of their collective lungs. Elizabeth was tempted to put her hands over her ears, but she smiled instead. Noisy kids were a part of her very near future.

Brendan came in from the deck, carrying a plate. "Hey Elizabeth," he called in greeting before coming over to hug her. "I can barely get my arms around you anymore."

He grinned when Elizabeth swatted his arm. "I'll have you know that's your niece or nephew you're disparaging."

He laid his hand on her belly. "Hello, Peanut. Uncle Brendan here. Can't wait to meet you."

Her resolve wavered. She'd always had a soft spot for Brendan. Then she remembered Charlie's tear-streaked face. Elizabeth straightened up and pulled back her shoulders. "Girls, could you go outside for a moment? I need to talk to your Dad. Boring adult stuff." She winked at the girls.

The girls scampered out the door, faithful dogs following at their sides. His smile faltered. His shoulders tensed. "I have a feeling you aren't here for dinner."

Elizabeth pulled out a chair and sat. "Normally, I would pace, but I'm too tired."

His face softened. "Are you okay?"

She offered him a thin smile. "Not long to go. I'm worn out by the end of a day." She took a breath and held up her hands to him. "You know I love you, Brendan. But I love Charlie too, and you're being an ass."

"This has nothing to do with you, Elizabeth." He took a seat opposite her. The table between them may have been an ocean.

"But it does. I love both of you, and I can't stand to see you hurting. Surely, you can work this out?"

"She lied to me, Elizabeth. She knew about Jillian. And her rich family. She never told me about her own."

Elizabeth leaned forward, holding his gaze. "That's it exactly. You made no effort to hide your disdain for that. What was she supposed to say? 'Oh, by the way, my family is rich'?"

"And lying was a better option?"

Elizabeth closed her eyes for a moment and blew air out through her mouth. "You were both wrong, Brendan. Why can't you admit that and move on? Get past this?"

"I can't trust her now, Elizabeth." His eyes held a haunted look.

"If that's how you feel, then do her a favor and stay away from her altogether. Charlie's had enough pain for a lifetime."

She got up to leave, but he was quicker. He stood toe to toe with her. "What does that mean? Is she okay?"

Elizabeth tilted her head back to look up at him, hands clenched at her sides. "Why do you care? You've made it very clear she doesn't matter to you."

His nostrils flared. "I never said that. For Pete's sake, I just told her…"

"Told her what?"

Brendan took a step back and shoved his hands in his pockets. "I told her that I love her when we were away this weekend. Tell me she's okay."

Elizabeth would have missed his words if she wasn't standing next to him. Her shoulders sagged. "She is now. But she drank an entire bottle of vodka last night. Katie, Flynn, and I stayed with her to make sure nothing happened. It could have gone so much worse."

Color drained from his tanned face. "She doesn't drink."

"Normally, she doesn't. Even in our residency, we were the only two who didn't drink much. Running was always her stress relief. But that's not an option right now. Things went very wrong in Africa. Charlie has avoided alcohol at all since she started to find it too appealing."

"She never told me what happened over there. Not the details anyway. I didn't press her. Guess I thought she'd open up to me in time."

"It's her story to tell. But you need to know that there are wounds, both physical and emotional."

He nodded. "I know she's been seeing a doctor here in Windsor Falls. She has PTSD. I think it's great that she's getting help."

"It goes deeper than that."

He raised pained eyes to her. "Please tell me."

Elizabeth struggled with how much to tell him. He needed to know everything, but she didn't want to disrespect her friend's right to privacy. She decided. "Charlie can't have any children. Her injuries were life threatening. She had a hysterectomy."

She watched the emotions flit across his face; sorrow, shock, maybe even rage at what Charlie had suffered. She wasn't expecting what came out of his mouth.

"So, she thought she could buy my children?"

His voice held no inflection. Elizabeth had never heard him speak like this. "You can't believe that."

"She comes from money, Elizabeth. They're all like that. Have a problem? Buy your way out of it."

"If that's what you think, then I don't even know who you are anymore, Brendan." Elizabeth left the house before she said, or did something, they would both regret.

*****

Brendan watched Elizabeth go, not attempting to stop her. His mind raced. He couldn't get past the knowledge that Charlie came from a background very similar to Jillian. Deep in his brain, he knew Charlie was nothing like his ex-wife. Brendan pushed the thought aside. She had withheld that from him. And then went to see Jillian. And threatened to use her money. What was he supposed to think?

"Daddy, we're hungry," complained Abby from the slider door. Kerry nodded in agreement.

Brendan smiled at them, pushing thoughts of Charlie aside. He didn't have the time nor energy to deal with them now. "Who wants hamburgers?"

"We do. We do," cried both of his girls.

"Okay then, hamburgers coming up." Brendan walked out to the grill and turned it on. He felt a tug on his shirt.

"Daddy, when is Charlie coming back? We haven't seen her in forever."

"I don't know, girls. She's very busy at the hospital. We'll have to see."

"Did you have a fight, Daddy? You should say you're sorry if you did."

Brendan looked down into Kerry's solemn, green eyes. "It's not always that easy, honey."

"Is she not your girlfriend anymore, Daddy?" This from Abby, also with a somber gaze.

Brendan hunkered down to be on their level. "I don't want you to worry about Charlie and me, girls. That's a grown-up thing. Besides, we've always been fine. Right?"

The girls hesitated before answering, causing Brendan's gut to roll. They both hugged him, nodding their heads. It didn't make him feel any better.

*****

Charlie walked into the ER for a night shift the next night. She felt fine, unless you counted the lack of sleep. She hadn't heard from Brendan. Didn't expect to. Yet her foolish heart leapt whenever her phone chimed. She tried to tell herself she was better off. He had hang ups with money, and she couldn't change her family. It didn't matter that she lived a different life. He didn't want to hear it. He'd made his decision. She would learn to live with that.

But she missed him. She laid in bed remembering the feel of his body next to hers. His lips on hers. His hand tracing the line of her jaw. But it went beyond that. He was a good father and a good man. She loved spending time with him and his amazing daughters. She missed Kerry and Abby so much. Their infectious grins and little girl laughter.

This wasn't helping. She straightened her shoulders and marched into the locker room. After stowing her purse and keys in a locker, she went out to get report from Elizabeth. "There you are," Charlie exclaimed. She slid into the seat next to Elizabeth. "What have you got for me?"

Elizabeth didn't answer right away. She looked at Charlie like she assessed a patient. "How are you? Really?"

Charlie let out a nervous laugh. "Never could fool you. I've had better days. Not sleeping much. But, I'll be fine."

Elizabeth nodded. "Yes, you will. I don't suppose you've heard from Brendan."

Charlie shook her head. "Not expecting to."

Elizabeth sighed. "Stubborn man." She yawned, trying to cover it with her hand. "Sorry. These days are killing me. Let me tell you about a few patients so I can get out of here."

She gave report, nothing too serious, and left. Charlie watched her friend go before signing into the computer. She didn't know whether to hope for a calm or hectic night. She was exhausted but staying busy might be better.

"I know how to turn that frown into a smile."

She looked up and swallowed a groan. "Hey, Dan."

The overly confident surgeon beamed at her. "Seriously, we could have some fun."

She was tired. And in no mood for him. Her manners slipped a bit. "Dan, this is never going to happen. I thought I made that clear. So, stop. Now." She would rather be alone forever than with someone like him.

His smile dimmed. "Message received," he muttered before walking away. The headache that had been festering for hours bloomed. She rubbed her temples. Food and ibuprofen. That's what she needed. Otherwise, it was going to be a long night.

One of the nurses approached her. "Dr. Avery, medics called with a multi-vehicle MVA. We're getting at least three, one critical."

So much for food and pain relief. "Coming," she responded.

Chapter Twenty-Two

Charlie glanced around the deli section of the supermarket, not interested in the choices available to her. Fatigue leadened her steps. Her shift had been fine, eight hours with only one trauma and a variety of non-life-threatening cases. Her exhaustion had nothing to do with that and everything to do with a lack of sleep. Despite eating better and limiting her caffeine, sleep evaded her once again. And that had everything to do with Brendan.

Grabbing a rotisserie chicken, Charlie placed it in her basket and headed for the produce aisle. Her kitchen was bare. She just needed something for dinner tonight. She hoped a good meal, followed by a long, hot soak would be the catalyst she needed for a good night's sleep. She sighed and reached for some broccoli. That combination hadn't worked so far. Why would tonight be any different?

"Still eating trees, I see."

Charlie froze with the broccoli half way to her cart. She didn't turn around. She couldn't. No one else's voice sent shivers down her spine. Brendan. Her shoulders sagged. She placed the broccoli in the cart. Turning slowly, Charlie risked a glance at his face. And wished she hadn't. Seeing that rugged face she had missed so much hurt her heart. Her knuckles grew white on the cart handle. But at least the shopping cart held her up. Her knees threatened to buckle at any second.

"Hello, Brendan." The simple greeting was all she could manage. Emotion clogged her throat.

Brendan leaned in slightly, as though to touch her. He must have thought better of it. His hand hung at his side. "Hey, Charlie."

She stood there, in the produce section, and stared at him. The memories flooded back. His laughter. The touch of his hand on the small of her back. The feel of his body curled around hers in the darkness. Grief battled with anger. Everything they were building lay in ruins at their feet. And yes, she was responsible. But not entirely. He never even gave her a chance to explain.

"Windsor Falls is a small town. I was bound to run into you. Please tell the girls I said hello." She straightened her spine and turned away, generations of Averys giving her the strength she needed. At least they were good for something. Charlie reached the front of the store and kept going, abandoning her cart. Hot tears threatened. She held them at bay until she reached her car. Only then did she allow them to flow freely down her face.

She grabbed her phone and dialed the only number she could.

"Hey, Charlie. What's up?" Elizabeth's cheerful tone only worsened her mood.

At first, she could only sob into the phone. She took a deep, cleansing breath and tried for actual words. "I saw him. At the grocery store." She paused and blew her nose. "I knew it would happen, I would see him again one day. But I wasn't ready, Elizabeth. I may never be."

"Oh, I'm so sorry. I know that sucked. That's the problem with small towns. He's going to be everywhere you go. It will get easier, Charlie. I promise."

"I know. But right now, it hurts. All I wanted to do was wrap myself around him, Elizabeth. What am I going to do?" Her wails could be heard across the distance between them.

"All you can do is go on with your life, Charlie. You're a strong person. Today sucked because it was the first time. It will get easier. You have to believe that."

"Me too. Anything else is too depressing." Charlie grabbed a tissue and blew her nose. "But what if we're wrong?" Her voice was a mere whisper.

Silence reigned on the other end. Finally, Elizabeth spoke. "I'm not going to lie to you. I hoped that you and Brendan would end up together. And it sucks that he acted the way he did." Her heartfelt sigh crossed the distance between the friends. "But, Charlie, you are a survivor. Look at what you've already fought your way back from. You're going to be fine."

"Of course, I am. I just wish it didn't hurt so badly right now." For far from the first time, silent tears coursed down her cheeks. "I miss him." Three simple words summed up the pain and longing she had carried with her day and night.

"I know you do. It really will be okay. Eventually. For now, eat chocolate and avoid romantic comedies."

A reluctant laugh bubbled up from Charlie's throat. She wiped the tears from her face and sniffed. "Is that your prescription, doctor?"

"Yes, it is. Worked for me in the past."

"But you got Sam back. There's no chance of that for me. Brendan is too hurt and blinded by his past."

"To be honest, I don't even recognize this Brendan. His behavior is unacceptable. But you're still going to be fine."

The muffled noise of a door opening and closing came through. "Say hi to Sam for me. I should get home and eat dinner anyway. Early night for me, since I'm exhausted."

"Are you sure? You could always come here. A bitch session about the evils of men, Sam excluded of course, might make all the difference."

Charlie smiled for the first time since seeing him in the store. "I'm sure. Go hug your man for me. Talk to you later." She ended the call and started her car. Elizabeth meant well, and she appreciated the thought. But right now, she couldn't take being with the happy couple.

*****

One week had passed. Seven days. More hours and minutes than he cared to remember since seeing Charlie at the market. Brendan switched off the TV and threw the remote down in disgust. But he missed her. A lot. And it was mostly his fault.

The house was quiet, with the girls in bed for over an hour. He needed to shower and go to bed too, but he dreaded it. Sleep was a stranger since the fight with Charlie. When he did sleep, his dreams were about her. Hot, steamy ones that left him sweaty and even more frustrated.

Brendan switched off the downstairs lights and headed up. He walked to the girls' room to check one last time. Whispers stopped him in the hall. Usually, the girls were asleep the moment their heads hit their pillows. He was going to say something about it being past their bedtime when he heard Charlie's name. Brendan stopped and listened.

"Kerry, do you think we'll ever see Charlie again? I thought for sure she was going to be our new Mommy."

"Don't know, Abby. Daddy is sad. Maybe their fight was real bad."

"Maybe we did something wrong." The wobble in his daughter's voice almost did him in.

"Maybe Charlie doesn't like little girls."

"But she was always nice to us, playing with us and everything," came her twin's reply.

"Then why did she leave us?"

Brendan had heard enough. He entered the room, sitting on the edge of Kerry's bed. "Girls, please don't think that. Charlie and I had an argument. And it had nothing to do with you guys."

Abby scrambled out of hers and joined them. "If she's mad at you, then why doesn't she come to see us? Doesn't she like us anymore?"

He gathered both girls in his arms. "Charlie loves you both very much."

"We miss her," cried Kerry, burying her face in his chest. Her tears burned him. He never wanted the girls to be hurt by this. He shook his head at his own stupidity.

"I'm sorry. I never thought about how much you would miss her. Maybe she can take you guys to the movies."

Abby grabbed his hand. "But you miss her too Daddy. That's why you're so sad."

Out of the mouths of babes. "Yes, I do miss her. And that's why I'm sad. You guys are very smart."

"Then fix it, Daddy."

It suddenly seemed simple. 'Fix it', she had said. Yes, he missed Charlie. Yes, he was sad without her. He didn't agree with what Charlie had done, but he could understand why she had. He had been stupid and proud. And risked everything they were building, because of his disastrous relationship with Jillian.

Brendan jumped up from the bed and called his brother. Aidan answered after the third ring.

"Aidan, what are you doing?"

"Uh, now? Nothing. Why?"

"Yes, now! I need you to come over and watch the girls. I have to fix something."

"What? At a site? It can wait until tomorrow, dude."

"Not at a site, Aidan. I need to fix my life."

A second passed before it sank in. "Oh, you mean with Charlie. I'll be there in under ten."

Brendan slid the phone back his pocket. "Kerry, Abby, Uncle Aidan is going to come stay with you for a little bit so I can go talk to Charlie. Okay?"

Both girls shot off the bed, jumping up and down. Their screams of joy were enough to raise the dead. Fred and Ginger joined in, barking and wagging their tails. "Make sure you bring flowers, Daddy. Girls like that."

Brendan didn't want to know how they knew that. "I'm going to take a very fast shower. I need you guys to go back to bed. Okay? And be good for Uncle Aidan."

"We will," they cried in unison before slipping back into their beds.

Brendan leaned in to kiss them both. "Wish me luck."

"Go get her, Daddy!"

Brendan laughed and ran into his bathroom. He brushed his teeth and took the fastest shower ever. He threw on the first clothes he found. By the time he got downstairs, Aidan walked through the door.

He slapped him on the back. "Thank you, brother. You have no idea what this means to me."

"No worries. Don't screw up."

Brendan made a face. "Too late. Now I have to fix it."

He ran out the door and hopped into his truck. Brendan started the brief drive to her house. He wondered what he could say to make her forgive him. The look on her face had been devastating. The knowledge of what she had done afterward sickened him. He had caused that.

Without thinking of something brilliant to say, he pulled up to her house. The driveway was empty. Brendan jumped out and ran up to the door. No one answered. He looked in the garage. Empty. Raking a hand through his hair, Brendan considered his options. She might be working. But was that the best place to have this conversation?

He paced the width of the driveway, indecision his companion. He couldn't wait. He needed to talk with her. He had to fix things between them. Brendan got back into his truck and drove to the ER. Brendan found a parking space and entered through the emergency entrance. There didn't seem to be many people there, and he hoped she would take the time to talk with him.

"May I help you?" A woman in scrubs smiled at him.

Brendan smiled back. "I hope so. Is Dr. Avery working tonight?"

Her smile faded. "I'm sorry, sir, I can't tell you that. If you need treatment, I can help you."

Brendan ground his teeth. "I'm not a patient. I need to speak with Dr. Avery."

"Unfortunately, I cannot divulge that information to you, sir. I am sorry."

He didn't want to scare her, but Brendan was about to blow a gasket. How could he make her understand?

"Hey, Brendan, what are you doing here? Are the girls okay?"

Brendan turned to find Flynn standing a few feet away. Relief flooded through him. "Flynn, thank goodness. The girls are fine. I'm here to speak to Charlie, and this woman can't tell me if she's working."

The woman stood up and approached the two. "Dr. Reynolds, I followed protocol. I had no idea he knew Dr. Avery."

"No worries, Casey." He turned to Brendan. "She's right, you know. We don't release that information to anyone who walks in the doors."

Brendan turned to her. "I'm sorry that I put you in that position."

Casey nodded and went back to her post. Brendan turned to Flynn. "Now, can you get Charlie for me? Please?"

Flynn grimaced. "I was there last week, Brendan. I'm not sure that's a great idea."

Brendan's face flushed. "I know you were. And I appreciate it. Charlie needed you. And I know that's my fault. I need to make it up to her. Please."

Flynn stood his ground, eyeing Brendan. "I'll go back there and tell her you're here. The choice is hers. Understand?"

"Thanks, man."

"I'm marrying your sister. And I consider you a friend. So, I'm telling you this out of respect. Don't hurt her, Brendan. She deserves better."

Brendan nodded. "Understood."

Flynn walked away, badging himself into the treatment area of the ER. Brendan watched him go, hoping the other man could convince Charlie to speak with him. He paced back and forth, giving Casey a wide berth.

How had it gotten to this point? Where had it all gone wrong? He could strangle Jillian, but Brendan knew he was ultimately responsible. He didn't listen to Charlie. Hadn't given her a chance to explain. He would listen now. He just hoped it wasn't too late.

The doors swished open, and Brendan released the breath he hadn't realized he was holding. Charlie wore baggy scrubs. She wore her hair in a single braid. The darkened skin under her eyes told the story of sleepless nights. She looked beautiful.

"Flynn said it was important." She scanned the waiting area. "Are the girls okay?"

Brendan approached her, stopping feet away. He reached out to touch her but dropped his hand at the wariness in her eyes. "I have so much I need to say to you."

"So, say it, Brendan. I have patients waiting."

Brendan glanced around them before lowering his voice. "I'm so sorry. More than you'll ever know. I never meant to hurt you."

Casey, only a few feet away at her desk, harrumphed.

Charlie sent her a look. "This isn't the time nor the place."

"I know it isn't. But the second I realized I didn't want to live without you was the second I wanted to tell you."

This time, Casey sighed.

"For Pete's sake," exclaimed Charlie. She grabbed him by the hand, pulling him outside. When they were away from the doors, she turned to him. "You don't trust me, Brendan, and I get that. But it's not something I can live with."

Brendan blew out a large breath. "I do trust you, Charlie. Hearing about your family surprised me. From Jillian, no less. And I reacted like a fool. I realize now that I didn't make it easy for you to tell me. I'm sorry about that too. I let my past blind me."

"Yes, you did." She took a step closer. "But I should have told you. I should have found a way. So, I'm sorry also. And I should have told you about Africa. I would have eventually. I needed time."

Brendan closed the gap between them, placing a hand along her jaw. "Elizabeth told me a little about what happened to you. I'd like to hear the whole story. From you. When you're ready."

"Hey, Charlie."

Charlie glanced over her shoulder to the ER. The director, her boss, stepped out of the shadows. "Eric, what are you doing here?"

Eric smiled and walked towards her. "Well, I was leaving when a little birdie told me you might need coverage."

Charlie flushed. "Uh, no sir. I'm fine. Heading back in as a matter of fact." She shot Brendan a look begging his understanding.

Eric held up a hand. "Not necessary. I was young once." He approached Brendan. "You're Katie's brother, right?"

"Yes, sir, I am. Brendan Fitzgerald."

"Good family. I'm trusting you to not hurt our Charlie. I may be older than you, but I can hold my own."

"Message received."

"Good." Eric waved a hand at both before walking back inside.

Charlie turned to him and burst out laughing. "You've gotta love small towns. That would never happen in Chicago."

Brendan took her hand and led her to a bench. "I over reacted to things, and I'm sorry. Can you forgive me?"

"Only if you can forgive me. I should have told you about my family. But I was afraid of losing you. Before there was even an us. I came to Windsor Falls to start a new life, recover, focus on my career. Not to meet anyone. But there you were, day one, all worried sick Dad in the ER."

Brendan winced. "Don't you mean rude, obnoxious person?"

"Well, that too." She stopped at the expression on his face and burst out laughing. "Okay, you might have been a bit much, but I understood. And then I fell hard, and quick, and the last thing I wanted to do was jeopardize that. It was bad enough that you saw how fragile I still am."

He cupper her face in his hands. "Fragile? Because you have PTSD?" He shook his head. "Charlie, you're the strongest person I know. You survived something that most people would not have. And here you are, still helping others."

She blew out a shaky breath. "That's just it, Brendan. I haven't been honest with you. I'm not the same person who went to Africa. I lost part of myself over there." Her voice dropped to a whisper. "They took it from me."

"I love you, Charlie, for who you are. Right now. You're smart and funny, beautiful, and so sweet. I watch you with Kerry and Abby, and for the first time I thought they would have two parents after all."

Tears sprang to her eyes. "They are the sweetest little girls ever. And you're amazing with them. That's why I went a little crazy when Jillian threatened to destroy what you have. I couldn't stand by and let that happen. And I know it was wrong, but I'd do it again."

Brendan wiped the tears from her face. "Elizabeth told me that you can't have children of your own, Charlie. I'm so sorry."

"And that was the other thing I couldn't tell you. You saw the scars on my abdomen." She stopped and sucked in a shaky breath. Her eyes got a faraway look. "That last day started like any other. We had heard gunshots throughout the morning, but that wasn't out of the ordinary. No one knew what would happen. They came into our camp after dark, Brendan. Flames were everywhere. Then the shooting. It didn't matter who. Patients, staff. Whoever they could find. I tried to reason with them." She broke off and sobbed, wrapping her arms around her middle.

He folded her in his arms, rocking her. "Charlie, you're safe here. What happened wasn't your fault." He stroked her hair. "It's okay, honey."

After a few moments, she straightened up and continued. "I begged for my life. And the lives of my patients and friends. But they wouldn't listen. There was so much screaming and the sound of gunshots. And then it fell silent. So very silent. I lay where I fell, watching my blood seep into the dirt." She raised stricken eyes to him. "I thought I was going to die there, Brendan. But someone had radioed out when it all started. And help came, just too late for most of them."

Tears gathered in Brendan's eyes. "I cannot begin to imagine what you went through, Charlie."

She raised the hem of her scrub tip and traced her scars. "I don't even mind these. They remind me of what I went through. And survived. But they also make me sad. I wanted children, Brendan, one day."

"I happen to know two little girls who would love for you to be their Mom, Charlie." He smiled at her gasp. "And I also know there are many children out there who need a family. You can be a mom, Charlie."

"Are you asking me to marry you, Brendan?" Shock, and love, shone from her eyes.

Brendan laughed. "Well, I did imagine it would be a bit more romantic." He glanced around. "And probably not in the hospital parking lot. But yes, Charlie, I am." Brendan got down on one knee. "I don't have a ring, Charlie, and I know this has happened very fast. But before you, I didn't even believe in second chances. Will you marry me? And adopt Kerry and Abby? And whoever else comes along?"

She launched herself at him, knocking them both to the ground, and rained kisses on his face. "Yes, Brendan, yes! Of course, I will."

Loud whistles and a chorus of cheers erupted from the ER doors. Brendan looked up to see Flynn, Eric, Casey, and several others clapping. He stood, bringing Charlie with him. "Maybe we should go tell the girls before someone else does."

Charlie grinned. "You have the best ideas," she whispered in his ear.

The End

Help for Post-Traumatic Stress Disorder

Mental illnesses, Post Traumatic Stress Disorder or PTSD included, are often overlooked in our society. They are underreported and often dealt with in private and in shame. There isn't any reason for this. I hope to see a day when they are treated like any other chronic illness, such as heart disease or diabetes. No one chooses to have a mental illness. But choosing to get treatment can make all the difference.

The National Institute of Mental Illness estimates that 3.5% of American adult and 4% of 13-18-year-olds suffer from PTSD. The National Center for PTSD reports that 7-8 of every 100 people will be affected by it. It's hard to say how many of those are receiving the appropriate treatment.

We think of soldiers in active combat when we think of PTSD, but it can, and does, effect many others. Any traumatic experience can cause PTSD, including but not limited to: emotional, physical, or sexual abuse, acts of terror or violence, accidents or natural disasters. It can also be caused by the sudden death of a loved one.

The good news is there is help. If you or a loved one is experiencing PTSD, please get help. The following websites are the first step in getting help:

US Department of Veteran Affairs: https://www.ptsd.va.gov/public/PTSD-overview/basics/how-common-is-ptsd.asp

PTSD Survivors site: https://ptsdsurvivors.info/

PTSD United: http://www.ptsdunited.org/

Dealing with Infertility

The National Center for Health Statistics estimates that 12.1% of women between the ages of 15-44 suffer from impaired fertility. There are many reasons for this infertility. The NCHS also reported 600,000 hysterectomies in the United States alone every year, making the second most common major surgery for women.

Having a hysterectomy not only takes away a woman's fertility but can also lead to poor emotional health and altered self-esteem. The following agencies can provide women with support and assistance:

Hyster Sisters: http://www.hystersisters.com/
Resolve: The National Infertility Association: http://resolve.org/
Fertile Thoughts: http://www.fertilethoughts.com/

Acknowledgments

Shout out to romance writers everywhere. I've never encountered a group of people who were more welcoming or kind. I've met so many amazing authors over the past year. Not even once has someone said, "I had to learn the hard way, so do you." Thank you all for being so supportive.

There aren't enough words for the magnificent Jeni Burns. I lost my previous editor in between books two and three. I was at RT and panicked. What was I going to do? Jeni stepped right up and offered. I worried because Jeni and I are friends. Would that be awkward? Would it work? I'm happy to say that it wasn't and it most definitely did!! Working with Jeni was fabulous. I am so appreciative of her insights. Thanks for keeping me on track, Jeni.

As always, I am thankful for the design genius of Rebecca Pau, The Final Wrap. At each signing, I get comments on my covers. For Second Chances, we struggled, trying to find what I knew I wanted. Thanks, Rebecca, for sticking with it and coming up with this beautiful cover.

My family is always number one, even though they probably don't feel that way this year. It's been a busy time for me, heading off to conferences and signings. Thank you to my husband, Mark, for picking up the slack while I'm gone. And thanks to my children, Jordan and Lucas, for understanding. How many soccer games, XC meets did I miss? Probably too many. Thank goodness for texting!

How to Help an Indie Author

Review, reviews, reviews! Even if you didn't love Second Chances, please take the time to review it on Amazon and/or Goodreads. Reviews are so much more important than you could ever imagine.

Follow me on social media:
Facebook: https://www.facebook.com/profile.php?id=100012114317732
Twitter: https://twitter.com/K_OMalley67
Instagram: https://www.instagram.com/kimberleyomalley67/

***

Miss Windsor Falls already? Here's a sneak peek into Saving Quinn, due early 2018. Who will be the next two to fall in love? It's Quinn's & Paige's turn. They just don't know it. Saving Quinn is a work in progress and is therefore subject to change.

Excerpt from Saving Quinn

Paige Harrington blew the blonde wisps out of her face while she waited for the light to change. Glancing at her watch only told her what she already knew. She was going to be late. Again. A sigh escaped her. She wasn't a morning person. And although many people understood this, sadly her boss was not amongst them.

The light finally changed, and she moved forward into the intersection. Although she would have loved to rev the engine in her sporty little coup, the rain slashing against her windshield made her think better of it. The late spring storm showed no signs of stopping. Just another of the seemingly endless circumstances plotting against her this morning.

First, the storm must have knocked out power when she was sleeping, since her alarm never rang. She knew her friends would laugh at her and point out this was just another reason to join the twenty-first century. Paige was helplessly 'old fashioned' as they put it. She used an actual alarm clock.

After waking more than 45 minutes later than expected, her day continued to spiral downwards. No power meant the shortest and coldest shower on record followed by no coffee. Really? The shower she could take, but the lack of caffeine killed her. Then she discovered her new puppy, Finn, had mistaken her favorite pair of flats for a chew toy. Her laundry was seriously behind as well, which would explain the rather questionable outfit she was wearing. Thankfully the average six-year-old didn't care.

Paige taught kindergarten at Windsor Falls Elementary School. This was her dream job, and she loved the daily challenges she faced. What she didn't love was that it started at eight o'clock in the morning. It was supposed to. Right now, it was already past that. Thankfully, her best friend Amy Windsor, who happened to also be the other kindergarten teacher in the building, had the classroom right next door to hers. Amy would cover for her, bringing all the children into her own classroom until she could get there.

Fierce winds shook her small car. She tightened her grip on the steering wheel until her knuckles whitened. She tried to breathe deeply to calm herself. She never liked to drive in storms. She especially didn't care for it when she was already running late. Paige tried to think happy thoughts. Her puppy's soft, furry belly. Lying in a hammock under a palm tree while George Clooney fanned her with a palm leaf.

Paige grinned at that last image. Whew! That was certainly a happy thought. He might be much older than her 26 years, but she wouldn't hold that against him. Silver foxes were all the rage these days. The technique was working already. She felt calmer, especially since she knew she was less than a mile from the school. She loosened her white knuckled grip on the wheel just a fraction. *What else could possibly go wrong*, she wondered.

She briefly winced as the words still rang in her head. Hadn't her grandmother always warned her about putting ideas like that out there into the universe? Paige grimaced at the superstition and decided she would be okay. She was intelligent and educated. Nothing was going to happen just because she had asked that.

That was her last thought as another car came out of nowhere, slamming into hers on the passenger side and sending it spinning across the road. Her small, passenger car finally came to a halt wedged up against a light post. The sound of metal wrenching filled her ears like the roar of an oncoming freight train. Blood trickled down her face and blackness engulfed Paige.